UNTRUE TILL DEATH

Master Mercurius Mysteries
Book Two

Graham Brack

SAPERE
BOOKS

UNTRUE TILL DEATH

Published by Sapere Books.

20 Windermere Drive, Leeds, England, LS17 7UZ,
United Kingdom

saperebooks.com

ISBN: 978-1-913518-92-9

My wife Gillian has accompanied me as I wander round Dutch towns and cities researching these stories without ever quite knowing what I am looking for. For her patience, and for so much more, she deserves this book dedicated to her.

It is customary to say that the characters in a story are all imaginary and no resemblance to anyone living or dead is intended. That is true, but there is a character in this book who was inspired by my friend Ben Salfield, whose concerts (details of which are found at **www.kernowconcerts.co.uk**) we have long enjoyed. When I approached Ben for permission to use his name, he agreed provided that the character was sufficiently disreputable. I hope that he will be satisfied with the result. Beniamino is not Ben; he may, however, be a person Ben would like to be.

PROLOGUE

Now that I am advanced in years, the time has come to set down my memoirs before senility sets in and I can no longer remember what happened. I have had, by the grace of God, a long and exciting life. This is a small country, and as I have traversed it I have met many of the great and good that you, dear reader, will only have encountered in history books. Of course, much of my work has been devoted to the service of the University of Leiden, which God preserve, where I have worked my way up from juvenile student to even more juvenile professor. Although there was a new Rector every year (except that in difficult times nobody could be found to take the job and the old one had to continue) I never made it to the Rectorship, which is probably just as well, for I had some notions of reform which were too radical even for Leiden. Things like paying humble lecturers enough to live on, for example. The astute reader may notice that the matter of salaries is mentioned occasionally in these memoirs but let him not worry — there'll be blood enough to sate anyone's tastes sooner or later.

Whenever a man publishes his diaries there are always naysayers keen to tell him that he has misremembered. No, I haven't. I was there. It all happened exactly as I set it down. I am, after all, a man of the cloth. I don't lie.

I just get things wrong now and again, that's all.

CHAPTER ONE

I was enjoying a glass of wine with the Rector when there was a commotion outside. I cannot quite recall the order of events, but there was a woman's scream, the sound of rushing footsteps, a period of quiet, and then a stampede of feet on the stairs followed by an urgent hammering at the door. Before the Rector had given the command to enter, one of the kitchen boys threw the door open and rushed in.

'Rector, sir, you'd best come. There's been an accident.'

The Rector put his wine down and beckoned me to follow him. Quickly, but without running, we followed the boy downstairs and along the corridor towards the dining hall. Just before its doors we turned to the left, where a small crowd had gathered. The Rector demanded passage and the bystanders stepped aside to allow him through. I followed like a lapdog, with no authority of my own except the right to follow my master.

On the stairs was a man who had evidently tumbled down and broken his neck. The Rector gently eased the head towards us, and I found myself gazing into the staring eyes of —

Just a minute, Mercurius. You're getting ahead of yourself. Shouldn't you begin at the beginning?

I realise, gentle reader, that you probably want to know all about the body, but I pray you be patient. There will be bodies enough in time. I wish it were not so, but it is. Let us go back a bit.

Van Looy had a way of looking at you that made you feel he regarded you as slightly lower than a snail's belly.

'Ah, there you are!' he said.

'Indeed I am,' I replied.

'The Rector sent me to find you. Of course, I should have known you wouldn't be in the university library.' He looked around the interior of the inn on the Langebrug where I do most of my reading.

I find the silence of the library oppressive, and they don't serve drink there, so I pass much of my free time in the inn. At the moment when he interrupted me I was trying to finish Spinoza's *Tractatus Theologico-Politicus* as a matter of some urgency, since it had just been banned. Spinoza had backed the wrong side in the argument between the De Witts and the Prince of Orange. The De Witt brothers ended up being lynched by the mob, whereas the Prince of Orange became Stadhouder, which seems a pretty conclusive win to me.

Anyway, Spinoza's work defended democratic and constitutional government, which was not in fashion in the Netherlands in those days. The Reformed Church condemned his treatise, and therefore it was not a good idea for a lecturer of the University of Leiden, a Reformed institution if ever there was one, to be seen reading it. Fortunately, most of the customers at Steen's inn couldn't read, but Van Looy would undoubtedly have reported it if I had not quickly closed it as he spoke.

'Why did the Rector want me?' I enquired as levelly as I could, given my belief that Van Looy was one of those people who would look good impaled on a pike.

'I believe he has a task for you,' Van Looy responded, with just enough incredulity in his voice to make clear that he personally would not have entrusted me with peeing on a fire.

9

Although, come to think of it, if Van Looy were in flames nothing would give me greater pleasure.

I drank up, paid my bill and followed Van Looy through the streets of Leiden back to the Academy building on the Rapenburg. Conversation was sparse, which suited me perfectly. I concentrated on thinking holy thoughts, just to annoy Van Looy.

When we reached the door, Van Looy held it open for me, bowing slightly and saying, 'After you, Master.'

I politely responded, 'Thank you, mijnheer Van Looy,' just to rub in that he did not have a higher degree. I was rewarded with the distinctive sound of grating teeth.

The Rector was busy writing at his desk. His ink consumption must have been astonishing, because I rarely caught him doing anything else. He was a small man, neat, precise, tidy and very, very clever. Dressed as always in austere black with an old-fashioned white collar and a little black wool skullcap, his piercing blue eyes noted my arrival and he smiled slightly. The Rector liked me. He must have done, or he would not have allowed me the latitude that he did.

'Master Mercurius! Welcome! Please seat yourself.'

I humbly selected the bench along the wall.

'No, not there, man. Take the chair.'

That was a good sign. If you were in his bad books, the bench was your natural place. Errant students could pass an afternoon there as he harangued them.

'No doubt you are wondering why I sent Van Looy for you.'

I was, of course. A secondary question was why a man of sense would send Van Looy for anything.

'We have a considerable responsibility, Master Mercurius, standing, as we do, *in loco parentis*. Our charges are impressionable young men, many of them living away from home for the first time, and some of them in funds to a greater extent than ever before in their lives. One can understand the temptations that lie in wait to ensnare them.'

This was, no doubt, a reference to the whores who hover outside the university gates each evening. There is a fascinating thesis waiting to be written about the economics of prostitution, but even the simplest courtesan has mastered the law of supply and demand and realises that the best customers to court are those who have money. And while Leiden is a prosperous town, it has become so largely because its burghers place a high emphasis on thrift and saving. Which leaves the whores looking for business from the students, who take a different view of life.

All in all, 1674 was a hard time in Leiden. It was, however, the hundredth anniversary of the famous siege of the city, so plans were in hand for a celebration in October at which, I was sure, a re-enactment of the starvation of the population would not be a feature.

One happy result of the collapse of the 1574 siege had been the foundation of the University of Leiden in 1575 by the Prince of Orange, who wanted to reward the city for its heroic resistance, although what exactly is heroic about choosing not to drop dead is unclear to me. But it neatly returns us to the Rector's study, and the problem posed by importunate whores hanging around in the street outside. Incidentally, I had no vested interest in this. The whores have never been a problem for me, because they know how much we lecturers are paid. Those who fall within my price range are not at the select end of the market, so I would rather spend my money on beer and bread. Erasmus famously said that he spent his money on books, and if he had any left over, on food. I disagree. You can always borrow books, but you can't eat a loaf and give it back.

I realised, belatedly, that the Rector was still talking.

'I need hardly stress that the recent contretemps with the civic authorities is not in keeping with the best traditions of the university. We must do what we can to curb the high spirits of our young men, both for their sake and for that of the university's reputation.'

I began to see where this was leading, and I did not particularly like it. Staging uplifting moral lectures in the evening is not my preferred occupation. In any event, I was convinced that in a contest between my moral philosophy seminars and an evening between the ample breasts of Fat Lysbeth, I was unlikely to come out on top, if you'll pardon the expression.

'Tomorrow we have a general convocation of students, and I shall use the opportunity to deliver a few remarks *ex cathedra* to remind them of their responsibilities. But I am under no illusions, Mercurius, as to the likely success of that proposal. You, on the other hand, are much nearer their own age.'

I suppose when you're nearly seventy, someone of my age seems not much more than a teenager, though in fact the students would probably have viewed me as a relic of the Golden Age. I was, after all, almost thirty-six then.

'I intend to introduce you to them, and then withdraw so that you may address them privately, man to man. Mercurius, I'm too set in my ways. You speak their language.'

He was wrong there. Nobody speaks their language. They shamble around the lecture theatres grunting. Ask them a direct question and the likely answer is "Uh?"

'I'll try, Rector,' I replied, 'but what exactly would you like me to cover?'

'Well, I don't want to be too prescriptive, Mercurius. Perhaps a general reminder of their privileged position, their responsibilities to their family name, the shame they bring to their mothers by their antics, the duties of a Christian gentleman, a review of the seven deadly sins and the ten commandments, all of which are endangered by such goings-on, the evils of prostitution, venereal disease, gambling, excessive drinking, riotous and noisy behaviour, and the importance of observance of the Sabbath. That should do it.'

If that wasn't prescriptive, I don't know what is.

I said that I would retire to compose a suitable charge to the students, and bowed gravely. As usual, I attempted to walk backwards out of the room in a respectful fashion, and as usual I got a door handle up my arse for my pains. I would have sworn that the Rector sniggered, but when I raised my head he had his usual composed and benign appearance.

My first thought was that this required a couple of tankards of strong ale to inspire the muse, but it was growing late, so I sneaked down to the kitchen to see if anyone was around. Mechtild, that angel in human form, wife of Albrecht the master cook, who rescued her husband's "cooking", smiled when she saw me and wiped her hands on a towel.

'Master Mercurius,' she cried, 'what brings you below stairs?'

After a few minutes of light conversation, I was on my way up to my room with a jug of ale when I met Van Looy coming downstairs.

'Not going to the inn, Master?' he asked.

'No, I'm preparing a speech for the Rector,' I answered, hoping he wasn't going to look in the jug. 'But don't let me stop you,' I added cheerily.

'Hardly my preferred way of passing the time,' he responded. 'I shall sit in my chamber with an improving book.'

A book that improves you? Well, you won't be short of choices, I thought, but inclined my head and ascended to my own room to compose my thoughts. And eat the fig tart Mechtild had slipped in my sleeve.

Leiden is a university devoted to traditions, some of them utterly baffling. The students were formed up in pairs and paraded in the public streets to the Hooglandse Kerk, where they suffered a sermon from the minister which was not improved by substantial untranslated quotations from the original Greek New Testament. The students were then marched back to the Academy where the Rector addressed them vigorously and directly. He then introduced me and withdrew.

I waited until the doors had closed behind him, and then began my disquisition along the lines the Rector had laid down. I reminded them of the need to save a small fraction of their money for food, made passing references to a number of aspects of morality (but told them they would have to attend my lectures to get the detail) and warned them that God's grace is irresistible and that those whom God has unconditionally saved would face divine chastisement — and then moved on to whores and venereal disease.

It was at this point that I think I made my greatest impact. I recalled that the late Franciscus Sylvius, vice-chancellor of the university and professor of medicine, had once described to me a man who contracted the Spanish disease and whose *membrum virile* had fallen off. This seemed to make a profound impression on my audience, several of whom shifted uncomfortably and one of whom took a sly peek down his breeches. I omitted to mention that the detachment had occurred *post mortem* as his body was being wrapped in a winding sheet, but it was one of those stories that simply cries out for as little corroborating detail as possible. I think it quite likely that by the end of my talk the subdued response of the students was due to their resolve to visit a physician with all speed.

The students departed, and I collected my remaining notes and my bible with a view to reporting to the Rector. It was then I noticed that one student had not left the room.

'Thank you, Master,' he said, 'for that valuable advice.'

I dipped my head in gratitude for the thanks, and asked his name.

'I am Jan van der Horst. My father was here a generation ago.'

'Ah,' I responded, 'sadly I wasn't.'

'No matter. I believe the Rector taught him, but of course many of his other teachers are dead now.'

'No doubt. How have you settled in here?'

'Very well, thank you. Hearing you describe the city's whores and taverns, I almost regret that I have had nothing to do with either.'

'How very upright of you,' I said, thinking all the while what an insufferable little prig this fellow was.

'It's not moral rectitude, Master. It's the knowledge that my father would flay my hide with a strap if he found out I'd been doing it.'

'A fear of punishment is not a bad reason for forswearing sin, mijnheer Van der Horst.'

'No, perhaps not. But we ought to do the right thing simply because it is the right thing to do, wouldn't you agree? Forgive me, I'm keeping you. I look forward to our next meeting.'

He bowed politely, and was gone, leaving me to wonder why he had bothered to wait behind to converse. Had I missed something?

The Rector had received a report of my talk already by the time I stood before him. Since it was favourable to me, it cannot have been provided by Van Looy, yet I had seen no other member of staff there.

'One of the law students was good enough to wait upon me to convey his father's greetings and took the opportunity to tell me how uplifting he found your talk.'

'Van der Horst, by any chance?'

'Yes, that's him. I taught his father, you know. Old Van der Horst is now a minister somewhere near Haarlem, I believe.'

'I am surprised his son is not following him to the cloth, Rector.'

'The older son has. The younger one has been allowed to make his own way, and has chosen the law as a career. So many gifted young men do, you know.' The Rector rose from his chair and walked round the desk towards me. This was ominous. 'Since you have acquitted yourself so well, perhaps I may raise another subject with you, trusting to your sense of discretion.'

'Of course, Rector,' said my mouth, though my brain was already telling me this was getting worse by the minute.

'It concerns the university staff stipends.'

My heart sank. I could guess what was coming.

There was a scale of pay within the university, but some faculties did better than others. Needless to say, philosophy ranked right at the bottom. The scale was varied, of course; Professor Sylvius, whom I mentioned earlier, was employed at double the standard salary of a professor. Adriaanus Heereboord, one of my illustrious predecessors, had — during one of his increasingly infrequent sober moments — complained bitterly about the salary, and finally announced that since they were only paying him half the money he was worth, he was only going to work half the week. I never did work out which half that was.

However, Heereboord's point was that whereas lawyers and physicians could augment their salaries with private work, that option was not open to the masters of the school of philosophy because, by and large, people do not go out and hire a personal philosopher. It was therefore unjust, he claimed, that the university preferentially rewarded those who already had more earning potential. Much to my surprise, the authorities had finally conceded the point. No doubt they found it easier to do so now that Heereboord was dead. Anyway, the outcome was that some of us had received a very nice pay increase. Now, I supposed, the Rector was going to ask us to give it back.

'How can I help you, Rector?'

'The fact is, Mercurius, that at least a part of the recent controversy came about because the pay scale is so transparent. Everyone can work out what everybody else gets and that simply engenders envy, covetousness, and wrath. As you will appreciate, I cannot be a party to the encouragement of sin in my academic staff, any more than I can turn a blind eye to it amongst my students. So what I want you to do, Mercurius, is to come up with a system that is much more complicated. Of course, nobody who is here now will be disadvantaged, but we want to ensure that the Regents have much more … flexibility … in future appointments. We don't want to be seen to be making special cases all the time.'

'Don't you need a Jesuit for this?' I asked. 'They're good at this kind of thing.'

'Perhaps so, but we don't have any, and if I commissioned one to do the work for us I think he would smell the largest of rats.'

'I'll do my best, Rector,' I said, and began to lever myself out of my seat.

'There is one complication,' came the reply.

Of course. There always is. Nothing in my life is simple, except the lad who waxes my boots, preferably on the outside.

'The Stadhouder himself wants to approve the reform before it is promulgated. He has taken a keen interest in the affairs of the university and is distressed by the past instances of disorder.'

I told you that the Rector was very clever. Note the cunning way he had managed to shift the Stadhouder's potential displeasure onto someone else even before the work was done. And yet I still liked the man.

'How long do I have?' I asked.

'Oh, there's no rush. It's much more important to spend time getting this right than doing it quickly just to get it finished. Shall we say the end of the month?'

If I had protested it would have been to his back, since he immediately broke eye contact and turned away from me. So many little tricks I had to learn!

'And Mercurius…'

'Rector?'

'When you give the philosophy department the pay rise that will undoubtedly seem reasonable to you, may I suggest moderation?'

'Of course, Rector.'

'And discretion. It's probably best if nobody knows you're doing this.'

There's no "probably" about it, I thought. 'No-one shall hear it from my lips, Rector.'

'Excellent. The only people who know are you, me and, of course, Van Looy.'

I must have shuddered at the mention of his name or made the sign of the Cross or some such solecism, because the Rector continued: 'He is not a member of the teaching magisterium and therefore not included in your plan, but I have seen no reason to tell him so.'

Oh, what fun I shall have, I thought. Three whole weeks of Van Looy thinking that I'm setting his salary. That must be worth some favours. Or at least a bit of respect.

CHAPTER TWO

Coming from chapel a couple of days later, I chanced upon mijnheer Van der Horst again, in company with a couple of others of his age. One was a dark-haired man, possessor of a sparse beard and sallow skin, introduced to me as Molenaar. The other was a spotty youth with sandy hair and hardly any beard at all. While Molenaar seemed reserved and cautious in his speech, the other seemed angry about everyone and everything.

'You must forgive mijnheer Terhoeven, Master,' Van der Horst said with a faint smile. 'He finds much in the world in need of reform.'

'As do we all,' I answered. 'What is the point of the gospel, if not to change the way the world works?'

'My point exactly,' agreed Van der Horst. 'There is change ordained by the Almighty, and there is chaos. We must distinguish the two.'

I almost added there is change brought about by the authorities, which was usually a mixture of the two, but I let it pass. In those days you still had to guard your tongue to some extent.

'We all appreciated your little speech the other day,' said Molenaar.

'I cannot imagine why young men waste their time and money on wenching when there is so much to be done in the world,' added Terhoeven.

'Quite, quite,' I agreed. 'Though, of course, I am not well placed to judge what pleasure there might be in the company of a young woman.'

'A young lady is a very different thing to a whore,' offered Terhoeven, and was rewarded with a shudder from Molenaar at the very mention of the word whore.

Whatever this little group was, I was inclined to think that Molenaar was its brains, Van der Horst its mouth, and Terhoeven its heart. He was all energy and action, Van der Horst was suave and elegant, while Molenaar was made of caution. I suspect the first word he uttered as a child was "perhaps".

'I fear that we are giving you a misleading impression, Master Mercurius,' Molenaar said. 'We were on our way to the chapel to practise our music. Do you play?'

'Barely,' I answered, and even that was an exaggeration. My father bought me a viol when I was young, but I gave up when it could not be mastered in an afternoon. 'I sing a bit.'

Van der Horst's face lit up. 'You're not a bass, by any chance?'

'No, sadly not,' I replied, 'just a reedy tenor.'

'Ah, we already have one of those,' Van der Horst announced gravely, accepting a peeved buffet from young Terhoeven who had belatedly recognised the slight he had been offered.

'I hope, Master,' Molenaar interrupted, 'that you are not offended by the playing of music. It seems to us that so goodly an art cannot have been forbidden us by a God who is the source of all human gifts and knowledge.'

I understood his concern. There were those of a puritanical cast of mind who regarded music and musicians with suspicion. In the case of musicians this was understandable, since a more lascivious bunch of reprobates has not walked the earth, but anyone who has heard the great choral music of our age cannot object to its use by pious men and women. It was not many years since the Puritans of England had banned Christmas, the maypole, theatres and dancing, not to mention bear-baiting, of which they disapproved not because the bear did not enjoy it but because the spectators did. There were plenty of churches in the Low Countries without music, but others that cherished it. Within Leiden, the Marekerk had a fine organ, though in need of a bit of refurbishment.

'I certainly have no objection to music, mijnheer, any more than I reject art. The gifts bestowed by God can be used for good or ill as man chooses.'

Molenaar appeared almost enthused by my response. 'May we ask, Master, when you next preach? We must make sure that we are there.'

The ordained staff were wheeled out now and again for the edification of students. There were a lot of us, and since we employed a chaplain it was my view that he should do the bulk of the work, but the occasional sermon was unavoidable.

'31st October,' I replied.

'All Hallows' Eve! How splendid!' chuckled Van der Horst. 'It will be one for Satan to remember, I'm sure.'

He bowed politely, and his companions followed suit, though I think I detected that Molenaar was displeased at any teasing of Satan, and quite right too. It does no good to tweak the Devil's tail unnecessarily.

I took a long draught from the tankard and signalled for another. A sailor by the fireplace was in the middle of a highly entertaining and inventive story about a woman of the East Indies which was distracting me from the task in hand, namely, the devising of a system of remuneration for the magisterium that would defy any attempt at understanding.

The potboy put down my tankard and asked if I would be supping with them. As part of my employment, I have the right to eat in the university hall free of charge. Unfortunately, this arrangement does not include covering the physician's bill that would undoubtedly arise if a man were reckless enough to eat Albrecht's food every day. For that reason, a few coppers spent in the inn was often well invested.

'What's for dinner?' I asked.

'Rabbit stew,' came the answer.

There had been a certain monotony to the menu for a little while, so I should not have been surprised to hear this. The fields were filled with rabbits, and since a country that depends heavily on food it grows locally must be threatened by their incessant nibbling, rabbits were regularly hunted and the markets were full of the proceeds. Rabbit stew was cheap and nourishing, but you can have too much of a good thing.

The curious question was why there were so many of the large-toothed larcenists that year. A late summer was usually blamed, but I was inclined to the opinion that the flooding had killed many of their natural predators, allowing them to increase in numbers.

I declined the offer of supper, deciding instead to brave the incinerated delights of Albrecht's kitchen whilst hoping — I confess my sin — that he might burn his hand again and have to let Mechtild cook instead.

It was then that inspiration seized me and my prayers were answered. Whether this was the work of the Holy Spirit or three jugs of ale I leave to my readers to judge, but I found myself musing on the spectacular multiplication around us and the explanation offered by Master Hubertus, who taught mathematics to a small band of students who found such things interesting, often because they wished to become bankers in the hope that one day they would outstrip the Fuggers of Augsburg in their acquisitiveness. Holy Scripture tells us that the love of money is the root of all evil (First letter to Timothy, chapter six, I believe), which I have always thought a bit harsh on bankers and rather lenient on lawyers. Be that as it may, Master Hubertus introduced us to the rules of compounding, which is to say that rabbits do not simply multiply, but as more rabbits are around, the rate of rabbit production accelerates. If each pair of rabbits produces five baby rabbits who in turn produce five baby rabbits per couple, the increase can be precisely calculated. Not by me, of course, but Master Hubertus knew how it was done, so I gathered up my papers and headed for his room.

Mijnheer van Looy crossed my path as I proceeded thither. The man turned up everywhere. One would almost think he spent his days lurking in corridors.

'Your pardon, Master!' he said as I raced past him. 'You seem to be in a hurry?'

'I'm going to learn about compound interest,' I announced.

'Indeed? I'm sure any moneylender could explain it to you.'

'I'm sure they could, but I don't know any. Do you?'

We bowed politely and went about our business.

Master Hubertus conformed to all the stereotypes one can imagine about a university lecturer. His hair was unkempt and he made extravagant gestures with his arms as he explained things. If he had not worn a cleric's gown, he might well have been taken for a lunatic. Even so, he looked like a clerical lunatic.

His chamber was more untidy than mine, a circumstance which would have astonished many of my friends. The sense of disorder was heightened by the large slate hanging on the wall upon which he chalked his calculations, continuing along the wall when he ran out of space. I had seen such boards used by choirmasters but never by a mathematician, which led me to feel new respect for one who was such an early adopter of teaching technology.

'I hope I'm not disturbing you,' I said, indicating the abrupt end of the scribbling on the wall.

'Ah, no,' replied Hubertus. 'It continues over there.'

He pointed to a further area of scrawl behind the door. If a child had done this, we would punish him severely. The university, by contrast, had just promoted Hubertus.

'Are you interested in mathematics?' he enquired.

'Who isn't?' I responded, with my most encouraging smile.

'Most of my students, sadly,' he answered. 'They're only interested in double entry bookkeeping and calculating gambling odds correctly.'

'Shocking!' I tutted. I can tut with the best of them. It goes with the moral philosophy turf.

'What can I do for you, Master?'

'Rabbits!' I announced.

'I don't have any, I'm afraid.' He gestured about him to prove his point. He was quite right; his room was marked by a complete absence of lagomorphs.

'I'm not being clear, Master Hubertus. You told me once about a method for calculating the number of rabbits in a country after a period of time.'

'Compounding, yes, I recall. It has more practical uses too,' he added.

I sensed this would be a long visit and looked about me for a stool. Hubertus lifted some papers to reveal one and invited me to sit. Before doing so himself he poured two beakers of wine, managing to soak his cuff in the process.

'Let me lay out my problem for you, Master Hubertus. A certain man has some servants. He wishes to reward them for their service. He could simply divide the sum he has in mind between them, but that would reward the newest equally with the longest-serving. Then he recalls that a friend —' and here I raised my beaker to salute Hubertus — 'has recently explained to him how compounding can reward them more equitably.'

'Why doesn't he just give them one or two guilders for every year's service?' Hubertus asked.

'He could! Indeed he could!' I answered, having failed to think of this myself. 'But he wishes to honour his friend's ingenuity and adopt a more subtle approach.'

Hubertus took a draught from his beaker and stared into the distance. 'You — your friend — might apply an incremental rate and compound it according to the years of service, I suppose,' he murmured.

It was obvious that he considered this a complete explanation and proposed to say no more, so I was compelled to coax it from him.

'Which means?'

'Ah, you — your friend — will proceed thus. Let the man's portion be one.'

'One what? One guilder? One ducat?'

'One whatever. The unit is unimportant.'

'I think it's important to the recipient.'

'I am viewing it as a mathematical matter, Master. To me, the unit is unimportant. The calculation does not require to know it.'

'I beg your pardon,' I said, inwardly thinking that mathematics is a nonsense if it thinks that.

'Then let his portion at the outset be one. For each year of service, let his portion be increased by a fraction of one that we shall call x.'

'What is x again?'

'The incremental fraction.'

'Yes, but what number is it?'

'Any number you like. It might be a tenth or a twentieth part, for example.'

'Ah. I beg your pardon,' I said again, and indicated that he might continue.

'Then, after one year, his portion will have increased to one plus that twentieth part.'

'I see.' Surprisingly, I actually did. If you set a sum to increase by an increment of one twentieth part each year, after one year it will be one twentieth part larger.

'Now, after two years, how large will it be?' Hubertus asked.

'Two-twentieths?' I stuttered.

'No!' he cried, as if I were the greatest dunce in Christendom. 'That is the beauty of compounding! That would be to ignore the increment of the first year. After one year our man has not one guilder, but one guilder and one stijver, and you must increment both parts by that twentieth part. For the guilder he receives another stijver, but he also receives a twentieth part of his new stijver.'

A twentieth part of a stijver would be such a tiny sum that it would not be worth having, but I judged that to say so would expose me as a mathematical fool, so I just nodded sagely.

'And, in general, we may say that the man's portion after n years can be expressed as $(1+x)$ to the power of n, where x is the incremental rate.' Hubertus bounded up and wrote this formula on a corner of his slate. I hoped he would remember to rub it out before he included it in whatever calculation he was undertaking on the rest of the slate.

'So if we set x to be a twentieth part, how much would a man get after, say, thirty years?'

Hubertus set to with a will. 'About four and one-third guilders for every one he had at the outset,' he announced.

I could not imagine that the Rector would stand for a man's stipend being four times as large at the end of his career as at the start.

'What if it were a fiftieth part?'

Hubertus gulped, but reworked his calculations. 'One and four-fifths,' he finally announced, and finished off his beaker to recover the animation of his spirits, which must have been depressed by his efforts.

'I think my friend would be well satisfied with that result,' I exclaimed, patting Hubertus on the arm before I remembered his cuff was wet.

The intelligent reader, if such a man would deign to peruse this volume, might be asking himself why I have lavished so much attention on this mathematics. And, being intelligent, he will then recall that the Stadhouder himself had expressed an interest in my plan.

I took it to the Rector, suggesting a base salary for each grade of teacher, an augmentation depending on the subject taught, and then compounding to reflect the lecturer's length of service. This resulted in a number that could not easily be recalculated by anyone who had not had the method disclosed to him.

'This is splendid,' enthused the Rector. 'Logical, yet utterly opaque.'

'Thank you, Rector.' I bowed humbly again, and once again received a door handle up my arse for my pains, though in this case it was due to Van Looy abruptly opening the door.

'You asked me to remind you of your meeting with the Mayor, Rector,' he said.

'Thank you. But surely it is nowhere near midday yet.'

'It is not quite eleven o'clock, Rector.'

The Rector thanked and dismissed him. 'Why on earth tell me an hour early that I have an appointment? It makes no sense,' he grumbled.

It does if all you wanted was an excuse to come in and eavesdrop, I thought, but said nothing.

Thus it was that two days later I found myself boarding a barge that would take me to The Hague for an audience with the Stadhouder. I am bound to confess that I was rather excited. The Stadhouder is not exactly a king, though nobody had told William that. The office is bestowed on someone by each province, usually for life, but we had just concluded a long period without a Stadhouder. William's father had died when he was very young, so he had not succeeded to the title. The country passed into a sort of regency, but with time, power became concentrated in the hands of two brothers named De Witt. As I mentioned earlier, one day the mob turned on them, and they were lynched and their bodies treated abominably. I met a man once who claimed that he had Johan de Witt's penis. It presumably was some compensation for not having one of his own. I have met men who kept the skulls of animals displayed on their walls as trophies, which, I suppose, might testify to their bravery in the face of such creatures. I could not imagine what having a politician's penis on your mantelpiece might speak to.

Anyway, it is likely that William and his cronies incited the mob to act, because the outcome was that William found himself installed as Stadhouder, whereupon he ensured that the leaders of the mob received the most derisory of punishments.

I may as well say at this point that William's mother was the sister of the English king, Charles II, and William had spent some time in England where the king reputedly found him serious, pious and patriotic, and generally such dull company that he declared war on us. However, this little family tiff seemed to have been put behind us, and Charles had been at pains to point out that the argument was really with the De Witts and that he had liked his nephew all along. William, for his part, was too polite (and too clever) to call his uncle a barefaced liar.

When the barge drew up alongside the quay in The Hague, a troop of soldiers immediately approached to ask us our business. I had not been to The Hague for a couple of years, but I was struck by the fact that there seemed to be soldiers everywhere.

'I have been asked to appear before the Stadhouder,' I declared, and displayed the letter given to me by the Rector, sealed with the seal of the university. I suppose one seal looks much like another to a near-illiterate, so the soldiers merely nodded me through and two were deputed to lead me to the Stadhouder's quarters.

At the doorway to the Oude Hof, I was handed into the care of two other soldiers who insisted on inspecting my satchel for weapons. Albrecht had given me a pie for dinner which caused them some concern.

The older soldier hefted the pie between his hands. 'Feel the weight of that!' he said. 'You could kill someone throwing that crust at them.'

'I'm more worried about the filling,' I replied. 'Goodness knows what Albrecht has put in it.'

'Maybe we should keep it here,' said the sentry. 'You can collect it when you leave.'

'You won't eat it?' I asked, more in hope than fear.

'My teeth wouldn't cope,' he grumbled.

They ushered me through and told me to report to two more soldiers at the top of the staircase, who opened the grand door and announced me. If I thought that was all there was to it, I was swiftly disabused by another pair of soldiers inside the door who marched me to the far end of the room, where the Stadhouder was talking animatedly with a couple of officials.

He turned to greet me. 'Master Mercurius! Thank you for coming to The Hague. Did you have a pleasant journey?'

'Yes, thank you,' I replied. These people never want to hear the truth anyway.

'Would you like a cup of water?' he asked solicitously.

I had heard that he was a brave man, but I had never realised that he was sufficiently reckless to drink water. No wonder he was a martyr to piles. (There are some who attribute that affliction to certain practices, which I will not name here, involving young men of his court. I am bound to say that I saw no evidence of such predilections. If anything, the Stadhouder seemed to be indifferent to fleshly pleasures of any kind. However, I believe him to have been genuinely fond of his wife and cousin, Mary, and he was melancholic when she died at a young age.)

The Stadhouder was slightly built and rather short. He made up for this lack of physical presence by wearing a large black breastplate and strutting around armed to the teeth. He had a high hairline and a long, rather hooked nose. I know his portraits show such a nose but, believe me, the artists toned it down. It was much more misshapen than most artists were prepared to depict.

There was a brass bowl containing herbs sitting over an unlit brazier. I learned later that William suffered badly from asthma, and therefore such a bowl was always nearby so that the herbs could be warmed quickly in the event of an attack and he could then inhale the vapours to gain some relief. I surreptitiously sniffed the contents once, and on balance I think I would rather have taken my chances with the asthma.

I declined the water, and offered him a scroll on which I had laboriously copied the mathematical explanation described by Master Hubertus. The Stadhouder accepted it without breaking the seal.

'I think it best if we continue this discussion in my private chamber, Mercurius. Come with me. No, Pieters, you are not required at present.'

This last remark was addressed to his secretary, a man who appeared to have been chosen because his physique made his master look like a giant. If he had not possessed a sparse brown beard, he might have passed for a boy of ten.

We adjourned to the inner room where, to my great surprise, William dropped the scroll on his desk and completely ignored it thereafter. 'Remind me to break the seal on that before you leave, Mercurius.'

'I'm sorry, Stadhouder. I thought you wanted…'

'I wanted *you*, not *that*. It was merely a subterfuge to get you here without having to tell anyone why. Oh, I genuinely have an interest in the management of our universities, and I fully intend to read this at some time, but not now. We have more important matters at hand. Do sit.'

I waited respectfully until the Stadhouder had taken his own seat, then descended as gracefully as I could into the chair offered. I doubt I had ever sat in anything as luxurious in my entire life. It was covered in crimson silk embroidered with small gold lions, each lion having a little blue tongue. I have never seen a live lion, but I doubt that the blue tongue is an accurate representation.

The Stadhouder was speaking energetically. 'I need a trusted man to undertake a difficult task. The Rector suggested that you were the best he could offer, and told me about an incident in Delft that you managed very well.'

'Not everybody thinks so, mijnheer. Some people regret that the perpetrator was not hanged.'

William nibbled at an apple and waved his hand airily. 'You can never please everyone. I above all people know that. You found out why the girls were being taken, recovered two of them and restored the public peace. To my mind, that's a job well done. And it's exactly the kind of job I want you to do again.'

'Find missing girls?'

'No, Mercurius, restore the public peace. You will be aware that my coming to power roughly coincided with a popular uprising against the De Witt brothers.'

For "roughly coincided with", you could read "was a direct result of".

'The De Witt faction may lack its heads,' said William, who might, perhaps, have chosen his words more carefully, 'but it still exists. I am not blind to the fact that there are people who would be very happy to see me treated the same way as the De Witts.'

I judged that any protestations on my part would be misplaced. I had nothing against William — in fact, I might well have favoured him over the De Witts — but what he was saying was undoubtedly true. The breastplate was not just an item of fashion in his case.

'To that end,' he continued, 'I maintain a little army of informants around the country who do their best to ensure that I know what is going on.'

I could not resist. 'Even in Leiden?'

'Especially in Leiden. Education is a wonderful thing, but it sometimes encourages people to think on matters which are unsettling for them. It makes them unhappy and restless. I have a deep care for our universities, but they are the likeliest places for rebellion to fester, Mercurius.'

There was something in what he said. If you are working every hour to feed your family, you tend not to spend a lot of time plotting. But if your whole professional life is concerned with arguments and disputation, as mine is, then plotting could be second nature.

'Do you know a man called Gijsbert Voet?' asked William.

'Of course,' I said. How could I not? Voet, or Gisbertus Voetius, to give him his Latinized version, was a household name. Or, at least, he was in households where they talked a lot of religion and philosophy.

'Voet's family have long been loyal supporters of my family. His grandfather was imprisoned for backing my great-grandfather and died there without betraying us. His mother's family lost everything they owned in following us. I have absolutely no doubt about his loyalty. As you'll know, he is a professor in Utrecht and keeps me informed about matters there.'

Voet was a militant Calvinist who liked a good argument. Whereas some ministers had difficulty reconciling God's forgiving nature with His omniscience — strict Calvinist teaching held that if He knows everything, He knows whether you are damned or saved from the moment you are conceived, and nothing you can do can change that — Voet unflinchingly told us that in any clash between divine powers and human free will, there was only one winner, and that the only reason there was any debate about it was that some of his colleagues were flabby thinkers. The problem was that he insisted on telling people that to their faces. As a result, he was forced out of Leiden and eventually made his way to Utrecht, where he divided his time between lecturing and preaching in the Dom, Utrecht's cathedral.

'But surely Master Voet is a great age now?' I ventured.

'Past eighty, certainly,' said William. 'And that is part of the problem.' He selected another apple and offered me the bowl. It looked like this was going to be a longer audience than I had expected if I needed sustenance at this stage. 'It appears that just before Christmas, Voet collapsed in the pulpit of the Dom. It had only just been returned to us when the French invaders withdrew, and he was determined to preach there again at the first opportunity. Anyway, I hear he has not preached since, though he claims he has made a complete recovery. What I need to know, Mercurius, is whether he really has regained his full powers. If he hasn't, I need to find another loyal person to be my agent in Utrecht. Inevitably that will have to happen soon, but he could select his own successor.'

I found myself liking this assignment less and less with each sentence.

'The other thing that troubles me is that Voet's allegiance is well known. If I were plotting against me, the last thing I would do is go anywhere near Voet. So it may be that when he says the province is solidly loyal to me, he doesn't really know.'

'But surely you were only installed as Stadhouder there a couple of months ago?'

He waved his hand testily. 'That proves nothing except that a few important men thought they could force that through, whatever the opposition. I would go to Utrecht myself and face my enemies down, but I have pressing duties here. That's why I sent for you.'

If my heart could sink further than it already had, that was the moment.

'All you have to do —' Isn't it strange that as soon as you hear that phrase, you know what follows is well-nigh impossible? '— is go to Utrecht. Your cover is that I'm very happy with the work you've done in reorganising the salaries at Leiden, and now I want you to do the same for the university in Utrecht. Report to me on Voet's health, and if you find him hale and strong, by all means work with him to select a lieutenant who can take over from him. He won't like it, but I'll give you a letter saying it's my will and that there's no question of replacing him while he is well, but we must prepare for the inevitable.' He reached behind him and plucked a document from his desk.

'Forgive me, Stadhouder,' I stammered, 'but isn't this my report to you?'

'What? Oh, yes. One moment.' He rummaged through the papers and finally produced a pouch. 'Letters for Voet, for the university, the mayor and anyone else I could think of. Pieters thinks it's all about the salaries. Only the one addressed in my own hand to Voet tells him the real reason for your visit.'

It was as well he told me it was addressed to Voet, because I would never have deciphered his handwriting. I just hoped an old man with fading eyesight would be able to read the contents.

'If you find him failing, you have my commission to find someone else. Use your initiative. And I want an honest account of the loyalty of the public too. No gilding of the lily, Mercurius! I'm a plain man and I like plain talking.'

I felt like doing a bit of plain talking myself, in which the words "shove" and "backside" might have featured, but it would have put the Rector in a difficult position.

William handed me a small bag. 'Money for your expenses. Keep anything that's left at the end. Any questions?'

I decided that there were none. It seemed best. Instead, I took my leave and made for the door. Since I was in an unfamiliar place I didn't attempt to reverse out of the room, and William didn't seem to expect it, but just as I reached the doorway, he spoke one last time. 'Oh, Mercurius, just remember that Voet has a reputation for prickliness. Try not to antagonise him. I'm relying on you to be tactful.'

I could picture my dear mother falling off her stool with laughter at any suggestion that I might have to be tactful. I nodded my understanding of the request, closed the door, and marched off to find the nearest inn where nobody knew me and I could get outrageously drunk.

CHAPTER THREE

My resolve failed me. A habit of sobriety is difficult to shake off, even under the pressure of the kind of diplomatic mission to which I was supremely ill-suited, so I just had a couple of beakers of ale and picked at the calf's liver I was served for meat.

It was a sombre journey back along the canal that evening, and I was in a dark mood as I arrived at the hall just in time to see Albrecht removing the last of the dinner plates. I was weighing up whether this was a blessing or not when I spied Mechtild swiftly laying a place in a corner.

'Bless you, Master, we thought you wouldn't be back in time for supper,' she said.

I am sure I heard Albrecht mutter "He isn't", but he seemed to unaccountably knock his shin on something as he passed Mechtild.

'The best is gone,' she added, 'but you'll take some bread and a piece of the roast, I hope?'

It was quite difficult to identify what particular species of animal had been subjected to the fiery furnace of Albrecht's oven, but I think it might have been mutton. Anyway, it was very welcome, especially when Mechtild produced some fresh bread, a jug of her beer and a fine pear to round it all off.

A miserable day was capped off when I looked up from my plate in response to a shadow falling over my food to discover Van Looy standing over me. If you had set his remaining hair alight, he would have made a passable lighthouse.

'The Rector saw that you had returned, Mercurius, and hopes that you will find it convenient to report to him soon. Shall we say ten minutes?'

'Shall we say when Hell freezes over?' was what I wanted to reply, but I just nodded meekly.

The Rector was sitting reading by his fireplace when I arrived. 'Mercurius! Come in and sit down. A glass of wine, perhaps?'

There was no uncertainty about it. I accepted with alacrity.

'Did it go well?'

'Very well, thank you, Rector. In fact, the Stadhouder has asked if I might be permitted to travel to Utrecht to repeat the exercise at the university there.'

Given that I had no idea who was watching whom, nor who was under suspicion, and that I had been strictly charged to keep my task confidential, I did not mention my real motive for going to Utrecht.

'I know,' said the Rector. 'He wrote to me. The postboy was quicker than you were, though I suppose he had a horse. Well, it redounds to the credit of this university that you have been selected for this duty, so well done, young man!'

He raised his goblet in a toast, which I acknowledged. I had no idea where the Rector got his wine, but it plainly was not the same stuff we quaffed downstairs. This was like liquid silk, whereas the wine served at the hall dinners was more like fruit juice mixed with vinegar.

'When do you propose to leave?' he asked.

'The Stadhouder is keen to have the matter concluded quickly,' I began, 'so perhaps I should go first thing on Monday.'

'Do you have any duties that I must give to some other lecturer?'

This was always a tricky one. The work of a lecturer is not, on the face of it, especially arduous, but if I told the truth it might cause someone to wonder what we were paid for. Someone like Van Looy, for instance. Whatever I thought of him, it could hardly be denied that he put the hours in. Whatever hour it was when I came to the Academy building, he always seemed to be around.

'I have a lecture to give tomorrow, Rector, then I must mark some assignments on Saturday. I can leave them with Van Looy for the students to collect, if you will permit.'

'Yes, of course. If they have any questions, I'm sure we can find someone to answer them.' He sipped his wine and gazed into the fire. 'Van Looy himself is not an imbecile.'

I was about to say 'You surprise me' but judged better of it. 'What makes you say that, Rector?'

'Hm? Oh, he makes himself out to be just a competent secretary, but I have seen him reading English books with apparent ease.'

'Where did he come from?'

'I think he had been working as a family tutor somewhere. I was persuaded by a friend to give him a trial as secretary. Of course, when the French came a number of families fled and could no longer support all their servants.'

'That would have hurt his pride.'

'Which is considerable. But perhaps there is such in his past as makes it understandable, Mercurius. Well, your plan is approved. I understand you have been given some expenses.'

'I have.'

'Then I'll let you get on with whatever you need to do before you go.'

He stood, so I did the same, not forgetting to drink the last of my wine. It was too good to leave. As I reached for the door, he spoke again, as if in passing, though I suspect it was the main question he wanted to ask.

'Did the Stadhouder say anything about this university?'

'Only that he takes a keen interest in it, as he does with all our universities. He said nothing critical, Rector.'

The Rector nodded. 'Good, good. There is a lot of change going on, Mercurius, and some of us adapt to it better than others. Personally, I have never been a lover of novelty, but I must breast the tides or be dashed on the rocks.'

Rather than wait until Saturday, I decided to complete the marking of the assignments on Friday, however long it took, so that I could leave for Utrecht at the earliest opportunity. To save as much time as possible I took my meals in the hall, despite the obvious risk to my digestive system posed by taking two of Albrecht's meals in a single day, and I am pleased to report that the midday meal was surprisingly palatable, hinting that Albrecht was out somewhere.

Fridays are a problem for me, because I am a Roman Catholic and therefore I do not eat meat. However, because I am a secret Roman Catholic I have to try not to draw attention to the fact that I am not eating meat.

While Catholic students are admitted, the University is a pillar of the Reformed (that is, Protestant) faith, and my job depends upon my being an adherent; which I was, when I was appointed. However, for reasons which have nothing to do with this tale, I converted to Catholicism and was ordained a priest in 1664, with strict instructions not to reveal the fact to anyone. The reason for this injunction was the fear of my bishop that all his priests might be rounded up and burned, in which event it is a good idea to have some spares to hand.

It had become clear to me about three years earlier that the Rector had somehow detected my dual life, but had chosen to say nothing about it, thus earning my complete respect and obedience, not to mention my suspicion. Why would so intelligent a man turn a blind eye to something he must have found troubling and objectionable?

Anyway, I could see no answer to that question, so let me simply remark that my usual habit on a Friday was to take as little meat as possible, and just leave it on my plate. Readers of my first memoir may recall that on one Friday I departed from this custom, concealed the meat in my sleeve and was attacked by a stray dog. On this particular Friday I bumped into Mechtild in one of the passageways and, once I had regained my equilibrium, I arranged to have some bread and cheese set by on a platter for my supper.

'Don't trouble yourself to come down, Master,' she said. 'I'll bring it to your chamber just before we serve the meal to the others.'

I thanked her again and returned to my work, marvelling, not for the first time, at the ability of our undergraduates to both fail to grasp an idea and to express that deficit in poor Latin. I am regularly told, and I believe it to be true, that our graduates are the equal of any in Christendom, which leads me to ponder what happens to men as they pass from undergraduate to graduate, because if our undergraduates are the equal of their European counterparts then the future of learning is bleak indeed.

The afternoon slipped into a glorious summer evening, giving me plenty of light but tearing me away from work. It would have been so pleasant to have been at leisure, strolling along the canals and enjoying the sun; I might even have enjoyed vespers, unlikely as that sounds. Nevertheless, I plodded on, turning page after page of juvenile twaddle. I exempt one or two students from these strictures (as I must, since one of my former students is now Rector of the University) but it was a depressing experience, and I was glad when I completed the pile shortly after seven o'clock.

I gathered up the papers with a view to delivering them to Van Looy as agreed, but it occurred to me that he might have gone to the refectory, so I detoured in that direction first. Not finding him, I thought to leave them in his office. In the normal run of things, that would require me to go back to the main hallway and up the staircase, but since I was at that end of the building I decided to take the back stairs used mainly by the servants, which would be quicker. There was a risk that Van Looy would descend by the main stairs and we would miss each other, but I can't take two staircases at once so why not take the nearer one?

I arrived at the top, not without some effort, and had paused to compose myself when I overheard Van Looy's voice. The stairs opened onto the passageway to the side of Van Looy's office, so he would not have seen me there.

'I know my duty!' he snarled. 'But these things must not be rushed. In my own good time I will strike, but that time is not yet come.'

'We cannot wait indefinitely,' came the reply, delivered in a gruff voice that I did not recognise.

'I do not expect you to. You may tell our master all is in hand. But I want to be sure that all the fish are in the net before I lift it. Who knows what mischief even one survivor could do?'

There was silence for a short while, then the gruff voice spoke resignedly. 'We must accept your way of doing things.

After all, it is your neck that is at risk. I will meet you again in a month.'

'Gladly, but not here. Send word when you arrive and I will suggest a meeting place. Now, be off, and Godspeed.'

The stranger stepped out into the corridor, and you may be sure that I ensured that I was out of the corridor and safely tucked around the corner. When I was sure he was heading the other way, I sneaked a peek and saw the back of a man wearing a short black cloak, a broad-brimmed black hat, apparently with no wig, and a sword at his left hip in a scabbard with a gold mount at the top.

My curiosity being piqued, I decided to retrace my steps to see if I could arrive at the foot of the main staircase at the same time as the visitor, but having my arms encumbered with papers, not to mention a rather greater distance to cover, I failed. Arriving there, I thought I might as well carry on up the stairs to approach Van Looy's office from that side, which I duly did. It was locked.

Growling at being thus thwarted, I returned to my own room, just in time to see Mechtild returning to the kitchen with my supper. I called her and was pleased to see her attempting to turn in the narrow passage, hampered to some degree by a large board bearing bread, butter, cheese and a fresh egg custard.

'I didn't see egg custards on the tables below,' I remarked.

'You wouldn't have done, Master,' she replied. 'But there was space in the ovens to bake a few for my special gentlemen.'

I unlocked the door and offered to take the board from Mechtild, but the restricted space meant that I was no help to her, so she suggested that she should just carry it into my chamber.

I have, I hope, some virtues but I also have some vices. One of them is a certain lack of tidiness which has beset me from my childhood years. I had not noticed that one of my boots was in the middle of the floor. Mechtild, unable to see her feet due to the large board that she carried, tripped over it. With great presence of mind she held the food in front of her so that it survived the fall, but she came to rest face down on the floor with her skirts tangled about her knees. I stooped to pick her up, but she was a substantial woman and I needed to move my hands several times before I achieved a good grip under her armpits. I had succeeded in pulling her about halfway to her feet when a cough distracted me.

Behind us stood Van Looy in the doorway. 'I heard a noise,' he explained. 'I beg your pardon. I did not mean to intrude.'

He turned to walk away, whereupon I belatedly realised that a man grasping a woman from behind with her skirts disordered while she leans on a chair to support her weight was open to the most appalling misconstruction. I let go of Mechtild to chase after Van Looy, causing her to flop across the chair head first with a groan.

'Van Looy! Van Looy!' I cried. 'It's not how it appears.'

He stopped in the corridor, turned and stood with a horribly understanding look on his face. 'Don't worry, Master. I am discreet.'

'But I wasn't doing anything! Well, nothing discreditable anyway.'

'You are an unmarried man, I believe, and therefore free to take such pleasures as you will; but you will forgive my observation that our cook's wife does not enjoy such liberty.'

'I had no liberties in mind. Mechtild offered to bring supper to my room so I could complete my marking before I have to go to Utrecht.'

'Then let me not keep you from it.'

'I've finished it. I just tried to deliver the papers to your office but it was locked.'

Van Looy frowned. 'Just now?'

'Yes.'

'I had a visitor and escorted him to the door.'

Well, that's a lie for a start, I thought, but I was hardly in a position to argue with him. Instead I thought there was an opportunity to show that I knew it to be untrue, but was prepared to keep it our mutual secret, so long as he dropped this Mechtild nonsense. 'A gentleman with a fine gold-topped scabbard? I saw him leave as I was coming up the stairs.'

I declined to say which stairs. If Van Looy assumed I meant the main stairs, that was his misapprehension. I had not lied, which put me firmly on the higher moral ground in this conversation.

'I fear you are mistaken, Master,' Van Looy suggested. 'I had no such visitor. Perhaps the poor light in the upper corridor —'

'I am not mistaken, Van Looy. I saw him clearly.'

Van Looy looked me up and down for a moment like a farmer appraising a young ox. 'I suggest we both go about our business,' he replied. 'Your supper is waiting and I have some work to do. Maybe I can do you a service by taking those papers with me?'

I went back into my room to collect the papers. Mechtild was sitting in my chair, holding her hand to her brow. I had completely forgotten to check that she was unhurt. She glanced up at me and made to rise.

'No, don't!' I cried.

She flopped back into the chair, and I suddenly realised why she had a red patch on her shoulder.

'Van Looy! In here, man!'

Van Looy's face displayed the greatest possible consternation, but he acted swiftly. Taking Mechtild's legs, he ordered me to help him place her horizontally on the floor, and placed his folded coat under her hips to raise them a little.

'Have you a cloth or towel, Mercurius?'

I found one, and he soaked it in the water from my jug before holding it tightly to Mechtild's head.

'Find a surgeon. The gash is deep.'

I ran to the refectory and found one of the medical faculty. He appeared unwilling to leave his soup until I told him his patient was Mechtild, at which he grabbed his robes about him and sprinted for the stairs, explaining to me as we went that if anything happened to her we should have an unrelieved diet of Albrecht's fire and brimstone cuisine.

Within a few minutes the surgeon had staunched the bleeding, dressed the wound and returned to his meal. Van Looy offered to help me tidy my chamber, but I thanked him and gave him the assignments to hold for the students to collect.

It was only as I sat tranquilly at my desk that two thoughts occurred to me that had been suppressed in my excitement. One, that I had never before been addressed by my name by Van Looy; two, that someone had opened the Stadhouder's pouch.

I sat watching the last of the sun's rays flicker away, a goblet of wine in my hand, my bags packed by my feet, and my desk blessedly clear for once.

There were only two people in the room when the pouch was opened, and one of them was lying on the floor with a cold compress on her face, which, to my simple mind, strongly hinted at the guilt of the other. Admittedly the pouch was embossed with the Stadhouder's arms, so its origin was hardly a secret, but it had been sealed with a thin leather cord that ran through eyelets to draw the bag shut. Why had Van Looy not resealed the pouch when I would never have known that he had looked at its contents? He had not taken anything; indeed, he had not broken any of the seals on the documents. All he knew was that I was carrying letters from the Stadhouder to various persons in Utrecht. Even the money was untouched.

Now that I had calmed down, I was very grateful that none of those letters had been abstracted, because I would not have relished having to return to The Hague to ask the Stadhouder for a new set.

Suddenly I realised why Van Looy had not resealed the pouch. You only need one hand to untie a bow, but you need both hands to re-tie it, and one of his hands was pressing on Mechtild's brow to stop the bleeding. When I returned to the room, his hand had been on my desk as he knelt on the floor, after which he must have felt that he could not pick the pouch up to secure it without drawing attention to what he had done earlier.

I returned the supper board to the kitchen — the egg custard, by the way, was superb, if a little asymmetrical due to Mechtild's nose having struck the pastry at one side when she fell — and found Albrecht sharpening his knives in the large pantry.

'Master Mercurius, I would have fetched it later,' he said. 'It would have waited until the morning.'

'Ah, but I am off to Utrecht in the morning.'

From the look of awe on Albrecht's face, you might have thought I was about to sail to the Cape of Good Hope in a barrel. 'Utrecht, you say? That's a fair step.'

'Above ten leagues. But I'll take the canal boats down the Oude Rijn and Leidse Rijn through Harmelen. I'll be there by late afternoon, God willing.'

'God willing indeed, Master.'

'How is your wife?' I asked, and was rewarded with a dark look as if I had been branded across the forehead with the word "Wife-tripper".

'She has something of a headache, Master, and has taken to her bed.'

'I'm sorry to hear it, Albrecht. I won't disturb her, then, and wish you both goodnight.'

CHAPTER FOUR

There is rarely any difficulty finding a bargemaster who will take you down the Oude Rijn. They already have a cargo, so any fee they collect from a passenger is pure profit. While there are regular passenger barges, they start at a time more convenient to the moneyed classes, whereas I am happy to set out early. When I say "happy", I use that word in its loosest sense, because I have never been one for rising any earlier than necessary. One of the key reasons why I have not sought ministry in a church is the iniquitous practice of having early services, by which I mean anything before nine o'clock. However, I prefer to arrive at an unfamiliar destination in daylight, so shortly after six I was on the quay looking for a barge heading towards Utrecht and was rewarded at my second attempt. For once, the barge was not carrying any noisome cargo, if you exclude a man in an old woollen cloak who smelled like a wet sheep, and when it began to rain the master produced an oiled cloth and connected it to the gunwales on each side to make a small tent under which we could shelter.

The tow-horse kept up a steady pace, and soon we were free of the city and heading roughly eastwards. The rain stopped and the sun was shining into our faces as we passed through the fields and hamlets until we came to Hoorn after about an hour and a half, where the horse was rested and we had the chance to take some breakfast, which the locals were only too willing to sell us at hugely inflated prices. From Hoorn to Utrecht is about six hours, so with one more break for food we arrived in the late afternoon.

One of the advantages of being a minister is that you rarely have to look too hard to find the local branch office. The Dom towered over the other buildings, so it took me no time at all to present myself at the main door and ask for directions to Voet's house.

'Why, bless you, Dominie, it's just beside the square,' answered the verger, and walked me to the door so that he could point it out. I thanked him and presented myself at the front door, where I was greeted by a young maid.

'I am Master Mercurius, of the University of Leiden,' I began. 'Is your master at home?'

'Yes, Master,' came the reply. 'Who shall I say is calling?'

'Master Mercurius, of the University of Leiden,' I tried again. 'Wait — I have a letter of introduction. That may help.'

She closed the door, then immediately reopened it to invite me to wait in the hall while she took the letter to her master. After a while, she returned to say that her master would be pleased to see me in the library.

I have a library. For many years I could not afford one, and even now it is really just a corner of my suite of rooms. Voet, however, had a library worthy of the name. When the door was opened, I gasped.

I learned later that at his death he was reckoned to possess 4,777 books. He even had some he could not read, written in languages he had not yet learned. Since he was eighty-five when I met him, time to learn new ones was not plentiful, but he kept trying. He spoke languages that I did not know existed.

The old man was sitting in a large chair, his eyes bright and inquisitive. In some respects he reminded me of our Rector. Their taste in clothing was similar, black and white being favoured and each wearing a black skullcap most of the time. Voet was clean-shaven and had rather sunken cheeks. As a result of having lost some teeth, he occasionally emitted an involuntary whistle as he spoke.

'Master, welcome! Sit ye down. Anna, some refreshment for our guest!'

I thanked him and selected a stout chair by the wall.

'Bring it nearer, young man. My hearing is not as sharp as it once was, and there's no sense denying it. I see you have the approval of the Stadhouder. That is no mean achievement.'

'You have it yourself, Professor,' I replied politely.

'I have, I have, God be thanked for it. His family were ever a blessing to us, and I thank God that I have lived long enough to see the French gone from this city and a member of the House of Orange restored to his family's rightful place. He fares well, I hope?'

'Yes, I believe so. He suffers from asthma but otherwise seems healthy.'

'I have read his letter. Do you know its contents?'

'No, Professor. I have, of course, received commands of my own,' I added, lest he should think I was a mere messenger boy.

'Well, I see no harm in telling you what I read here. The Stadhouder tells me that you have come on a secret mission at his command, that I am to give you every assistance and that you will tell me what you are here to carry out. He also tells me that, for public consumption, it is to be announced that you are conducting an inquiry into the stipends paid to university lecturers.'

'I have recently conducted such an exercise in Leiden,' I said, 'so the explanation is plausible.'

'Excellent. Now, how may I be of service?'

I had to think quickly. You may be sure that throughout my journey I had been thinking how to break the news to an old man that his master thought he might die at any moment and therefore a substitute must be found. There is an axiom which says that if you have to break bad news, a little good news first sweetens the palate. It seemed as good an approach as any. 'The Stadhouder wishes me to say first that he was distressed to hear of your indisposition and asks me to enquire of you how you feel now.'

'If he is worried that my powers are diminished, he need have no concerns. I am as sharp as ever.' I did not doubt that. 'I will admit,' he continued, 'that I find standing for prolonged periods to be a strain, but my faculties are preserved, God be praised.'

'Amen,' I swiftly answered. 'The Stadhouder will be delighted to hear that, and I can see myself that it is true.'

Voet visibly relaxed before me, and his frown smoothed away.

'He also wishes me to express his profound and heartfelt thanks for all that you and your family have done for him and his family.' Admittedly he had not actually told me to say that, but it was undoubtedly true, and it was well received by my audience of one. 'And, in view of the high regard that he has for you, he desires me to ask for your help in finding men of discretion and loyalty who will be able to assist you now and, when it pleases God to take you to your well-earned reward, maintain the honour of the House of Orange in Utrecht.'

I thought this speech, whilst a bit flowery for my liking, and perhaps open to the stricture that I had laid on the flattery with a trowel, was sufficiently emollient not to cause offence. I was wrong.

'I am to be replaced?'

'Not in your lifetime, Professor. The Stadhouder was most insistent on the point. He merely felt that your illness had shown him how much he depends upon you, and bearing in mind that none of us is immortal, he is anxious to secure your invaluable advice on others who can be trusted when the need arises. Which, pray God, will not be for many years.'

Voet was not exactly mollified, but he looked less likely to leap from his chair and belabour me with a volume of his collected sermons. 'If I knew such men of unquestionable loyalty, do you not think I would have lightened my burden already?' he growled.

'I am at your disposal to help you find one or more,' I said.

'My grandson, Johannes, son of my deceased son Paulus, although only twenty-six years of age, has just been awarded a Professorship here.'

I knew nothing of Johannes, but I had heard of Paulus. While unswervingly loyal to the House of Orange, Paulus had written a treatise, *De Statutis*, in which he had argued that a citizen was not obliged to follow the order of a sovereign if it was contrary to the law of God. Our beloved Stadhouder regarded this as near treason, and had Paulus not had the good sense to die early he might have expected some consequences of his publication. As it was, William regarded Paulus' son with suspicion, as tainted by his father's opinions. But how could I explain that to the old man?

I am not noted for my cunning. I am a plain man and I do not take naturally to underhand or deceitful methods. [Memorandum to self: my clerk, Van der Meer, snorted when I dictated this. I must not forget that.] 'The Stadhouder will, of course, be delighted to see that your family's tradition of loyalty and service is to be maintained,' I said. 'But he was anxious that if his opponents are temporarily in the ascendancy, it could mean real difficulties for your kin and lead them into some danger.'

'They understand that. Johannes will not shirk his duty.'

'I am sure, and I look forward to meeting him. But perhaps we should have a name in reserve, just in case?'

Voet looked doubtful. 'I wouldn't want my grandson to be overlooked,' he began.

'Nor would I,' I chipped in. 'The Stadhouder is not going to question your judgement.'

He fixed me with a stern, appraising gaze. 'Where are you sleeping tonight? You are welcome to stay here if it suits you.'

'That is very kind,' I replied, bowing my head to acknowledge his gracious offer. There was no point in telling him I had a letter from the Stadhouder in my pouch ordering him to accommodate me.

'Then I propose to invite my grandson to dine with us. That will give you the opportunity to see what a fine fellow he is, and we can continue this discussion then. And now you will no doubt wish to wash off the dust of the road.'

This was an entirely transparent way of telling me to leave him in peace.

Voet rang a little bell to summon Anna. The maid appeared at speed, wiping her hands on her apron and attempting to curtsey while still moving, a feat of co-ordination which appeared to be beyond her powers and which led her to stagger as she came to a halt.

'Please show Master Mercurius to the rear chamber, where he will be our guest. Tell cook there will be two more for supper. Then go to my grandson's house and tell him I will be gratified if he will sup here tonight.'

Anna's lips moved as she silently repeated her three tasks, instilling no great confidence in me that all three would be remembered and accomplished, then headed for the front door.

'Anna!' Voet called. 'Master Mercurius first, if you please.'

The room was comfortable, though not luxurious, and furnished by a man whose guests were usually very like he was himself. It sported a desk under the window and a shelf on which some books stood. I noted that they were arranged in alphabetical order of their authors' surnames, and therefore obviously not by Anna, who was probably acquainted with the letters A and N but not much else.

In fairness to her, I must observe that she was solicitous and brought me a bowl of hot water to wash in. Needless to say, she forgot the towel and had to go back for it.

You can learn a lot from servants, so I make it my practice always to engage in some light conversation with them when I can, and I did so when she returned with the towel. 'Thank you, Anna, you're very kind,' I said, and smiled in what I thought was a benevolent way. She immediately grasped the top of her apron as if I meant to deflower her on the spot. 'What time will supper be?'

'I don't know, Master. I could ask the cook?'

'Please don't bother. I just wanted to be sure I wouldn't keep the family waiting. Do you know Professor Voet?'

'Yes,' she answered. 'I work for him.'

I realised my mistake. 'I meant his grandson.'

'Oh, the young professor. Yes, Master, he comes often. He likes to see that his opa is doing well.'

There was something about her use of opa rather than grandfather that I found touching, and I wondered how Johannes would address the older man.

'To be a professor at such a young age he must be very clever.'

'He must,' agreed Anna. 'He can do writing and everything.'

The idea that anyone could become a professor without being able to read and write had not, I confess, occurred to me, but I suppose if you have little use for writing in your life you might be impressed by those who do it. Though not, one assumes, by the Stadhouder's scrawl.

Anna bobbed a curtsey and left the room, though not, apparently, the house, because I heard Voet shouting to her to remember her visit to Johannes' house. The back door slammed at once and I could see Anna running across the lane. It cannot have been far because she did not take a cape or shawl.

I sat in the chair and considered the options. The Stadhouder had not expressly forbidden the employment of Johannes. His notes expressed some reservations about his father's views, certainly, but his bigger concern was that anyone ill-disposed to the House of Orange would at once lock up Gijsbert Voet and probably the rest of his family for good measure. While I had tried to imply that William was concerned about their safety, I doubt the Stadhouder cared much about anyone's safety but his own. However, he was a very practical man, and the difficulty of having his party in Utrecht hampered so easily would certainly have occurred to him.

Having been instructed to be discreet about my visit, I had not been able to do any useful research among colleagues at Leiden, some of whom might well have known Johannes, but I knew the bones of his career. Having graduated from Utrecht (and how it must help a student's prospects if his grandfather is Rector of the university!), he went to work in Germany. Around the time of the liberation of Utrecht he returned to take up a professorship in law (and how it must help a lecturer's prospects if his grandfather is Rector of the university!). I do not cast any aspersions on his ability — as I came to realise, he was a gifted man — but I wonder how different my life might have been if my grandfather had not been doing whatever it was he should have been doing when he was in the tavern. I have never been exactly sure what his trade was, but that literacy was seemingly not involved is attested by my grandmother's repeated applause when I write something in front of her. When I successfully defended my Master's thesis I thought she should have the first bound copy, and took it to her. She wept tears of joy, opening it at random and looking at the pages with delight. It rather spoiled the moment when I turned the book the right way up.

The alert reader will recall that the alleged justification for my presence in Utrecht was to review the salaries of the university staff, so I occupied myself before supper by walking to the university offices and presenting my credentials. To my great delight these caused immediate and gratifying consternation, and it seemed to me that I was to be indulged in almost any whim that came to mind. In no time they had found me a chamber to use, provided me with a small lockable chest for my papers and enquired solicitously about any feelings of hunger or thirst that I might have. I am fairly certain that if I had asked for six nuns to be sent to my bedchamber they would at least have made the effort.

As I anticipated, the salaries at Utrecht were generally lower than ours. While Leiden's university dated from 1575, Utrecht's was founded in 1636. It was therefore only a little older than I was myself, and its scale was smaller. The French occupation had caused it some inconvenience and some of the staff had fled, leaving it short of competent lecturers, though this does not explain Johannes Voet's appointment. As I hope will become clear, he had great gifts.

I locked the papers in the chest, placed the key in my pouch, and returned the room key to the clerk in the office, who shot to his feet as if a small devil had attacked his fundament with one of those red-hot pokers we hear so much about.

'Thank you for your co-operation. I shall return tomorrow.'

'Tomorrow? But tomorrow is Sunday.'

I had completely lost track of time or I would not have said something so stupid, especially given that I was wearing clerical costume. No doubt the clerk was wondering what kind of churches we have in Leiden where even the clergy don't go on Sundays.

'Forgive me. I meant Monday.'

He sighed with relief and rushed to hold the door open. I was so unused to such a display of servitude that I almost put a few coppers in his hand as a tip.

I draped my cloak over the end of the bed, rinsed my hands and stepped downstairs to the parlour. Voet was still in his chair, scribbling furiously, but the stack of paper beside him had grown perceptibly in the time that I had been out.

I could see no sign of Johannes Voet. It crossed my mind that his grandfather's invitation — or summons — might not have been convenient and that I would be denied the opportunity of meeting him.

'My grandson will be here on the hour,' announced the ancient professor.

'I admire punctuality,' I remarked, without adding 'in everyone but myself'.

'It is a matter of practicality. If he leaves his house on the first stroke of the bell, he will be here as the last stroke dies.'

That probably doesn't work as well if he comes for lunch at one, I thought, but said nothing.

'You'll take a beaker of wine?'

'Thank you, Professor.'

'So will I. You'll find it on that table by the fireplace.'

I poured two beakers, though the word beaker is generously applied here. I've seen bigger thimbles.

'I trust you received every courtesy at the university,' Voet began.

'Indeed I did. The clerk was most co-operative.'

'Excellent. He is a good man. Scrupulously loyal.'

"Loyal" was drawn out as if to emphasise it to me.

'I have made arrangements to continue the work on Monday.'

'Very good, very good. I have been giving your comments much thought. I can see that if anything were to happen to me, it would be unfair to give Johannes the additional burden of political duties when he is managing the family's affairs.' I sighed with relief. He had seen the light. 'Therefore, I think it important to take him into our confidence now, while I am around to provide some support.'

'That is very wise,' I stammered, while praying that the Almighty would regard this as merely a little white lie.

'Please speak freely in front of him. I will vouch for his discretion.'

'I would not dare to doubt it, Professor. And the Stadhouder himself bade me to take your advice.'

Voet smiled. Either that, or he had heartburn; but I think he was pleased.

It seemed only a few moments later that the clock struck the hour. I was gazing out of the front window when the back door opened and Johannes entered, an event signified by Anna's dropping of a wooden platter.

Johannes strode through from the kitchen, fixed his cloak to a peg in the hallway and bowed to me. 'Good evening, Master; good evening, Grandfather,' he said. His voice was pleasing, richer than his grandfather's, though we must allow for the old man's great age.

Johannes was a little taller than me, with brown hair and eyes and a ready smile. Even in repose there was a slight upturn of the mouth at each corner that suggested an incipient display of pleasure.

'This is Master Mercurius, of the University of Leiden,' Gijsbert announced. 'He has come by order of the Stadhouder to review the university's stipends. And one or two other matters.'

'Of Leiden? I trust you had a good journey, Master.'

'I did, thank you, Professor.'

Johannes laughed gently. 'I have been appointed, but not yet installed. But let us be less formal. Please call me Johannes.' The older man made no such offer. 'What do you teach at Leiden, Mercurius?' Johannes enquired.

'Moral philosophy and ethics. And you?'

'Law. But from a moral perspective, I hope. Too many see the law as an obstacle to circumvent rather than as a guide to live by. A people's law should reflect their beliefs, do you not agree?'

'Indeed, it should. A man should not need law to guide him if his morals are perfected.'

'Well said! Grandfather, I am pleased to hear that Leiden is as orthodox as we are ourselves.'

Gijsbert gave a grunt that might have been interpreted as 'that remains to be seen', but eased himself out of the chair. 'We dine in the room beyond, Master. My wife will keep her own room so that we may discuss business.'

'Forgive me. I had not realised your wife was still … here.'

'She does well, but she keeps out of the way while I am working. I am afraid I am not sociable when about my work.'

I briefly pondered whether I was expected to protest and decided I ought not.

'Now, Johannes will lead the way, and I will follow as I can.'

'No, Grandfather, lean on my arm and we will go together.'

Gijsbert did as he was bid and patted his grandson on the arm. 'You're a good boy, Johannes.'

It was clear that while the apoplexy had spared the old man's faculties, it had left him with a weakness in the legs. One foot seemed to drag as he walked slowly through the house, and by the time he reached his chair his energy was spent. He dropped into it thankfully and took a few moments to compose himself again. 'It pains me that I cannot preach,' he admitted. 'But I can still think and write, God be praised. And my son Nicolaas is a fine expositor of God's word.'

When one considers that Voet had been ordained for sixty-three years, it is not surprising that he felt the deprivation keenly. Even at his great age he was the acknowledged leader of those who wanted what was politely termed "Further Reformation" or, to put it in layman's terms, militant Puritanism. Voet firmly believed that God knew exactly who would be saved and who would be damned from the moment that He created the universe. This was also the required belief of ministers of the Reformed Church (like me) but inimical to Catholic priests (like me). The Calvinist notion that a man cannot improve his prospects however godly he lives was a major reason why I had been attracted to the Catholic faith. If you ask me how I squared these two points of view, the answer is that I didn't, and if I had been unwise enough to keep my sermons you might have noticed an area of belief that received very few mentions while I was in the pulpit. You may be sure that I was keen that our conversation should not linger anywhere near this topic for long.

'Did you never think of following your grandfather, Johannes?' I asked.

He laughed. 'No, I could never have matched the example. My father took to the law, and I have done the same. But I serve the church in my own way.'

'Johannes is a deacon,' his grandfather interrupted, 'with responsibility for managing the alms and oblations.'

'It's simple enough,' answered Johannes, 'for a man who can count.'

Anna entered with the first platters which she had successfully carried from the kitchen. The cook herself bore the leg of pork that was the centrepiece of the meal, no doubt fearing the consequences if Anna lost it on the way between the kitchen and the dining room. The old man said grace and we fell upon the delicious meal. Conversation was stilted as we chewed happily.

When the plates had been cleared, old Voet told young Voet to tell Anna she would not be needed for a while and to close the door.

'Now, Master, I think the simplest approach is for you to tell my grandson what transpired when you met the Stadhouder and the true reason why you are here.'

'The Stadhouder had heard of your grandfather's brief indisposition,' I began, inserting the word brief to curry favour with the old man, 'and was concerned for his health. At the same time, it brought home to him how much he has relied on your grandfather's support and how difficult his position would be if your grandfather were no longer able to supply it.'

'He means if I were dead,' snapped Gijsbert.

'Lamented as it will be, it must come to us all, Grandfather,' Johannes said. It seemed that he could get away with anything where the old man was concerned. If I'd said that, I'd have expected to be belaboured with a walking stick and thrown out on the street.

'The Stadhouder is presently unable to come to Utrecht,' I continued, 'but he has asked me to obtain your grandfather's valued advice as to those upon whom he could rely in the event of any further indisposition.'

'Or death,' added Gijsbert.

'Let's not be morbid, Grandfather!' exclaimed Johannes. 'You say yourself that your strength is not what it was, so we must find willing legs to run where you cannot, and you can concentrate that excellent mind on issuing orders and providing guidance.'

'The chief amongst those legs must be yours, Johannes. But I fear that we may have difficulty persuading the Stadhouder of that in the light of your poor father's views.'

I saw my opportunity. 'I think, Professor, that I can overcome those reservations, provided that we have a second name to offer the Stadhouder.'

Johannes smiled. 'You mean a spy who can report to The Hague if I become an ardent Republican?'

'That's one way of putting it,' I smiled back.

'Well, that's just being prudent,' Johannes answered.

I was warming to Johannes. Personally, I had no doubt that he could fill his grandfather's shoes if need arose, and I hoped that the Stadhouder was pragmatic enough to take the advice of one who had visited Utrecht and seen for himself — I mean me, by the way — and not pose unnecessary obstacles. But the Princes of Orange were notoriously stubborn men, and I was

— and am — an atrocious judge of character, as will become clear as my tale unfolds.

'What about De Zwart?' posed Johannes.

'De Zwart? Well, the man is loyal enough, but timid. He rarely leaves the Dom's precincts.'

The Dom was the name used locally for the great cathedral of St Martin that dominated the central square of the city. To be honest, a man could live his life on and around the square and not miss much that was going on.

'But if his role is to keep an eye on me, he doesn't need to,' Johannes answered.

'If that is his only role, well and good,' replied the Professor, 'but he would be small help to you in gathering the intelligence you need around the city. We need someone more mobile.'

'Then Van Leusden is your man,' announced Johannes, at which the old man's face brightened, leading me to suppose that this suggestion was a good one.

'Do you think he has the intellect to fulfil the role?' Gijsbert pondered.

'He can read and write, after a fashion, and the man is a born gossip,' said Johannes. 'His work takes him all round the city and into the nearby towns and villages, and as a young man he fought for the Prince's father.'

It seemed so obvious a choice that I was astounded that nobody had suggested him before. 'What is his work?' I enquired.

'He's an undertaker,' laughed Johannes. 'Strictly, he's a carpenter who happens to spend most of his time dealing with burials. But he knows everyone, and between funerals he spends a lot of time talking to people. Grandfather, why don't I take Mercurius to meet Van Leusden now? Perhaps I can show him a little of the city afterwards and you can get back to your work.'

I suspect it was the last part of this proposal that produced his grandfather's ready agreement, but thus armed with approval Johannes and I gathered up our cloaks and stepped out into the street. 'Isn't it a little late to go calling on people?' I asked.

'Not on Van Leusden. We'll find him at home, at the Dom, or at the inn. And since they're within a few paces of each other, it won't be hard work.'

We strolled through the streets, Johannes pausing at intervals to point out some landmark of interest, until we came to a small alleyway down which we passed. I had thought it lined with mean cottages, but suddenly we found ourselves in front of fine iron gates enclosing a small but pleasant garden and a neat house.

Johannes opened the gate and rapped on the door. 'Is mijnheer Van Leusden at home?' he enquired of the maid.

'I'll ask, if you please to wait,' came the reply.

It was clear that the maid did not need to ask Johannes' name, and within a few moments we saw a man of about fifty years of age advance towards us as he buttoned his tunic. 'Mijnheer Voet! A pleasure!'

'Bartholomeus, I'd like to introduce you to Master Mercurius, of the University of Leiden.'

Van Leusden looked me up and down and then, once satisfied that I did not have four heads or a forked tail, he nodded a greeting, which I returned.

'I wonder if we might have a few words with you, Bartholomeus. In private.'

'Of course, of course. If you don't mind sitting in my workshop, we can avoid disturbing the ladies.'

I learned later that Van Leusden had a charming adult daughter and an equally uncharming wife. If I had been married to her, I would have spent a lot of time in my workshop too.

Van Leusden showed us to a room at the back of the house, ushered us inside, then went to fetch some more candles. Upon his return, I could not help noticing that we were not alone.

'I hope you do not feel uncomfortable among the dead,' he said nervously. A shrouded figure lay on a board across two trestles, while two more occupied coffins whose lids had not yet been fixed down.

'Business is thriving,' murmured Johannes.

'The unseasonable hot weather leads to agues and fluxes,' Van Leusden replied. 'That poor chap there —' he pointed to one of the coffins — 'was right as rain at breakfast, felt poorly at midday and was dead by evening. It is a reminder to us all that we must keep our relationship with the Almighty in good repair, because we may be called to meet him at any time.'

'Amen to that,' Johannes said fervently. I ought to have been just as fervent, but I fear I sounded a bit half-hearted since my first concern was whether I ought to be so near people who have died of a pestilence.

'Do not fear, Master,' Van Leusden was quick to assure me, 'all are agreed that the dead are not dangerous to us once they grow cold.'

I nudged the candles a little nearer to me in case letting the corpses warm up would restore the danger.

'Perhaps, Dominie, you would say a prayer over them before you leave?'

The only possible reply to this was 'of course'. It's what we ministers do, even if we have no idea at all whom the deceased might be. 'No time like the present,' I said, feeling that I would like to get it over with before any foul vapours in the air added to their number.

All present duly removed their hats and bowed their heads.

I am not the best extemporaneous prayer in the world. There was a fellow I met in Leiden once who could manage half an hour without even seeming to think about it. And during the late war against the French, I had enjoyed a tour de force by one of our local clergy who produced a commination against all Gallic persons and things that was simply majestic in its breadth and depth. If God answered even a tenth of his prayers, then 1673 must have been a really bad year to be French, what with the droughts, famines, failures of conceptions and plagues of boils that were called down upon them that day.

Nevertheless I set to, borrowing extensively from the book of Job and the burial service, and ending with the uplifting piece from the epistle to the Romans, chapter 8, verse 39, which has often been a great comfort to me, especially if I have been reading too much of the book of Job.

At the end, my Amen was answered by two male voices and an unexpected female one. Raising my eyes, I discovered that a comely young woman had entered the room. The presence of the departed did not seem to concern her at all.

'What is it, Janneke?' asked Van Leusden.

'Mother thought your guests might welcome a little wine,' she replied, offering us fine goblets on a tray.

I have mentioned earlier that I was ordained a priest in the Roman Catholic church, and if there is one thing that everybody seems to know about priests, it is that they are forbidden to marry. Actually, they are forbidden to do many things, but let's preserve decorum and speak only of marriage for the moment. This does not mean that young men, such as I was at the time of these events, are immune to the attractiveness of young women; and Janneke van Leusden was an attractive young woman. In fact, I can feel my heart stirring even now as I recall her.

It was not so much the blonde hair and blue eyes, the rosy complexion, deep pink lips, or white smile that reduced me to melted wax, but the demure way that she cast her eyes down and then raised them in my direction. I have always been susceptible to a demure woman, and if Janneke van Leusden had suggested an immediate elopement, there is every chance that I would have discounted my Catholic ordination as a clerical error and decided that there was a lot to be preferred about the Protestant ministry. It might be doctrinally confused, recently coined and austere, but it allows its ministers to marry women like Janneke van Leusden, and that might be worth an extra spell in Purgatory. [Manuscript note: My clerk is shocked. But then he didn't see Janneke in the bloom of her youth.]

Her father introduced us, and she bobbed prettily to each before returning to the parlour and closing the door behind her, no doubt on her way to recount what she had seen to her mother who had despatched her. The mother would have been burning to learn who might be taken at once to the workshop but could not be seen to be curious, and had therefore devised this little piece of theatre so that she could inform herself. What she made of discovering a couple of university lecturers were in her house, I cannot say; what her daughter was saying about them was, I confess, something of the keenest interest to me. I hoped that I had made a good impression. After all, I might not be a priest forever. (All right, according to Psalm 109, I am — *tu es sacerdos in aeternum*, it says. But maybe there is something in the small print...)

I need not describe the remainder of the discussion in detail. Johannes explained my mission, and Bartholomeus assured us that he would be honoured to serve the Stadhouder in any capacity within his power. We celebrated with another goblet of wine, this time in the parlour, where we paid our respects to the mistress of the house. If I had been thinking of the potential joys of marrying Janneke van Leusden, this introduction to a future mother-in-law would have poured cold water on my ardour at once, though, on balance, there was still much to be said for the young lady's hand, particularly if her mother could be persuaded to keep eating the sweetmeats that explained the difference in their physique. One did not need to be a master carpenter to detect that building a coffin for mevrouw van Leusden was going to be a test of anybody's joinery skills, not to mention the strength of the pall-bearers.

We took our leave and Johannes walked me back to his grandfather's house.

'I trust I shall see you in the morning,' he said. 'I normally walk my grandparents across to Divine Service. It takes a while now, but Grandfather says a carriage would be an extravagance, bless him.'

'If I can help, I gladly will,' I replied.

'If he allows it, you'll know you have his seal of approval,' laughed Johannes, and bade me goodnight.

CHAPTER FIVE

I had two dreams that night that I can remember. In the first, Janneke van Leusden and I were having a picnic in a green meadow alongside a tinkling brook. She sat under the shade of a willow tree while I reclined with my head in her lap. There is a feature of dreams that I have never understood, which is that they can completely ignore any references to reality, so in this dream I was playing the lute and singing to her. I do not possess nor play a lute, nor do I understand why or how we had taken a small harpsichord with us on a picnic so that she could accompany me; and even if we had, I do not understand how I could play the lute with my head in her lap while she played the harpsichord. She fed me luscious fruit while telling me of her deep desire to marry urgently so that she could give herself to me completely.

The second dream? Ah, yes. That involved my being tied to an iron bedframe while little devils lit a fire underneath it and plucked at my tenderest parts with red-hot tweezers. When I woke, I had no doubt that these two dreams were connected and that if I courted Janneke it would involve a brief period of earthly paradise followed by an eternity of misery at the hands of Satan and his minions. But it was still very tempting.

At some unearthly hour around dawn there came a knock at the door, and Anna entered with a pitcher of hot water for my shave. She threw open the hangings to reveal a bright summer morning and a number of vindictive birds hollering their lungs out just outside the window.

I am not a morning person. One of the finest institutions of the Roman Church is the anticipated Mass, under which a

Mass on the Saturday evening counts as if it had taken place on Sunday morning, because I am rather livelier on Saturday evening than I am on any morning.

Having shaved and gone downstairs, I discovered that the reason for the early start was that the Voet household had its own prayers before the church service. Gijsbert read a passage from the bible then led some prayers before the servants returned to the kitchen and we could eat our breakfasts.

About an hour before the service started, Johannes arrived to help his grandfather make the walk to the church. This was not because the walk would take so long, but because the proud old man did not like people to see how frail he had become. For the same reason, we entered by a side door that allowed us to seat him at the front with the minimum of fuss.

It was clear by the way people addressed him that he was respected. It was also clear that people were very willing to share information with him. Within about half an hour I had overheard at least three accusations of adultery, one of theft and a particularly lurid one alleging the *peccatum Sodomiticum*. There was, however, nothing touching on any threat to the Stadhouder or the governance of the state.

The preacher spoke on the sixteenth chapter of the gospel according to St Luke, recounting the story of the rich man and the poor man, Lazarus, who begged outside his gate. It is curious how the popularity of that passage is inversely related to how much money the hearer has, being very much enjoyed by the poor and leaving the rich shifting uncomfortably in their seats. Van Leusden appeared to be fascinated by the stitching on his gloves during this sermon, but I observed his daughter watching the preacher intently, her sapphire blue eyes fixed on his face. Her mother, meanwhile, made short work of some kind of confectionery in her muff. I had suspected there might be some such item in there, because it was a hot July day and yet the woman had both hands firmly inside a barrel of fur, looking for all the world like an apprentice furrier coming to grips with an elderly cat.

At the end of the service, I raced around the back of the pews so that I could accidentally encounter juffrouw Van Leusden once more, albeit in the company of her father and mother, if that is what the spherical object in a dress was.

'Master Mercurius!' Janneke said brightly. 'How did you find the sermon?'

I opened my mouth to offer a witty and learned critique, but it seemed unaccountably dry and my brain seemed to have fallen into a deep slumber. 'I — well, it is a well-known story — hard to find anything new to say — very striking delivery…' I stammered.

'I am sure it is a lesson you would not need,' she offered generously. 'You have no use for worldly riches, I'm sure.'

I wouldn't have put it quite that strongly myself. If I had ever had them, I might well have wanted to keep them, I suppose. 'Some things are more valuable than money, juffrouw,' I replied.

'Such as?' She cocked her head in that endearing way some young women have of indicating that they are keen to hear your answer.

'Friendship, loyalty, honesty, love,' I suggested. I put love lower on the list lest I appear too enthusiastic.

'I am sure you are right, Master,' she replied. 'Though I am just a silly woman and not learned, it seems to me that these things must be precious, being so rarely met with.'

'I would not describe you as a silly woman,' I insisted, doing my utmost to convey that this was not mere gallantry but an indication of the respect in which I held her.

Her mother began to walk towards the door, so we followed.

'I wonder, juffrouw,' I asked, 'do you play a musical instrument?'

'Why, yes,' she said. 'At least I try. I play the harpsichord.' So my dream was not pure imagination after all! My heart was lightened at the thought. 'Did you not see it in our parlour last night?' she asked.

I was keen to return to Leiden on Monday, so I agreed with Gijsbert Voet that I would take copies of the papers I had been lent and work on them there. This was sensible because I would have to show my conclusions to the Stadhouder in The Hague, and Leiden is much closer to it than Utrecht is. I know he did not want to see them, but they were my cover for visiting him so we had to go through the process to make the story credible; which meant, of course, that I actually had to do the work, but I reasoned I could do that on Tuesday, travel to The Hague on Wednesday, tidy up my Leiden desk on Thursday and be back in Utrecht for Friday to present my results and take the weekend to brief the Voets on the Stadhouder's views.

The alert reader might wonder why I was so eager to leave given that I had enjoyed the company of Janneke. I will confess there was an attraction, but I was wary of being absent from Leiden for too long at the end of the academic year, otherwise my esteemed colleagues would take the opportunity to shift all the heavy work for the new term onto me. I was well aware that one of them was scheming to pass the lectures on the Ten Commandments in my direction, and he would not be the only one trying to lighten their load. Besides which, I was rather hoping to get someone else to take on the moral teachings of Peter Abelard, which I had taught for so long that

I was finding it hard to present them in a balanced and constructive way, given my belief that the man was an utter charlatan and an unprincipled blackguard to boot. I can get away with saying that in a Protestant setting, but I have to be more circumspect when there are Catholics around. And you never know when there are: occasionally I sit in a meeting and think, *Well, I know I'm a secret Catholic. I wonder if anybody else here is.* It just goes to show me how difficult it would be to plot against the government of the day — not that I intend to do so, I hastily add.

I collected the papers from the university office, but the look on Gijsbert Voet's face made it clear that working on the Sabbath was completely out of the question — which is strange, because as a minister I am very accustomed to working on the Sabbath. I think most church elders would take a dim view of a minister who asked for his day off to be a Sunday. Looking on the bright side, this offered the prospect of strolling over to the Van Leusden house to see if Janneke would care to go for a walk.

I did, and she did, and her mother came too to act as chaperone. I realised that I could hardly take them to an inn, and any coffee houses that Utrecht might boast would be closed on a Sunday, but mevrouw van Leusden supplied the deficiency for me when she threw into the conversation that if we walked up to the Janskerk, she knew of a place where we might find a dish of hot chocolate and a cake. Having found it, she became so engrossed in sampling the wares that I would swear a lesser man might have ravished her daughter on the table without distracting her from her delights.

I am sure that a few readers are asking whether I was trifling with Janneke's affections, knowing, as I did, that we would never marry; to which I reply that I did not know it. I entertained fancies, foolish though they may have been, of recanting on my conversion. As a minister of the Reformed Church, I could marry at will. And since I was an underground priest and did not have to report to anyone regularly, it could be a long time before the Catholic Church knew that I had left. But then it dawned on me that there would be a record somewhere of my ordination, and I wouldn't put it past them to send a copy to my employers, who would immediately dismiss me, just to discourage anyone else from doing the same thing. That's the trouble with bishops; they take religion too seriously.

The journey back to Leiden took a large part of Monday, despite an unreasonably early start, but eventually we berthed at the butter market and I was able to get back on dry land; or what would have been dry land had it not been pouring with rain.

As a result of this deluge, I ran across the city to the Academy building and was shaking off my wet cloak in the doorway when I was addressed by the Cerberus of the university, Van Looy. (All right, I admit he had only one head, but I suspect he had three pairs of eyes to know so promptly of my return.)

'Master Mercurius, welcome back. How was Utrecht?'

How did he know I was in Utrecht, I wondered? But then I hadn't made any secret of it, I suppose. 'Drier than this, Van Looy. Has all been well here while I've been gone?'

'Surprisingly we have been able to keep going despite your absence,' he replied. 'Shall I inform the Rector of your return?'

'Please do. I'll just find a dry gown and then I'll wait upon him.'

'Excellent. He will be pleased.'

I thought I detected a slight emphasis on the "he", as if to indicate that there was no accounting for individual taste.

I dried myself off in my room and found a change of clothes, though it was clear that I was in need of some new underlinen, my stocks having been seriously depleted by just a few days away. All this gallivanting was messing up my laundry timetable. There were laundrywomen attached to the university, but I had never really felt comfortable about getting them to wash my small clothes, so I preferred to do that myself. This meant that my room was often festooned with drying underwear, a matter which militated against holding tutorials there as other lecturers preferred to do; though, thinking about it, Master Hubertus did not seem to exercise himself too much about the state of his room before allowing students to enter. Maybe I was fretting about nothing.

Thus costumed, I made my way to the Rector's office. As I approached, Van Looy oozed into view.

'I have informed the Rector of your intentions,' he said, with all the distaste that I might have expected had I been a dancing master about to give a private lesson to the Rector's daughters.

Van Looy helpfully knocked for me, and on the command to come he opened the door, as if I were too imbecilic to do it for myself. We both attempted to bow politely to each other in the cramped doorway, resulting in the very satisfying outcome that he headbutted my shoulder as I turned into the room.

The Rector greeted me civilly and invited me to sit beside the fire. To my surprise, he then walked over to the door and threw it open suddenly before looking out in each direction. 'Just wanted to be sure we weren't being eavesdropped,' he explained. 'How did your mission go?'

'Very well,' I answered. 'The technique we used here at Leiden should work just as well for the university there.'

'Don't treat me like a fool, Mercurius,' he snapped. 'I mean your real mission.'

I smelt danger. I smell danger a lot of times when danger is not there, but that's better than being blissfully ignorant when it is. 'Rector,' I answered carefully, 'if I had a mission other than the public one — which I'm not admitting — surely I would be sworn to secrecy about it and could not discuss this mission, if it existed, with anyone who did not already know about it?'

'And surely if the Stadhouder asks me to send him my most cunning lecturer for some special task, I am aware that the special task exists even if I do not need to know what it is?'

I could not resist it. I am a philosophy lecturer, after all. 'Forgive me, you would know that it might exist, but not that it assuredly does exist.'

'Rather like your job here then,' he answered. 'It might have a future, but it does not assuredly have a future.'

I gulped.

'For Heaven's sake, man!' blazed the Rector. 'I'm not asking what it is, just whether it went well. The favour of the Stadhouder is important to us. I just want to know that he's going to be happy.'

I gulped again.

'Spit it out!' the Rector commanded.

'Well, it's a little difficult to explain the difficulty without divulging the mission.'

'Which you mustn't. And I am alarmed by your use of the word "difficulty", Mercurius.'

I took a deep breath and decided to try a different tack. 'May we approach this hypothetically?'

'If it would help resolve the "difficulty".'

'Then, let us suppose that a certain person in a position of responsibility wanted to reassure himself that another person in whom he had reposed great trust was physically well enough to be able to carry out those duties.'

'That would be only prudent, especially when the other person had a very public collapse just a few months ago.'

This was getting a bit too close to reality. 'In this *hypothetical* example,' I continued, 'let us assume that the certain august person's agent was tasked with lining up a replacement with a view to any future incapacity.'

'Again, that would be only prudent.'

'And suppose the august person had a list of unacceptable candidates which happens to coincide closely with the preferred choices of the person in whom that trust had been reposed.'

'I see.'

There was a long pause.

'Do you have any suggestions, Rector?'

'How can I? It's just a hypothetical example, isn't it?'

I should have anticipated such a comment. He is far too clever to give an opinion on a topic like that.

'I suppose,' he continued, 'that the agent's advice might depend on the view the agent had himself formed of the candidates' merits. If he were convinced that the august person was troubling himself unnecessarily, he could say so. After all, he has met those concerned, whereas the august person has not. And what was he chosen for if not to form his own judgement?'

'You don't think that the august person might think the agent was a fool who has ignored a clear direction given to him?'

'Not unless the august person were himself a fool. And very few fools get to be august persons.'

I might have taken issue with him then, because I could reel off a pretty extensive list who had, a surprising number of them being leading figures in the church, but I let it go.

'Thank you for this little chat, Mercurius,' the Rector said. 'No doubt you will wish to visit The Hague at the earliest opportunity to discuss the matter.'

I had been hoping not to spend another day sitting on a barge, but I could not argue with the idea. There was some urgency after all.

'I happen to know that the Mayor has been summoned to The Hague for a meeting tomorrow morning. I shall send Van Looy to see if he would find it convenient to take you in his carriage.'

'That is very kind, but his meeting may end before the Stadhouder can see me, and I would not wish to keep him waiting.'

'You won't. He'll leave when he's ready. There are barges, Mercurius. You can't expect luxury all your life.'

CHAPTER SIX

Van Looy came over to me at supper to give me the wonderful news that I was going to have to be ready to go just after dawn on the next morning. The Mayor was going to be kind enough to bring his carriage past the Academy's door, which was a signal mark of favour. This involved a detour of around two hundred paces from the direct road out of town towards The Hague, but I must not be churlish.

Being on official business, the Mayor had not brought his wife and sons with him, which was a great blessing. His wife was an elegant woman, the perfect hostess and a lady whose beauty had been considerably enhanced by the discovery that she came with a thumping dowry from her father, leading there to be a frenzied competition for her hand. The fact that the elder of her two sons was born eight months and a week after her wedding led to some speculation about the tactics that the Mayor may have used to win her hand, though the midwife attested that the child was very small due to his early birth.

I had met the younger son recently, because he was now eighteen years old and his father was very keen that he should have the benefit of a university education. The only supervening obstacle was that no faculty wanted to take him on, because he was, without a shadow of a doubt, one of the stupidest boys I have ever encountered.

In the end, the Rector suggested to the Mayor that perhaps if the lad attended a few lectures and wrote an essay or two it would meet the case, since it would be unhealthy for a spirited young man like his son to spend years indoors studying for an actual degree. The Mayoral ambitions were satisfied by this plan, so the younger son occasionally sauntered into a classroom to while away an hour. He came to a lecture I was giving on Giordano Bruno ("The tormented soul of the believer", since you ask) in which I expatiated on Bruno's view that the desirable union of the soul with God could not be achieved during an earthly lifetime but could be consummated after death and that true believers were therefore destined for earthly disappointment followed by heavenly bliss.

I spoke for nearly an hour, then asked if there were any questions. I had dealt with a couple when I saw his hand shoot up.

'This Bruno fellow — was he a Dago?' he asked.

'He came from Italy,' I replied.

The fool just shrugged as if that explained it all and there was little point in attempting to understand his thinking since he was a foreigner. I heard afterwards that in the theology class he correctly identified Luther as a "cabbage-eater".

Anyway, neither boy was in the carriage, so I sat opposite the Mayor and spoke when I was spoken to. The Mayor showed no great interest in my reason for going, and I reciprocated heartily, though I could see that he faced the prospect with some trepidation.

We arrived at the Binnenhof where the courtyard appeared to be filled with the carriages of dignitaries from various cities and towns in the district. This brightened the Mayor considerably since he now knew that he had not been particularly singled out for contumely, and he headed for the large hall with a certain jauntiness of step while I presented myself at the guardroom, once more anticipating a lengthy wait.

The sentries recognised me at once.

'You're the fellow who left that pie behind,' said one. 'We've still got it here somewhere.' He began to rummage through a chest on the floor.

'Do me a favour,' I said. 'When you find it, please heave it in the river, ideally where no poor birds will attempt to eat it.'

'They'd have to dive for it,' he answered, 'because it sure as hell won't float.'

I gave my name and was marched to a door when I was handed to another pair of soldiers. The officer of the watch took my details and went on ahead, so I had only had time to be handed on once more when he came running back.

'Not that way!' he exclaimed to the guards. 'Take him through the corner door and up the back stairs. He'll be met at the top by the Stadhouder's secretary.'

This intelligence sharpened up the guards considerably, who must have decided that I was much more important than they had previously believed, because we marched at a fair lick to the doorway. Their attempts to march up the back stairs alongside me were doomed to failure, so finally they adopted my suggestion of proceeding up the narrow steps with one before and one behind me.

My brother Laurentius was a naval officer, and I began to understand how pleasant it must be to give commands to people who obey them without dispute. I could imagine that it would become quite addictive were it not for the great disadvantage of military rank which Laurentius also experienced, being killed at the Battle of Lowestoft in 1665.

It is curious to see how the paths of brothers diverge. My brother was always a lively, daring boy, the first to climb trees or swim across a canal. For myself, I preferred indoor pursuits, books and prayer, none of which played a big part in Laurentius' life. Shortly before he died, he hinted to me that he had a sweetheart but we did not know whom it might be, and nobody came forward when his death was known. I could only hope that she had somehow learned his fate and was not saving herself for a man who would never return.

If I had shown any inclination to follow Laurentius in his martial pursuits, our mother would probably have prevented it. Having lost one son she had no desire to sacrifice another, which was exactly how I felt about it, so I returned to my studies and mourned him quietly, but nine years later I still found myself occasionally hoping that the reports were mistaken and that one day he would bound up the stairs, throw my door open and lob his hat upon the table in the old, familiar way. Ah, poor Laurentius!

As the upper door opened I found Pieters, a small weasellylooking individual in a black suit, waiting for me.

'Good day, Master Mercurius,' he said. 'I will conduct you to the Stadhouder.'

I may have mentioned that the Stadhouder, while undoubtedly impressive, was not the tallest of people, and in Pieters he had contrived to find one of the few men markedly smaller than himself. As we passed his desk, I found myself pondering how the secretary was able to climb up on his chair, but our arrival at a large pair of doors interrupted my thoughts.

Pieters composed himself, strode forward and waited for the sentries to open the two doors, which they did in perfect unison, allowing us to pass within. I had assumed we would be coming into a receiving chamber, but instead we seemed to be in a small dressing-room of some kind. It was empty.

'Master Mercurius is here, my lord,' announced Pieters.

'I'll be there presently,' came a voice from behind a folding wooden screen, and in a short time the Stadhouder appeared, buttoning his breeches and wiping his hands on a towel. 'The chamberpot needs emptying, Pieters,' he said, which the secretary rushed to do. I was just asking myself whether the Stadhouder would be offended if I did not kiss his hand when he indicated that we should sit without undergoing such formalities. 'How did your visit to Utrecht go?'

'Very well,' I answered. 'Voet showed me every courtesy. He was a little reluctant to accept that his powers were in any way diminished, but accepted that he can't go on forever.'

'And are they diminished?'

'Mentally he is as sharp as ever, but he has a weakness in the legs that precludes standing for a long time and makes his movement quite slow. His grandson tells me he is improving, and they still hope he may regain his full vigour.'

The Stadhouder sniffed. 'I see. And this grandson — is he sound?'

I took this to be a reference to his potential loyalty to the Orange cause rather than a comment on his physical state. 'He is a very accomplished young man, soon to be a Professor of Law at Utrecht University.'

'I don't suppose his grandfather being the Rector influenced that in any way?'

'The two of them are very animated by any such suggestion. In fact, they are so sensitive to the idea that Gijsbert has offered to maintain his grandson for the first two years, during which he will draw no salary.'

'How public-spirited of him. I wish more of my people would offer the same. I should send you to count the money in my treasury, Mercurius. It won't take you long.'

I have no knowledge of high finance, but one thing is for sure. If the Stadhouder counted the contents of my treasury, it would take him a lot less time. 'I suggested that if enemies of your cause were to gain the upper hand in Utrecht, both of them would probably be arrested, and that therefore it would be good to have an alternative outside their family.'

'Good for you. How did they receive that?'

'The younger man persuaded the elder that it was likely to be so, and suggested a fellow called Van Leusden. I have met him, Stadhouder, and he seems entirely suitable.'

'What's his profession?'

'He is an undertaker.'

'Excellent. Even during enemy occupations, undertakers are rarely restricted in their work. They're normally among the first to be given a pass to go wherever they need. You've done well, Mercurius. Care for an apple?'

He held the bowl towards me, so I selected one and thanked him while hoping this was not going to be the entire extent of any reward. I did not know what I was hoping for, though following New Testament precedent I might have asked for Van Looy's head on a platter.

'I have also brought my proposals for the Utrecht salaries. They are the same as the Leiden ones.'

'Good. I shan't have to read them, then. I'll write to the Rectors today to tell them to put them into effect. I'll call Pieters in and we'll do it now, so you can take the two letters with you.'

I had expected him to have a small bell or some similar contrivance, but he simply strode to the door, flung it open and shouted for Pieters. The rapidity with which the secretary appeared strongly hinted that he had been somewhere near the keyhole when summoned.

'Pieters, I will dictate two letters to you which you are to write out in your fairest hand and deliver to Master Mercurius here so that he can take them this afternoon. Ensure that Mercurius gets some dinner while he's waiting, give him ten guilders from my privy purse and whatever he needs for a barge back to Leiden. And you'd better write out one of those letters that tells people he is my official and not to mess with him.'

That all seemed very satisfactory to me, though the look on Pieters' face betrayed his belief that I was not the class of person who should be receiving letters like that. However, like the good and faithful servant he was he just bowed so low I expected his breeches to rip at the back and indicated that we could leave now with a sweeping gesture of his arm. I bowed to the Stadhouder and made to follow Pieters from the room.

'Good man, Mercurius. You've done well. I won't forget this.'

I thought that was just one of those things important men say. Unfortunately, he meant it.

You can imagine that there was a certain jauntiness in my step as I left the barge and returned once more to the Academy to report to the Rector and give him the Stadhouder's letter. I had ten guilders in my pouch, and while money was not something that I coveted, that is much easier to say truthfully when you already have some.

The Rector opened the Stadhouder's letter and read it carefully. Like all such letters, it was designed to be displayed in public and therefore could be represented as a mark of approval of the university; and since it held out the prospect of pay rises for many of the staff, it was bound to be a popular achievement that would redound to the Rector's credit. He was a modest man, a fine man, a fair man, and I do not believe for a moment that he planned to take personal pride in this, but you could see at once that he was happy.

'This is splendid!' he exulted. 'Mercurius, you have done wonderfully well! Sit down, man, and let us share a flask of wine to toast your achievement.'

I attempted to brush away the praise, but such half-hearted efforts were easily deflected.

'Oh, don't be so self-deprecating, Mercurius. You have exceeded all the expectations I might reasonably have had. Let me fill your goblet.' He sat opposite me, sipped his wine and stared reflectively into its mulberry red depths. 'I will open my heart to you, Mercurius. I feared the worst. It is impossible for a man in my position not to attempt to maintain friendly relationships with the powers that be. I was never close to the De Witts — I barely knew them — but universities need stability, which means that I was bound to support them when opposition arose.'

The Rector was an honest man, and I had no reason to believe that he was dissembling, but I confess that I could not think of a single word he had uttered in favour of either side in the great dispute.

'Naturally,' he continued, 'when the current Stadhouder claimed his office, I feared that he might seize the opportunity to cleanse the Augean stables, and that anyone who had done any service for the De Witts could expect to be removed. And when he began to interest himself in our finances, I thought my fears were entirely justified. I was sure he would pretend to have found some small irregularity and cast me out in shame. I could withstand the loss of office, Mercurius. I have my books, and it would afford me time for my own work which has been neglected far too long. But a man loses everything if he loses his good reputation.'

He took another draught of his wine. I tried to think of something apposite to say, some comforting word to share with him, but my mind had gone utterly blank. Fortunately he supplied the deficiency himself.

'I am not a man to fawn over the mighty, Mercurius. Power is transitory, and the great men of today are the jailbirds of tomorrow. But I will confess I submitted to any whim of the Stadhouder's in the hope of deflecting his wrath. And when he said he wanted to meet you, I was only too happy to make the arrangements.'

'He asked for me, Rector? By name?'

'Not exactly. He asked for the man who solved the abductions of the girls in Delft. He has a high view of your abilities, Mercurius, as I do myself. And you have justified it. I feel that the clouds have lifted from above our heads.'

Just then, there was a commotion outside. I cannot quite recall the order of events, but there was a woman's scream, the sound of rushing footsteps, a period of quiet, and then a stampede of feet on the stairs followed by an urgent hammering at the door. Before the Rector had given the command to enter, one of the kitchen boys threw the door open and rushed in.

'Rector, sir, you'd best come. There's been an accident.'

The Rector put his wine down and beckoned me to follow him. Quickly, but without running, we followed the boy who led us downstairs and along the corridor towards the dining hall. Just before its doors we turned to the left, where a small crowd had gathered. One of the lecturers was comforting Mechtild, leaving me in no doubt as to whose scream we had heard. The Rector demanded passage, and the bystanders stepped aside to allow him through. I followed like a lapdog, with no authority of my own except the right to follow my master.

On the stairs was a man who had evidently tumbled down and broken his neck. The Rector gently eased the head towards us, and I found myself gazing into the staring eyes of Van Looy.

One of the advantages of a modern university is that it houses experts on every conceivable branch of knowledge, so when an emergency strikes the right person is close at hand. Admittedly, I have not yet met with an accident that has called for me to push my way through the crowd whilst yelling, 'Let me through! I'm a moral philosopher!' but it may happen one day.

In this case there were two medical men in the dining room who could certify that Van Looy was certainly dead, though if truth be told you did not need a medical degree to see that. When a man's head seems to be unattached to his shoulders, it is a fairly safe wager that he is not going to recover well.

I was marvelling at the realisation that two surgeons had just agreed on something, a rare event in my recollection, when I noticed that the Rector was speaking to me.

'I need to talk to you, Mercurius.'

'Rector?'

'There are matters touching on this accident upon which I would welcome your advice.'

I did not quite understand him at the time, and I assumed that he meant that he had doubts whether it was an accident, which is why I turned my mind to that line of thought.

'Two things puzzle me, Rector.'

'Speak on, Mercurius.'

'Can we encourage people to leave us alone for a moment?'

The Rector gently persuaded onlookers to retire to the dining room and await him there, dispatching one of the servants to inform the Mayor and, through him, the Sergeant of the Civic

Guard. Since the Mayor is responsible for law and order, he is also the person who investigates any unexpected deaths. A pair of gardeners were ordered to prepare a cart so that Van Looy could be transported with decorum, though none of us could be quite sure where his next destination would be.

I climbed the stairs and examined the panelling and the balustrades carefully before turning my attention to Van Looy himself. Fortunately, I am not a man given to squeamishness, so I felt no inhibition about turning the head slightly so that I could see the rear. I saw what I expected to see.

'You are thoughtful, Mercurius. What is it that disturbs you?'

'You knew Van Looy, Rector. Are you as surprised as I am that he should be on the servants' staircase?'

'It had not struck me, but you're right. He had a fierce sense of pride.'

'I never knew him to use it, even when it was the shortest route. He would always use the main stairs in preference. And then we come to the greater problem. Have you ever known a man to fall down stairs and make no attempt to save himself?'

'It sounds unlikely.'

'There are no scratches on the wood panelling, no damage to his fingernails, in short, no sign that he tried to arrest his fall. And while it is possible that he caused the damage to the back of his head on the way down, I can see no patch of blood on the stairs that corresponds to the wound on his head, but just round the corner at the top of the stairs there is a small smear on the floor.'

'Leading us to conclude that someone attacked him there and pushed him down the stairs to make it look like an accident?'

'I fear so, Rector. Van Looy was murdered.'

CHAPTER SEVEN

I think even the most doltish of my readers will have realised that I was not a great admirer of Van Looy. The man was proud, arrogant, devious, suspicious, and exuded as much warmth as a dead herring. But he was a child of God, and therefore his life was not to be taken away lightly.

Allow me to digress briefly to observe that there are certain difficulties about investigating a murder in a Calvinist milieu. First of all, some of my colleagues in the theology department will tell you that Almighty God ordains all things, and therefore decides who should be murdered and who should not. He has measured out a man's span of life, and some are allotted much and some less, and that's an end to it. For these men, asking why someone has been killed is quite pointless, because the only answer they can give is that the murderer was doing God's will. Any investigation of motive that keeps coming back to the notion that God wanted the victim dead is not conducive to a successful enquiry.

I will digress further to note that if you say to them that if the murderer is doing God's will it seems rather unfair to hang him, they will tell you that it is much more complicated than that and suddenly find other things they urgently need to do.

The Rector had left me to speak to those in the dining hall, and the servants were standing by to move Van Looy to wherever you take dead bodies as soon as I gave permission, but I wanted to fix the image firmly in my mind and assure myself that I had not overlooked anything.

The first thing I had overlooked, it seemed to me, was praying for this poor man, so I knelt by his side and placed a hand on his head as I said a short prayer.

'Where are you taking him?' I asked the servants.

'The crypt of the Hooglandse Kerk, Master,' one replied. 'At least until they tell us to take him somewhere else.'

I nodded and bade them get on their way. They lifted their melancholy cargo onto a board and then through the kitchen to the back door where the cart was waiting. Lying him there, they draped a black cloth over him, then one walked the horse while the other kept an eye on their load to ensure he did not slide off the open cart.

When I returned to the Academy, the Rector was waiting for me.

'I have something to discuss,' he reminded me, and we both ascended to his rooms where he closed all the doors and offered me no wine. This was obviously serious. 'We will need to inform the Stadhouder of what has happened,' he began.

'But surely it is enough to tell the Mayor,' I protested.

'There is more to this than meets the eye, Mercurius,' answered the Rector, at which point my heart did its customary wobbling. No good conversation ever starts that way. 'This is why I wished to speak to you when we saw the body. Whoever the victim is, I'm fairly sure he isn't Van Looy.'

My heart's callisthenics were joined by a slight thumping in the temples. 'No?'

'No. That is, I'm not sure there even is a Van Looy.'

'Forgive me, Rector, but this is a riddle to me.'

The Rector sighed deeply, composed himself, and began to tell the tale. 'Van Looy — let us call him that, as we always have — presented himself here last year bearing a letter from the Stadhouder. In it, the Stadhouder made an odd request. A request from the Stadhouder is not like that of ordinary men, Mercurius; one does not refuse it, especially if one sees what happens to those who do. I have no taste for a dungeon.'

Well, there was something on which we were agreed, and if I detected one was in the offing, I could be packed and on the road within the hour.

'He wished me to give Van Looy employment. He explained that Van Looy had specific duties to perform here, which were secret, but for which he required room and lodging and an explanation of his presence that would deflect curiosity. There would be no difficulty with his salary, because Van Looy would not require one. That is why I told you not to include him in your remuneration plan. Had you enquired at the University Treasury, you would have discovered we had never spent a stijver on him.'

'So Van Looy was the Stadhouder's eyes and ears in Leiden?'

'I don't know, but I would not be surprised. I'm sure part of his function was to report on my loyalty or otherwise. But he was a man of some gifts, and it seemed to me that the simplest option was to employ him as my secretary, so I did. In such a position he could go almost anywhere he wished without questions being raised by curious observers.'

I liked this less and less. I could not say anything to the Rector, but it occurred to me that what Van Looy was doing in Leiden was not very different to what I had been doing in Utrecht, and it had resulted in his death. I am not a coward — well, actually, yes, I am — but I am not martyr material either. On the other hand, it is not the done thing to tell the Stadhouder to take his job and shove it — never mind, my point is made. On top of which, he would probably want the ten guilders back.

'So you see why I say we must let the Stadhouder know what has happened, Mercurius?'

'Yes, Rector, I do.'

'Sound man. Off you go, then.'

'Now?'

'Well, you don't want him to hear from anybody else first, do you?'

I don't care, I thought, *but I can see that you do.* 'Isn't it rather late to be setting out for The Hague?'

'You can take my carriage. It has lamps and Adriaan is a good driver.'

'Thank you. I'll prepare myself.'

There may have been an hour or so of daylight left when we set out on our journey. You can walk from Leiden to The Hague in a little over three hours, so I hoped the horse might cut that time in half. It would be dark before we arrived and I was by no means certain that the guards would let me in, but there was no shirking the duty.

I might have felt more comfortable had I been walking. A clergyman on his own is self-evidently too poor to bother robbing, whereas a fine carriage with a coachman is asking for trouble, especially since there was nobody on the roof with a weapon. I thought briefly that I would feel safer if I rode on the roof, because people would then assume I was armed and leave us in peace. Against that, the presence of a guard might cause them to think that the carriage bore something worth guarding, and I recalled that the first person killed in a robbery is usually the armed guard, so I decided to stay where I was.

The road to The Hague is straight and well-kept, so we were able to make good time and it was not yet ten o'clock when we drove into the courtyard of the Binnenhof. The sentries raised their guns ominously as if expecting a large number of armed brigands to spring from the carriage, and seemed a little disappointed to see only one minister alight.

'My name is Mercurius,' I said, 'and I must see the Stadhouder urgently.'

'You obviously don't have an appointment,' said one of the guard.

'Well, no, but who would at this time of night? Nevertheless, my business is urgent.'

'And what is your business, Dominie?'

'I can't tell you,' I replied. 'It's secret.'

'But if you don't tell me, how do I know if it's urgent enough to disturb the Stadhouder?'

'Trust me, it is. I would not have driven here from Leiden without any supper if it were not.'

The mention of supper seemed to convince them, so one said he would just have to check with the captain of the watch. A few moments later a head appeared at an upper window.

'Oh, it's him with the pie. You can let him in.'

Albrecht's pie was plainly deeply engrained in their memories. As we walked through the corridors, the sentries returned to the theme.

'That pie was a corker. Who cooked it?'

'The kitchen master at the university.'

'What — someone who cooks for a living?'

'Yes.'

'Not your wife?'

'I'm not married.'

'Ye gods!'

I took this exclamation to be a commentary on Albrecht's nerve in accepting a chef's pay rather than on the fact that I had remained unmarried.

'We eat better than that, and the sergeant says we're the scum of the earth,' announced the younger guard proudly.

They arrived at the point at which one of them had to go ahead to seek entry, so I took some time to think how I would break the news to the Stadhouder. I have never been terribly good at breaking bad tidings, though I never sank to the level of a colleague who was sent to tell a woman her husband had been killed in an accident at work and simply blurted out, 'Mevrouw, you are a widow', raised his hat and left.

'They say you can go in,' announced a guard, and held the door back for me.

The Stadhouder was standing over a brazier of his revolting herbs, inhaling their smoke. He was wearing just his shirt, breeches and hose and appeared to be in some distress.

'Mercurius,' he wheezed, 'what is it?'

'Van Looy is dead,' I answered. So much for breaking bad news to him gently.

This may seem strange, but I swear that his asthma instantly improved. Perhaps it was the shock, but his eyes widened and he inhaled deeply before embarking on a bout of coughing such as I have rarely heard.

He dismissed Pieters with a wave whilst he gathered his breath.

The little secretary bowed to each and slipped from the room.

'Sit!' commanded the Stadhouder. 'My chest — still tight — can't talk well. Explain,' he continued.

I told him how we had found Van Looy, of my suspicions about the way that he met his end, and that the Rector had insisted that I must go at once to The Hague to tell him what had occurred.

'Did he say why?'

I am not a practised dissembler but I am a quick learner, so I judged it safer to say no. 'He said you would tell me anything you thought I should know.'

'Did he?' He took a draught of something warm and fragrant, pulled a face as it crossed his tongue, and flopped into a chair. 'That's better.' Here he launched into a colourful description of his illness that I do not propose to insert verbatim, but I suppose that being periodically starved of air by one's own lungs cannot improve a man's temper. 'This is serious, Mercurius. That they would dare to do this shows that they believe they are strengthening.'

'I don't want to appear stupid, but who are these "they" of whom you speak?'

'The De Witt faction, of course.'

I was unaware that people who had been dismembered by a mob could still have a faction, and you may be sure that I would have resigned my membership at the first sight of blood if I had been part of it, but it was clear that the Stadhouder was in earnest.

'You may find this hard to believe, Mercurius, but there are people around who prefer the De Witts to me.'

'Astonishing!' I wasn't sure I really meant that, but I knew what was expected of me.

'Their problem is that with both the brothers gone, there is no obvious figure around whom opposition can coalesce, but you may be sure that my agents are watching closely for the emergence of one so we can finish the job and give this country the stable government it needs.'

I took "finish the job" to mean something along the lines of "emasculating and hanging the alternative candidate".

'Van Looy, as you call him, was one of my best men. He was watching a conspiracy closely and had recently informed us that he knew most of those involved but was waiting for the identity of the leader to become known before making a move. Sadly, he has died before being able to give us his full report.'

I thought it my duty to point to a possible culprit. 'I should tell you, Stadhouder, that I overheard Van Looy talking to a man the other day who was encouraging him to strike quickly.'

'Did you see this man?'

'Not his face. But he wore a very elaborate scabbard, capped in gold. Van Looy denied that such a meeting had taken place, but I know what I heard.'

William pulled a face as if he had sucked a lemon. 'You heard correctly. That would be Adam van Kamerik.'

'Van Kamerik? I don't know him.'

'It's a long story. He styles himself Lord of Kamerik, but I've never seen any paper to support the title. He was a colleague of my uncle, Frederick Nassau de Zuylestein.'

Now, I had heard of *him*, and a nastier piece of work is hard to imagine, though I wasn't going to say so in front of his nephew, who got on very well with him. Frederick was the illegitimate son of the Stadhouder's grandfather and one of the fiercest supporters of the House of Orange. He married an Englishwoman and became William's trusted adviser. It was widely believed that De Zuylestein was behind the lynching of the De Witts, though William maintained he had received no advice at all about that, except possibly not to hang around The Hague that day.

De Zuylestein's influence had come to an abrupt end in October 1672 when he was killed in a battle, curiously enough at Kamerik.

'According to Adam, when my uncle lay dying he bestowed the honour of Kamerik on his faithful officer. It's just possible. They were of an age, and Frederick couldn't give him any money.'

'Do you believe the story, Stadhouder?'

William shrugged. 'We know that Frederick sent for him. And, to be frank, if Adam made the story up he'd have chosen a much better gift than Kamerik. It's a midden.'

'And you suspect this Adam was the man I heard arguing.'

'If he wore a scabbard with a gold top, it sounds like it may be. Besides, I sent him.'

This was getting murkier by the moment, and all my instincts were telling me that this was the moment to ask for a passport so I could go to Sweden to study some important theological papers, if I could think of any that were convincing enough. Or, if not Sweden, then maybe Poland. Scotland, if there were absolutely no alternatives.

There was a very awkward silence. In a conversation between equals, I might have felt at liberty to question the actions of anyone who had done this, but this was not such a dialogue. The Stadhouder did not have to explain himself to me; in fact, this particular Stadhouder believed that he did not have to justify his actions to anyone.

'I can see that you're puzzled, Mercurius. Very well — I'll tell you the whole story. But if I do, you must swear to hold it a secret. If you are to serve me well, there are things you must know, but it is only fair to point out that while I am a generous master to those who do their duty, so I am merciless to those who fail me.'

I thought that I was going to be given the chance to think about this and maybe follow my initial inclination, which was to get back to Leiden as quickly as possible and have nothing to do with any of this, but he continued at once, taking my acquiescence for granted.

'Have an apple,' he said, passing the bowl to me.

I like apples, but I was beginning to associate them with unpleasant missions, death and disaster. Besides which, I really wanted a proper dinner. Nevertheless, I thanked him and took one.

'You'll recall that my late mother of blessed memory was the daughter of the King of England, Charles the first of that name, father of the present king. When she came here she brought various ladies-in-waiting with her, one of whom married De Zuylestein. She also brought some lesser ladies, one of whom was her favourite seamstress. She also married, and her son was Van Looy. His real name was Dekker or Dekkers, something like that. He was brought up to speak English by his mother and Dutch by his father. As an only child, they concentrated their attention on him and he proved to be gifted. However, they hadn't the resources to send him to the universities, and this was twenty or so years ago. I was a babe, and my father was dead. He had nobody here to be a patron to him.'

William poured a tumbler of brandy and handed one to me without asking. I had assumed it would be diluted with something, but the first swig told me otherwise.

'You may have observed his pride. I knew his mother, who always insisted that she was paid for her work, as opposed to being a servant. This arose when she married and left the household, and she and her mistress came to some kind of arrangement for her to go on making her dresses in her own home. Thus he inherited this sense of status from his mother, and it was accentuated when his mother spoke to her patroness about him. My mother could not send him to England because the royal court was in exile then, but he became a member of the household of the King's brother, the Duke of York, at Breda, which did nothing to diminish his pride. When the English returned to their kingdom, Van Looy went with them, but he left when the wars between us and the English began and found work as a tutor in Germany, somewhere near Brunswick. So far as I know, that was where he came to the attention of De Zuylestein, who reintroduced me to him shortly before he died at Kamerik. So there you have it.'

I wished I had been able to make notes, but somehow the gist of it remained with me. De Zuylestein was William's man, and Van Looy was De Zuylestein's. 'And this Adam chap, Stadhouder?'

'It was difficult for Van Looy to leave Leiden to report to me. Had he come here and been seen, news might have leaked back there. Thus I employed Van Kamerik as a messenger between us. He is a good man, fiercely loyal, but he has no patience and he seemed to regard his role as managing Van Looy. That they argued does not surprise me. But he is not the killer, I assure you.'

'How can you be certain?' I asked.

'For two reasons. First, because it would displease me, and he would not wish to do that. Much more importantly, because if Van Looy was killed today, then it is impossible for Van Kamerik to be the murderer, since he is in Haarlem.'

'May I ask how you know he has gone to Haarlem, Stadhouder?'

'Because I sent him. But I get your point. At present, I suppose I don't. But he will return tomorrow with a report from the Mayor, and his arrival with it will prove his innocence. You'll stay here overnight and we can talk to him when he returns. Be a good fellow and call for Pieters, and I'll get him to give you a room. Do you need anything else?'

The conventional and polite answer would have been no. 'Some dinner would be nice,' I said. *And one without apples would be even better*, I thought.

CHAPTER EIGHT

To give Pieters his due, although the kitchens had retired an hour or so before, he rousted out a cook who produced a fine dish of eel for me, served with a mess of soft peas and a hunk of fresh bread. Years of living off Albrecht's fare had almost led me to forget that food could taste like this. For a start, none of it was black.

I am not sure how much sleep the Stadhouder (or, more probably, Pieters) got that night, but in the morning I received a dossier full of information about Van Looy — or, as I now knew him to be, Carolus Dekkers. His mother called him Charles and his father called him Carel, so it seems that they compromised by giving him a Latinised name, as happens to so many of us. I am pleased to say that nobody has ever tried to call me Mercury.

There were also a few leaves dealing with Adam van Kamerik. Since all the documents appeared to be originals, I could not take them away, but Pieters had provided a single page of summary notes for me to retain.

I passed the morning reading the information, pausing only to spring to my feet every time the Stadhouder came through to see how I was progressing.

'I want the killer found, Mercurius. Found and punished.'

'Yes, Stadhouder.'

'My uncle in England had the men who beheaded his father hanged, drawn and quartered. It hasn't happened again, Mercurius.'

You couldn't argue with that. There is nothing like killing all the culprits to ensure that they don't repeat their offences.

'Any ideas?'

'The first question I must solve, it seems to me, is who could have known that Van Looy was your man. He wasn't killed because he was a meddling secretary, after all.'

'It was a secret mission, Mercurius. Maybe he let it slip.'

'With respect,' I began — and I know that this introduction guarantees that what follows conveys no respect at all — 'if the Rector did not know exactly what Van Looy was doing in Leiden, I doubt if Van Looy himself was the source of the information. And if the Rector, who saw him every day, did not know, I doubt if anyone in Leiden could have done. I must make a list of everyone here who would have known.'

'Pieters will do that for you. It won't take long, because very few knew.'

The Stadhouder was right. When Pieters produced the list, there were only a handful of names on it.

The Stadhouder — well, obviously.

Adam van Kamerik — because he was the intermediary who collected and delivered messages between Van Looy and the Stadhouder.

William Nassau de Zuylestein, the son of the one I have been talking about, and now one of William's leading advisers.

Cornelis de Ring, the treasurer who was responsible for paying Van Looy's salary and expenses. While he was not formally told, he may have guessed what Van Looy was doing when examining his expenses claims.

Abraham Dekkers, the cousin of Van Looy. He had been told that Van Looy was absent from The Hague on state business when he came looking for him, but he was not told the assumed identity or the nature of the work Van Looy was doing.

Of course, any of these might have let the secret slip. I discounted the Stadhouder on the grounds that he had no reason to wreck his own plans, he was plainly shocked by Van Looy's death, and he was paying me to conduct the investigation.

The Stadhouder vouched for William de Zuylestein, though he would not have been the first ruler to be betrayed by a trusted lieutenant, so I decided not to scratch his name through (though it seemed prudent to let the Stadhouder think that I had).

That left Van Kamerik, who was taking his time returning from Haarlem, Abraham Dekkers and De Ring.

'Do we know where Abraham Dekkers lives?' I asked.

Pieters scratched his chin. 'Not precisely, Master. But they are a local family here in The Hague. I could make enquiries, if you wish?' He tipped his head to one side, smiled ingratiatingly and waited for my approbation. To my eyes he looked like one of those monkeys that hurdy-gurdy players have sitting on their shoulders in tiny suits with white collars about their necks. I half-expected him to rattle a tin cup in my direction.

'That would be kind, thank you.'

He wrote the task on his daily list of things that must be done. I could not help noticing that he left a few blank lines between that job and the one above it, as if he hoped that several more important duties would come his way.

'And where would I find this Cornelis de Ring?'

'Why, he is just along the corridor, Master. I will lead you to him, whenever you are ready.'

I shrugged. 'I'm ready now.'

'Then, if you will be so good as to follow me — that is, if you do not object to my preceding you?'

'Not at all. It is the only sensible arrangement.'

The fact that it was sensible did not mean, of course, that it would be the unvarying practice of the Stadhouder's court. I did not doubt for a minute that one or other of William's courtiers would have whipped Pieters thoroughly for preceding him through a doorway. We Dutch are an egalitarian people, and therefore ridiculously punctilious about things like orders of precedence. Almost all university ceremonies involve an unseemly wrangle between members of staff who think that they should go before someone else. My own preference is to go right at the end, not because I am extremely humble, but because the last one in is also the last one out and I enjoy watching the others getting wet when it rains.

Pieters was indicating a door, through which I stepped, to find myself in a magnificent chamber. Large book-cabinets lined the walls, a warming fire crackled in the hearth, and happy scribes sat at splendid desks. The university is comfortable, but this was quite a different setting, and I could imagine that a lifetime spent here would be as near to heaven as I expect to find on earth. All I needed to make my happiness complete would be young women moving between the desks dispensing free beer and keeping the occupants well supplied with tasty victuals.

An elderly gentleman with a long grey beard and a square black cap glanced up as I entered. I detected an element of suspicion in his countenance.

'Master Treasurer,' Pieters addressed him, 'I bring Master Mercurius of the University of Leiden, who has been entrusted with an enquiry by the Stadhouder. Could you spare him a few minutes?'

The old man laid his pen down carefully, stood and bowed gravely. I sensed no enthusiasm for the interruption but he doubtless knew that, as St Paul was told on the road to

Damascus, it is hard for him to kick against the pricks. That is just a poetic way of saying that he would be wasting his time, just as an ox prodded with a pointed stick may kick backwards but in the end he will have to walk on. I had no pointed stick, of course, but I could have a word with the Stadhouder, and nobody would want me to do that.

I had met men like De Ring before. Typically they come of good families but they are not the eldest son, so they have to find some way of earning a living, but it must be fitting employment for a gentleman. State service is ideal, because nobody would dare raise the tawdry question of any salary such a man might receive.

'How may I be of service?' he asked. That was the way he spoke. Circumlocutions and indirectness was his natural approach.

'I regret to inform you that a servant of the Stadhouder has been killed. I understand that you were forwarding his salary by some indirect means, and I wondered if you could tell me how that was done and who knew of it.'

'That is most distressing,' De Ring answered. 'It would assist me materially if you were willing to share with me the name of the unfortunate person involved.'

I was half tempted to refuse just to see whether his even temper could be shaken, but that would hardly have advanced my enquiry. 'He was employed at the university in Leiden. He was known there as Van Looy.' I was sure De Ring would know that name, because monies would be despatched to that identity.

'Indeed, I know the name. I am sorry to hear these tidings.'

'Did you know him by any other name?'

'I cannot say. I know a great many people, and I understand that sometimes a masquerade or subterfuge is necessary,' he replied, with a slight frown at the word "subterfuge" as if he found the whole idea distasteful. 'But I make it my business not to enquire into matters that do not concern me.'

'Presumably if Van Looy had been in service with the Stadhouder before, his payments under his real name would have to stop…' I began.

'Well, indeed they should,' De Ring agreed, 'but that would necessitate our knowing the relationship between the identities. We therefore arrange that those who prepare the payments in such cases are not the same people who forward the payments. My staff here would continue to prepare the salaries, but the person who forwards them would be instructed separately not to do so. At intervals the surplus funds are returned to us without attribution to any particular individuals.'

'If I may say so, that doesn't sound very efficient.'

'It lacks efficiency, but that is necessary to maintain secrecy. During the interval between Stadhouders an alternative method was tried, but it proved unsatisfactory.' He spoke as if this had been a period of a few weeks rather than twenty-two years. I could imagine him itching to turn back to the old system on every day of those years too. 'The difficulty that was experienced,' he continued, 'was that the new system involved a single person being aware of the double identities. This had unfortunate consequences when men died unexpectedly. As men are wont to do.'

Men were certainly wont to do so when they were too close to the De Witts or the Stadhouder, I thought. I was beginning to feel rather uncomfortable about my own position given how things had turned out for Van Looy who, I assumed, had rather more experience of this sort of thing than I had; whatever "this sort of thing" actually was. 'I understand,' I said encouragingly, though actually I wasn't sure that I did. 'But how were the monies forwarded?'

'In the case of mijnheer Van Looy, the arrangement varied somewhat from standard practice.' He winced at the thought of such an irregularity. 'Van Looy was paid by us rather than the university, and we provided the money quarterly.'

'And how was that achieved?'

'I believe that a courier delivered the monies directly to the Rector in person. The delivery would have been the responsibility of the Heer van Zuylestein.'

I was beginning to find these titles confusing, though their punctilious use was doubtless second nature to men of the court. The Heer van Zuylestein was the same person I knew as William de Zuylestein, the latter being a sort of family name and the former being his title, or at least a part of it. Of course the organisation of the delivery would be his responsibility, and he would employ Van Kamerik or some similar person to do the job. But, if so, then the Rector would have met the courier; and the courier would know that someone at Leiden was in the Stadhouder's pay. As did the Rector, of course. I just hoped that the Rector had waited until the courier was far from Leiden before he gave the purse to Van Looy in case the transaction had been observed.

My questions being concluded, I rose and was about to thank him for his help when my eye was caught by a painting on the wall behind him. 'That is a very fine work,' I said, although I confess that my knowledge of art is negligible.

De Ring turned and inspected it as if noticing it for the very first time. 'Oh, that,' he said. 'It is a view of Rubens' estate near Antwerp.'

'By whom, may I ask?'

'What? Rubens, of course. I bought it from the artist.'

'You own a Rubens?'

'Yes. I keep it here because I'm rarely at home. I would never see it if it were not here.'

'Aren't you worried that someone will steal it?'

'It would be easier to steal at home. This palace is much better guarded than my house. And any man would know that he who stole anything here would be hanged within a day of discovery.'

Strictly speaking, men ought not to be hanged until they have been tried in court, but Stadhouders have tended to regard this as an administrative inconvenience rather than a safeguard of their subjects' liberty. William was generally considered to be one of those most likely to follow the law, but I was sure that he could take a shortcut when it suited him. And if I could find whoever had murdered Van Looy, he could expect the minimum of delay before he was swinging in the breeze.

Despite Pieters' best efforts, I was not convinced that the list he had provided could be complete. Although Van Looy had not been sent to Leiden until the new payment system had been introduced and therefore nobody should have known his real identity, I had noticed that the clerks in the room worked with papers spread across their desks. I could not exclude the possibility that somebody had somehow seen two documents and put two and two together; but if that were the case, then the finger would have to point at somebody with access to the Stadhouder's offices. On the other hand, hundreds of men and women were walking around these buildings, and although there were sentries and checkpoints I presumed that from time to time guards could be distracted.

In the back of my mind I remembered the disappearance of a paper from one of the university offices which had never been guarded because, it was said, it would never be unattended, but then came a day when all the clerks except one were needed elsewhere, and he had to answer a call of nature, during which time an opportunist managed to slip in and "borrow" an item of correspondence. In my defence, I wanted to know whether I was going to be kept on as a member of staff after my probationary period, but it had taxed my ingenuity to think how to return the document. I had assumed that nobody would notice its disappearance for a while, but it was detected almost as soon as the clerk returned — how was I to know he had been working on it when he needed to leave urgently? — and I had to resort to pushing it under the locked door at night, giving it a sharp shove at an angle so that it was discovered in the morning under a desk near the corner of the room.

Obtaining an appointment with William de Zuylestein was more challenging than seeing the Stadhouder himself. It seemed that he had returned to his estate to deal with the eviction of some tenants who had not paid their rent. This was a duty that he took very seriously and liked to supervise personally, perhaps because he lived a fairly hand-to-mouth existence himself. He was required to put on a certain show as a senior courtier, but his lands had been severely damaged during the late war and it was rumoured that his income was much reduced. His tenants were struggling as much as any other lord's, but he could not be as accommodating as some others given the straitened circumstances of his own purse.

I was questioning whether anything was being gained by my continuing presence in The Hague when Pieters came to tell me that Van Kamerik had returned. I hastened to speak with him, and found him making short work of a roast chicken in one of the rooms where the guards ate.

I introduced myself and explained my mission.

'You won't take offence, I'm sure,' he replied, 'but how do I know that your mission is authorised? I can't talk to just anyone, you know.'

I was trying to think how I might prove my bona fides when Pieters chipped in.

'I am in a position to provide such assurance, mijnheer. The Stadhouder himself has commissioned Master Mercurius to establish the circumstances surrounding the death of mijnheer Van Looy.'

Van Kamerik stopped eating and stared at each of us in turn. 'Van Looy is dead?'

If he was dissimulating, he was very good at it; but then, I suppose it would be helpful in his work for him to be very good at it.

'I'm afraid he is. He was struck from behind and pushed down a flight of stairs,' I explained.

'The stairs near his office?'

'The very same.'

Van Kamerik leaned forward and spoke confidentially. 'I cannot say that I'm surprised. The last time I was there, I caught a glimpse out of the corner of my eye of some low fellow skulking there as I left Van Looy's room.'

I might have resented being described in such terms if it had not been important not to admit my presence. Then I recollected that there was no reason to conceal the fact now that Van Kamerik had admitted that he had been there. 'That was me,' I said. 'I was about to visit Van Looy myself when I saw that he already had a visitor. Your scabbard is distinctive.'

'I'm not ashamed of who I am.' He lifted the scabbard into view. 'This leopard has been the badge of my family for nearly two hundred years.'

I had completely failed to notice the animal, largely because it was the same colour as the scabbard and it was surrounded by gold mountings. I did not dare to ask whose badge the leopard was, because it was clear from Van Kamerik's face that I was expected to know that. But, in all truth, it was quite hard to tell it was a leopard. It might just as well have been a lion — or even a house cat.

I am not comfortable in the face of aggression, and Van Kamerik was distinctly pugnacious. There are bravoes who march around our cities challenging all and sundry to duels, and I could easily imagine Van Kamerik doing exactly that, but only if he thought he would win; and I had a strong suspicion that the customary rules of combat would swiftly have been discarded if the fight was going the wrong way. Van Kamerik had the look of one who would stick his sword-point between your ribs while you were politely saluting him.

'I heard raised voices,' I said. 'What were you arguing about?'

I expected him to tell me to mind my own business, but he was commendably direct on this point. 'He had evidence of a conspiracy against the Stadhouder which he had been gathering for some time. I urged him to use it to act at once, but he said that he believed that there were others who were party to the plot who had thus far escaped his detection, and therefore he proposed to delay in the hope of netting all the birds with one swoop.'

'Did he confide in you who these people were?'

'No, because he knew I would have run them through myself if I had known their names. I can't abide treason.'

He looked at me as if I might well be a traitor. I had not felt so concerned for my personal safety since the Bishop of Namur took exception to something in one of my homilies.

'I ask you, mijnheer, to think carefully. Did he say anything, at any time, that might help me to identify these villains and bring them to justice?'

My language was carefully calculated to excite his sympathy. It failed, because he plainly did not think that we needed to trouble a court if these names came to hand. Van Kamerik believed in direct action and would just have shoved them head first down the nearest well. At least, that is what he told me.

'And good riddance to bad rubbish,' he added.

Van Kamerik was able to give me one piece of information that I had not heard before. Van Looy had talked about a group of "at least five" plotters active in Leiden. It seemed incredible to me that so large a group had escaped detection, given the fever of activity that had resulted from the fall of the De Witts. On the other hand, despite my disparaging remarks about him, I could see now that Van Looy was not a fool. The man whom I had found repellent in almost every way was acting a part. This, of course, did not mean that he was not repellent anyway, but I was compelled to admit that I might have misjudged him. In any event, no man deserves to end his days in an undignified heap on a back staircase, and I was duty bound to do all I could to unmask his killer.

CHAPTER NINE

I presented my compliments to the Stadhouder, who asked me what I proposed to do next.

'I will return to Leiden and, with your permission, share what I have learned with the Rector. I will then see if any more has come to light about Van Looy's death. But in order to keep my cover intact, I must make the return journey to Utrecht soon to hand over my report on the university salaries and complete my task for you there with Professor Voet.'

The Stadhouder paced as he thought. Since he was wearing boots, this was not doing a great deal for the condition of his carpets. As usual, the Stadhouder was attired in a deal of armour which clanked as he passed back and forth. If I am ever haunted by a ghost dragging chains behind him, I expect it will sound much like the Stadhouder's perambulation that day.

'I approve,' he said at length. 'Tell Voet that I am grateful for his advice and I accept his proposal to have his grandson and mijnheer Van Leusden ready to support him. Tell him not to tire himself and that I am concerned for his health, all that sort of stuff. I'm sure you'll think of something. Let him believe that I am not concerned about any diminution of his powers but I do not wish to lose his valuable counsel by working him into an early grave.'

I was unsure how genuine I could make these sentiments sound, but I bowed to acknowledge the order.

'We can always think about replacing him in the spring,' William added.

I have been accused, at various times during my life, of an antipathy to great men. It is not so. I have known several, and

William III was amongst them. I would go so far as to say that he was, taken all in all, a good man. But I would not have wanted to devote my life to the service of such a master.

'Pieters, give Master Mercurius the same sum as before for his expenses. You heard what I just said. Write out a letter for Professor Voet in those terms and I'll sign it before Mercurius goes. Well, don't dither, man. The last barge for Leiden leaves within the hour.'

I had forgotten that Adriaan had returned to Leiden with the Rector's carriage.

'One last thing, Mercurius,' said the Stadhouder. 'Please tell the Rector I would be very happy for him to serve one more year, or at least until you have solved this mystery.'

I should have explained before how the university is managed. Each year one of the professors is elected Rector Magnificus. He chairs the Academic Board and is, in theory, the chair of the committee that awards degrees of all kinds. In practice, no man knows enough these days to ask sensible questions of all the candidates for doctorates in all the subjects, so a selection of deputies usually take on these roles. Occasionally a Rector serves more than one year or is re-elected at a future date.

As a result of the wars and general turmoil, the Professor elected Rector for 1672-73 had been unable or unwilling to take up the post, and nobody was very keen to stand for the job. Strictly, the man I have been calling Rector was filling in for his replacement, but to all intents and purposes there had been no change, and, to judge by the Stadhouder's words, there would be none next academic year either. I knew that the Rector would be disappointed. He wanted to return to his books and his teaching, and now the Stadhouder had explicitly tied that happy moment to my success. If I did not succeed, the Rector would be forced to carry on for yet another year. I suppose I could have concealed the message, but any man who did not pass on a command from the Stadhouder was either very brave or very foolhardy, and I am neither of these.

The barge glided to a halt alongside the Fish Market, and I hopped out and walked the short distance to the Rapenburg. My route took me past Steen's inn, and I was sorely tempted to slip inside and see how many beakers of beer were needed to make me forget everything, but I was worried that I might forget everything.

To my relief, the Rector had retired for the night so it was not until the following morning that I was able to wait upon him and recount what had passed at The Hague. It was all going very well until I got to the part about the Rector staying on for another year.

'So, if I am to understand the Stadhouder, I have to remain in office until you solve this crime?'

'So it would seem, Rector.'

'And if you don't solve the crime…?'

'The Stadhouder did not specify what would happen.'

The Rector broke eye contact and returned to his work, always a bad sign. 'Then I will specify it. I am growing old. No doubt I would need an Assistant Rector who would do the bulk of the work for me. I know just the man.'

This was no idle threat. The work of a Rector is arduous and conducted well into the evening. I might never get to Steen's Inn again.

'Permit me to observe,' I stammered, 'that the Rector is always a professor, which I am not.'

'Not yet,' agreed the Rector, 'but I'm sure I could find or create a professorship for the right candidate, should the need arise.'

My dear grandmother would be so thrilled to hear that I had achieved the rank of professor that she would overlook the fact that my life was irrevocably ruined.

'For example,' the Rector murmured softly, 'we currently have a vacancy for a Professor of Botany.'

'I know nothing whatever of botany,' I protested.

'Neither did the last one,' answered the Rector. 'That is why we have a vacancy.'

Van Looy was still in the crypt of the Hooglandse Kerk, covered with a white linen sheet. Nobody seemed to be taking any responsibility for burying him. I kicked myself for not having asked Pieters whether Van Looy's cousin Abraham had been traced, but whether he had or had not, Van Looy could not stay here much longer.

I said a few prayers at his feet and was just rising when I became aware of a sinister presence behind me. Turning slowly, I discovered the verger was standing there, which explained my creepy feeling. Vergers do that to me. They have a knack of sneaking up on you silently that must be part of their training.

'You're one of the gentlemen from the University,' he said firmly.

'I am,' I agreed. 'I am Master Mercurius.'

'I'm glad you're here,' he replied. 'We did as the Rector asked and washed and shrouded the poor gent.'

'Thank you,' I said, though that was going to stop me examining the body again.

'What should I do with the gent's things, Master?'

'His things?'

'Yes, his clothes and the stuff he had on his person.'

'I will take them for safe keeping and return them to his family. Do you need me to sign for them?'

'If you would, Master. The Minister's day book will do nicely.'

I followed him to the vestry where we wrote an entry in the Parish Journal and I signed it, whereupon the verger delivered a bundle to me.

'There you are, Master. Will his family be at the funeral tomorrow?'

'I'm afraid not. We have not managed to find them.'

'Ah.' He sounded disappointed.

'Is that a problem?'

'Well, the Minister was hoping to discover the gentleman's Christian name. It seems nobody in Leiden knew what it was.'

It was bad enough that he was perforce being buried under a false surname. I could at least ensure that the right Christian name was used. 'I can help you there. It was Carolus.'

The verger's face brightened. 'The Minister will be pleased to know, Master. I'll tell him as soon as may be.'

'Perhaps you can help me in return,' I said. 'I've been away for a few days, so I have not heard the funeral arrangements. What time is the service tomorrow?'

'Why, bless you, Master, at eleven o'clock. The body is being brought to the Academy tonight and will lie there before the procession.'

'He's to have a procession?'

'The Rector was insistent. He was a University official, after all.'

A procession meant that we would all be expected to wear full dress. In the case of Master Hubertus, his best clothes were not appreciably more elegant than the rags he normally wore, but the Professors of Law would be in their element, each bedecked with all manner of badges and sashes, enjoying every minute of the pomp. One of them, who had two doctorates, had been known to wear one cap and carry the other just to make a point. It would be tedious, but I suppose that the Rector was right; we owed it to Van Looy.

And a little voice in my head was suggesting that it was just possible that the killer would show up to crow over his success.

CHAPTER TEN

When my time comes, I wonder if I shall have a funeral as grand as Van Looy's. A number of staff and students had left for the summer, but the majority of the staff had been summoned to return, so as the bedellus lined us up in order of seniority there was a fine show of bright robes and elegant caps. As expected, the law professors were dolled up like peacocks on heat, strutting their way around the hall to ensure that their gowns were flowing in the most attractive way. Even Master Hubertus appeared to have combed his hair and beard, which is why I almost failed to recognise him until he spoke to me.

'Have you found those rabbits you were looking for?' he asked.

'Er — no. I've abandoned rabbit farming,' I replied. It seemed easier than trying to correct his ramblings.

Hubertus seemed content and dropped the subject, but remained beside me, obviously thinking of something else he might say to make polite conversation. I believe I may have been one of the few members of staff disposed to be polite to him.

'Did you know the deceased?' he enquired.

'Yes, I did. Didn't you?'

'I don't know. Name rings a bell, but…'

'The Rector's secretary.' Hubertus still looked puzzled. 'Tall chap, bald on top, fringe of brown hair.'

'Looked like he was sucking a lemon?' suggested Hubertus.

'That's him.'

'Ah! I'd wondered who had died. Can't have been very old.'

'He was murdered.'

Hubertus had evidently not heard this before. 'Murdered? You mean — killed?'

'Completely. Blunt object to the back of the head and pushed down the stairs.'

Hubertus frowned. 'Must have been a tall fellow.'

'Van Looy? Yes, he was.'

'No, I meant whoever bashed him. He was probably the tallest person in the university. Hitting him on the head can't have been easy.'

I stroked my chin in thought. The wound on the back of Van Looy's head was actually above the bit of the skull that sticks out at the back. You can tell I am no anatomist, because that probably has a name of some kind. Anyway, the blow had come down on Van Looy from above. Now, a long-handled club or weapon might have been used, so we could not deduce the height of the assailant, but another thought struck me. Van Looy was well built. I know he could have simply toppled forward, but if he had been pushed, you would need to give the great ox quite a shove to get him all the way down the stairs, given that there was a small landing.

To explain better, the stairs went up a few steps to the first platform, then turned left and went up again to a second landing before turning left once more and completing the ascent to the upper floor. Being servants' stairs, the turns were quite tight. The more I thought about it, the stranger it seemed that he had not stopped on the first landing or become wedged partway down.

I'm a fool! I thought. *How did I not see it before?*

Van Looy had been lying on the stairs and I had paid no attention to his clothing, but now I recalled that he was wearing his cloak. If I had thought about it at all I might have guessed that he was going out, but it had been evening and he rarely went out at night except to find me — and I was already there. And his cloak had not been clasped at the neck. I had assumed — if I had thought about it at all — that he had wrenched it open in the fall. But suppose he had been struck somewhere else, such as in his office, then wrapped in his cloak to make him easier to drag to the stairs, and thrown down by it. That would keep his arms in.

This line of reasoning was disquieting. If I had missed that, what else had I missed on first inspection? I resolved that as soon as the service was over, I would return to the staircase to examine it properly this time. And I would examine Van Looy's clothing which, by happy chance, I had kept in case his cousin turned up to the funeral.

My musings were interrupted by a tap on the shoulder.

'The bedellus is glowering at you,' muttered Hubertus. 'You're too high up the line for your seniority.'

He was right on both counts. I rushed to take my rightful place. And nobody can glower like a bedellus.

We paraded through the city to the Hooglandse Kerk behind poor Van Looy, who must have been getting bored of the journey by now, and I was touched by the number of townsfolk who bowed their heads reverently as we passed. Some even crossed themselves in the Catholic fashion.

The bedellus, who is a sort of jumped-up janitor, but who loves all the ceremonials of the university, showed us to our allotted places. The Rector delivered a eulogy of sorts, but that he could do it at all given how little we knew of Van Looy was quite remarkable. Looking back later, I could see that it was an all-purpose eulogy, which might have fitted any number of people but was cleverly crafted to appear personal to the corpse in question. After some prayer, the senior professor of theology delivered himself of a sermon. He took as his text the First Book of Samuel, chapter 2, verse 6: 'The Lord kills and makes alive; He brings down to the grave and brings up.'

Whether this was entirely appropriate for a victim of murder I leave to the reader to decide; unless, of course, it was an accusation of guilt, though I hesitate to think how the Stadhouder would take the news that Van Looy's death was an Act of God. I admit to a certain impatience during his address because I was keen to return to the scene of the crime to repeat my examination, more carefully this time, so it was a relief when the professor decided that fifty minutes was long enough and quit the pulpit.

A place had been found for Van Looy near the northern wall, but the actual interment was to take place after we had filed out. This was necessary because experience had told the church authorities that leaving a hole in the floor, however well signposted, was asking for trouble, so they would lift the slabs after we had left.

We duly lined up as before and processed past the coffin as it lay on the trestles, each pausing and turning to incline our head slightly in the direction of the deceased as we reached his heart. For some reason this affected me considerably, and I found myself silently promising Van Looy that I would find his killer.

I have a really bad habit of making promises when I have no idea how I will keep them.

My examination was delayed further when I discovered that the Rector had arranged a meal for us all in the dining hall which we were all expected to attend. The bedellus made sure we managed to sit in order of precedence as well, which meant that I was sitting very near the door.

I was delighted to see that Albrecht had been given some temporary help in the kitchen, so much of the food was edible. I noted the cook from Steen's Inn and one or two others as the doors opened to allow the food to be carried in, so I decided that if I was going to miss a meal today, this was not the one to avoid, and tucked in accordingly. I was hampered a little by the fact that it was a Friday, but fortunately there were plenty of non-meat platters from which I could serve myself, and in the general hubbub and confusion nobody seemed to notice that I was avoiding the meat. I did, however, take a large slab of beef and privily tucked it in my sleeve for consumption first thing on Saturday morning.

The bedellus rang a small bell and the Rector rose to his feet. He welcomed the guests, repeated some of the remarks he had made at the funeral about the sad loss of Van Looy, commented upon the difficult times in which we were living and the need to put old dissensions behind us now that the Stadhouder was firmly in charge, and then caused me to splutter over my wine as he somehow inserted the information that I had seen the Stadhouder only that week and had returned bearing the Stadhouder's greetings to the university and his commendation upon our work, not to mention a new pay scale for the staff.

I was conscious of many eyes turned in my direction, made worse when the Rector invited me to stand and be recognised; which doing, I glanced around the room, and found myself surprised to see Van der Horst in the doorway. He smiled as our eyes met.

It seemed that my examination of the scene had been better than I had feared, because I learned nothing new from it, except, perhaps, one thing. I had assumed that the killing happened when Van Looy had left his office and was facing the stairs. His assailant came up from behind, clubbed him, and then rolled him down the stairs.

There were obvious difficulties with this idea. Van Looy's office was in a long corridor, and the attacker would have to face Van Looy. As a result, he could not know whether anyone was watching. Why risk being seen in the act?

Second, it presupposed that Van Looy was wearing his cloak as if he were going out. But it was late in the evening for Van Looy to go anywhere, he being a man of regular habits, and he was always careful to lock his office door; yet my recollection was that the door was open when I examined the scene immediately after Van Looy was found.

For these reasons, I formed the alternative explanation that Van Looy had been assaulted in his office, probably with the door shut. The killer had then taken his cloak from the peg, wrapped the body in it to pinion the arms, looked out to see that nobody was about and dragged the body a couple of paces to the stairs. He had then probably used his feet and arms to shove poor Van Looy down them. This would explain the blood smear at the top of the staircase, where Van Looy's wounded head had rested.

If I was right, there should be some sign of a struggle in the office. I hastened to the Rector to request the loan of the key, and was gratified when he insisted on coming with me. Two heads are better than one, as they say.

We scouted the room carefully, and then we found it.

In the corner of the room under the window Van Looy had a strongbox, a sort of chest bound with hoops of iron and secured with a large lock. It was unlocked, though it had been carefully closed, and the contents were disarranged. Somebody had rummaged through them, and not in any systematic way.

'So whatever they were looking for,' said the Rector, 'they must have found and fled without bothering to secure the chest again.'

'I think not,' I answered. 'Observe, Rector, that the books on the shelves have been pulled forward. Our man looked for something there too; and since the strongbox was the obvious place to start, I conclude that he did not find what he was looking for there and continued his search elsewhere. After all, the papers in the strongbox all seem to me to be university papers. There is nothing of a personal or private nature there, so Van Looy must have had an alternative place for those. And since it is unlikely that Van Looy trusted entirely to memory, we might suppose that he had notes about the conspiracy against the Stadhouder somewhere, and I suggest that those notes were what the culprit was looking for.'

'And did he find them, Mercurius?'

'Well, Rector, if he didn't, we will.'

We had as much time as we needed, so we succeeded where the assailant had failed. I have no idea how long we had been looking when the Rector sat in Van Looy's chair to take a rest.

'Mercurius,' he said, 'there are papers in this cushion.'

He was right. We upended the chair and found that the underside was only lightly tacked in place. Prising it free revealed that the seat pad was resting on a small bundle of papers wrapped in canvas.

The Rector locked the door to the office. 'We must be careful. Somebody was prepared to kill to get these.'

It was a sobering thought.

Unwrapping the bundle we found a number of letters that must have been received from The Hague. I guessed that Van Kamerik had delivered these, though why Van Looy had kept them rather than burning them was an interesting point to ponder. So far as we could see, they mostly acknowledged packages received, beginning "The Stadhouder thanks you for your report…" but they contained no information as such. Perhaps he retained them as evidence that he had made timely reports.

The gem was a small piece of paper, barely a scrap, written in English. It bore a diagram rather like a family tree, with a grandfather, a father and three children, and underneath were words which I carefully copied onto another piece of paper.

'Does those words mean anything to you?' the Rector enquired.

'I don't speak English,' I answered.

'Neither do I, but there are plenty of people in Leiden who do. Let us find one.'

So saying, he made for the door and since he had the key, I was obliged to follow. We descended by the main staircase and the Rector marched resolutely onward. Within a hundred paces we found ourselves in front of the Pieterskerk, and the Rector pushed open the door of one of the workshops opposite. He made some enquiries and was directed to a man who was arranging the type in a small printing press, whom he addressed in Dutch.

'Mijnheer Cooper? I hope that you can help us.'

The small man looked up at us suspiciously. His face was smeared with ink, though I believe that his thick eyebrows were naturally jet-black. 'How so?'

'I am the Rector of the University and this is Master Mercurius. We have found a paper that we believe may be important but we have no English. I understand that you are English.'

'Scottish!' snarled the little fellow. 'I'm Scottish. But I have the English. Let me see.'

We handed him my copy, over which he pored for a moment before handing it back.

'It's nonsense,' he told us.

'But it must say something?' I persisted.

He translated it into Dutch for us.

'You do not need to grind the nest?' I repeated.

'That's what it says,' insisted Cooper.

'But that makes no sense.'

'I told you that, but that's what it says.'

The Rector plucked at my arm. 'Come away, Master. It must be a quotation or a cipher of some kind.' He thanked Cooper for his help and we stepped outside. 'Or the man is raving,' added the Rector. 'Let's find another English speaker and see if he believes it to say the same thing.'

The streets of Leiden contain quite a few English and Scots people, many of them Puritans who fled after Charles II returned and came to the Low Countries to find religious freedom. At Rotterdam they had their own church, but in Leiden they shared the use of the Pieterskerk, which is why it did not take us long to find another.

His name, though spelled Brough, was pronounced Bruff, he explained. I find English names very difficult to say sometimes. Why they can't have honest Dutch names like Terhoeven, Van Leeuwenhoek or Gijsbert Voet I have no idea. Anyone can pronounce those.

Mijnheer Brough inspected the paper and, with our leave, showed it to his daughter. We had overheard them speaking English to each other. He seemed to be a respectable man, a cloth merchant as he told us, and his daughter, while quite plain, was obviously intelligent.

'I cannot make much sense of it, gentlemen, but it appears to say "You do not have to grind the nest" or "You are not obliged", and so forth.'

The daughter concurred. 'Was the author in his right mind?' she asked.

'Indeed he was, juffrouw,' the Rector replied. 'Sadly it seems that he was done to death so that this paper could be destroyed, and he went to some trouble to conceal it.'

'Then, mijnheers, let us suppose it has a meaning, but not a plain one. If it were a code, it would require the recipient to have a code-book to uncover the message.'

'That would be very cumbersome, juffrouw. And the gentleman's chamber did not have any obvious code-book.'

'Surely he did not need one?'

'How so?' the Rector asked. His eyes were bright. Something was stirring behind them which I was not feeling. I was as much in the dark as ever I was.

'Well, if he intended to send this as a message, why had he not sent it? But perhaps it is a note to himself, and all that matters is that it means something to him.'

We thanked the Broughs politely and walked away.

'You know, Mercurius,' said the Rector, 'I think that young woman would be an adornment to our university. There is intelligence there, don't you think?'

'I do, Rector,' I agreed. 'But really — women students? Whatever next?'

CHAPTER ELEVEN

De mortuis nil nisi bonum. Speak nothing but good of the dead, or something like that.

I was beginning to feel that I had misjudged Van Looy. He was engaged on work of national importance, and he had adopted a persona that kept people at arm's length so that they were unlikely to stumble across anything incriminating. I could see now that he spoke to as few people as possible, so I should have felt honoured that he deigned to abuse me. Perhaps, I thought, if we had been given time, it was possible that we might have become friends.

No, that was pushing it a bit. But we might have grown to detest each other a little less.

I was sitting in De Vrede, Steen's inn on the Langebrug, with a tankard of ale in front of me. It was not my first, which might account for my maudlin disposition. Then, just to make my happiness complete, some idiot began to play the lute.

His name, I discovered, was Beniamino. Beniamino was a scheming, unprincipled scoundrel, with loose morals, unhealthy appetites and an utter indifference to the truth; but then I could simply have told you that he was a lute-player and saved myself a lot of words.

I don't know what it is about lute-players. I might, perhaps, exempt those who are the personal musicians of our great men, but the itinerant lutenists wander from inn to inn, frequently offering to play in exchange for food, drink and shelter for the night. As a result, they eat and drink lustily, to put it mildly, and that's not the only thing they do lustily. If I were the father of daughters, I should counsel them strictly to have nothing to do with anyone with a lute.

The problem is that they see themselves as figures of some celebrity. What in other men would look like a lack of deportment and questionable hygiene is viewed by young women as evidence of a louche and carefree lifestyle. There is undoubtedly some strange species of attraction between young girls and lute players that is like to bring about their ruin — the young women, not the lute-players — and there is many a maid in this land who has danced a horizontal galliard and has a little lutenist to show for it.

In Beniamino's case, this general shiftiness was enhanced by the fact that he was lately arrived from Italy, a fact that he casually threw into the conversation at least four times in the first ten minutes after he invited himself to sit at my table. Everybody else at the table left me in peace. He did not.

'Ah, a religious gent!' he announced, not much of a deduction given my clothing. 'I'm surprised to see a man of God in a low tavern like this.'

'There are much lower ones,' I replied.

'Don't I know it! I must have played in many of them. Still, a man must earn his living where he can. Is there a song you would especially like to hear, Master?'

'Yes,' I replied. 'Your last.'

He laughed heartily. 'Oh, there is wit in Leiden after all. I'll tell you what,' he continued, 'I'll sing a song for you anyway, no charge, just for keeping me company.'

He took up his lute once more and sang a song which, so far as I could gather, concerned a sailor who went away for many years and returned to discover that his sweetheart had married someone else. Broken-hearted, he returned to his ship and sailed away again, at which point I thought the story would end. But no, there were several more verses describing how, when his ship next docked, she was waiting on the quay for him with the happy news that she was now a widow, and they could marry. I expected to hear that they all lived happily ever after, but the story continued to describe how he went one day into the cellar of the house to investigate a foul smell and found the murdered body of the former husband with a handful of the torn dress he had seen in the closet in his wife's bedroom. Should he tell the authorities and see her burned at the stake? He decides he cannot, but never has a moment's peace in his life as he realises that a woman who has killed once may well do so again.

I cannot bring myself to describe his next song, except to say that it was filthy in the extreme and painted, if my brother's stories were in any way accurate, an overly romantic view of a sailor's life, given that it omitted any mention of flogging, sodomy or a watery death in favour of the attractions of a travelling lifestyle and a girl in every port.

There was a welcome pause in the music making at this point, but only because Beniamino reappeared at the table.

'Thirsty work, singing is,' he said.

One of the other customers poured a beaker of ale from his pitcher.

'Thank you, friend,' cried Beniamino. 'I think I may be here a few days.'

'That's unfortunate,' I said. 'Sadly, I must go to Utrecht the day after tomorrow.' I had only been thinking about when I should go, but the news that Beniamino was staying in Leiden had helped me to make up my mind.

'Ah, Utrecht! Nice city. Plenty of music lovers. Did you know that the city pays a man to make music for the citizens there?'

It was true. The city had employed a man called Van Eyck who was blind but could play beautiful music. He played on the square outside the Janskerk. Of course, this was about twenty years before, and he had passed away, but maybe it was still done. I decided I would find out while I was there.

The discovery that Van der Horst had been hanging around near the funeral had been preying on my mind, so I decided to see if I could find him. It was late July, so I would have expected the students to have gone home, in his case to Haarlem, but he was still in Leiden somewhere.

Students who intend to return are able to keep their rooms on, and Van der Horst was in his when I knocked.

'Master Mercurius! What a pleasant surprise. Please, come in.'

I thanked him and came straight to the point. 'I have been asked to investigate the circumstances in which mijnheer Van Looy died, and I noticed that you were in Leiden when others have gone home. I wondered if there was a particular reason for this.'

Van der Horst shrugged. 'I doubt that it bears upon your enquiry, Master, but the reason is simple. I have nowhere else to go. My father and I do not see eye to eye. I will, of course, pay him a short visit during the vacation, but when we are together for any length of time it usually results in high voices and strain.'

'I am sorry to hear that. We are instructed to honour our fathers and mothers in the Ten Commandments, of course.'

'Indeed. But we are also told to do no murder, and the temptation would be very great on occasion. I would rather break one commandment than two.' He smiled wryly. 'Do I shock you, Master?'

'Sadden, rather than shock. But I thank you for your honesty.'

'I hope all men will be honest, Master. The world will be better for it.'

'Indeed,' I agreed, though doubting whether I would ever see it come to pass. 'Are your friends still here?' I added, largely to make some kind of polite conversation.

'Molenaar is,' Van der Horst replied. 'He is an orphan, and relations with his guardian are strictly formal. As for Terhoeven, he has taken himself off home.'

'And where is home?'

'Do you know, I've never heard him say. But it must be quite a distance because he set off very early in the morning, I understand.'

Much of our country can be reached in a day if you can find a barge heading that way, but it may mean starting out before dawn.

'You were at the funeral?' I enquired.

'At the back. I thought it improper to insinuate myself into any part of the formal events. I would not have come to the dining hall except that I did not realise it would be used for a private function.'

That explained his presence. It did not explain the smile.

I had persuaded the Rector that it was important to examine the contents of Van Looy's rooms thoroughly, for which purpose he had given me the necessary keys. We had found nothing more in his office, but I had not yet found either the time or the appetite to search his bedchamber.

That room might yet have remained unchecked were it not for the sudden appearance of a messenger boy from the

Rector, bearing a note to tell me that Van Kamerik had arrived with the intention of searching Van Looy's rooms.

I fished in my pouch for a coin. 'What is your name, boy?' I asked.

'Cees, Master.'

'Well, Cees, I have a little extra task for you. Have you eaten?'

'No, Master.'

'Good. Well, not good that you haven't eaten, but good from the point of view of my plan.'

The boy removed his cap and scratched his head. It all seemed very straightforward to me, but perhaps he was a little backward.

'Go and have something to eat with this. Take at least an hour. Then return to the Rector with this note I'm writing. If he asks, tell him I wasn't in my room but you found me at the bookseller's.'

'But you are in your room, Master.'

'Yes, but I want you to tell him I wasn't.'

The boy looked shocked. 'You want me to lie, Master?'

'Yes. No! Not lie, exactly. Just … confuse the truth a little.'

'But I'll go to Hell for all eternity.'

'No, you won't.'

'Yes, Master, the minister told us all that Hell is full of liars and hippos.'

'Hypocrites?'

'That's the word. And if we tell a lie, the Devil will come and stretch our tongues with red-hot tongs and rub them with a burning coal forever and ever.'

Of all the children in Leiden, I had found one who had scruples about telling fibs. 'In some very special circumstances, God permits us to tell lies when there is a greater good. For example, if a burglar asks where your gold is kept, you can tell him you have none even when you do, because it's all right to tell a lie to a bad man.'

'Is the Rector a bad man, then?'

'By no means. But this message tells me that the man with him may be a bad man.'

This seemed to satisfy the lad's sense of honour. 'I thought he might be, Master. He looked angry.'

'So, take your time, and remember what I said. I wasn't here, but you found me at the bookseller.'

'But you won't be at the bookseller.'

'No,' I said as patiently as I could manage. 'How about this, then? After you've eaten you go to the bookseller, then, when you find I'm not there, you come back here?'

There was a short interval while he contemplated the implications of this deception, but at length he was satisfied and ran off, allowing me to slip along to Van Looy's room so that I could search it before Van Kamerik had his turn.

I did not expect to find anything of import, so I was not disappointed when nothing turned up. The only surprising thing was that there was absolutely nothing to hint at Dekkers' life before he became Van Looy. I had expected a miniature of his mother, or his first prayer book, but there was absolutely nothing. In fact, his room was commendably orderly, a task made easier by its spartan furnishings. All I saw were a few books, neatly stacked, including a couple in English, a bible, well-thumbed, a chest full of clothing and some blank paper but nothing else, a table with some more paper on it and a selection of quill pens.

I was just locking the room when it occurred to me that I had not seen something I would have expected.

There were pens, but no ink.

CHAPTER TWELVE

One of the advantages of working at a university is that there are experts around on everything. There are many things that we do not know, but all that is known is known by the staff of the University of Leiden, more or less. With this in mind, I went looking for someone who was well versed in natural philosophy, and the best person to start was with Theodorus Craanen.

You may have heard me mention Franciscus Sylvius, possibly the greatest doctor in Leiden's history, and certainly the best paid as a result of the very special arrangement that he made with a previous Rector, under which he pocketed double the usual salary of a professor. This Sylvius had studied under Craanen, but went on to eclipse him. Craanen was a professor of philosophy and mathematics but also a fervent follower of the French philosopher René Descartes. This set him at odds with some of the other professors, particularly Friedrich Spanheim, who would not normally rank mention here except that he was a close friend of the Rector and had a few years as Rector himself.

The issue was that Descartes held that the body and the soul were entirely disconnected and that any sensory information that the body provided could not be trusted. We know this is possible because we have experienced optical illusions, where our eyes tell us something that cannot be true. However, there is truth in the world, and the soul, being made by God, can identify truth provided the senses do not get in the way. Cartesians, as Descartes' followers style themselves, believe that scientific knowledge can be acquired *a priori* by deductive reasoning and that scientific experiments, which must involve observation (which, being dependent upon the senses, may be misleading), are unnecessary. Descartes said that God gives us our power of reason and that we can trust our reason even if observation suggests otherwise because God would not deceive us.

Even if the reader is not of a philosophical bent of mind, I hope it will be obvious that a scientist who believes that experiments are not necessary is out of line with the expectations of the world, and in 1673 Craanen was removed from his chairs, but managed to obtain a professorship in the school of medicine, because, as is well known, surgeons are dull beasts who do not need to think. I have heard it said that Craanen was such a fast operator that he could have amputated his own leg before he passed out with the pain, though, so far as I know, he never made that particular experiment either. At any event, Craanen would either know the answer to my question, or would know someone else who did. Whether he would tell me was another matter.

We Dutch have a completely undeserved reputation for being stubborn, but in the case of Theodorus Craanen it was, if anything, understated. He could be prickly, to put it at its lowest, and his temper was not likely to be improved by the knowledge that I was a member of the philosophy school staff and not, by any stretch of the imagination, a Cartesian. I had, however, overlooked one of the Christian virtues — pity.

Craanen pitied me as a person of inadequate philosophical training, and when I said I wanted to improve my knowledge of chemistry he at once volunteered the information that his species of natural philosophy was largely mechanical. To make his point, he led me to a tray upon which he had several metal spheres and a piece of fur. He rubbed the balls vigorously with the fur and demonstrated that they could then be used to pick up small pieces of paper. This power he attributed to something he called the "electric fluid". I have to say that I can think of much easier ways to pick up pieces of paper and that if this is all the electric fluid is good for I cannot see it amounting to much, but I said nothing at the time except to express myself impressed by the demonstration. This seemed to please Craanen immoderately, and he suggested that I might take up my enquiries with Carolus de Maets, the professor of chemistry.

You might wonder why I had forgotten that we had a professor of chemistry. To be perfectly honest, as I try to be, once I found de Maets I had to confess that I realised that I had seen him at staff meetings, but I had no idea what he did. For perfectly good reasons the experimental chemistry theatre was not housed in the main Academy building, but at a considerable distance, so we rarely saw the scientists. At intervals we heard small explosions, but the chemistry theatre was normally out of bounds to other staff — and, indeed, to students. The logic behind this was simple and has to do with the Cartesian theory I described earlier. The laboratory existed only for the use of staff, who were supposed to use it to verify the conclusions they had already reached by the exercise of pure reason. In this way Burchard de Volder, who taught physics, de Maets and their scientific colleagues were able to justify experimentation without infringing on their Cartesian beliefs. They did not experiment to gain knowledge, but to confirm knowledge that they had already gained. In fact, de Volder went as far as to deny that experimentation was science at all.

Although it was Saturday, I tracked de Maets to his sulphurous pit, where he was taking advantage of the lack of classes to do some work of his own. He was a young man and I confess to a fleeting sense of jealousy that one younger than me had been appointed to a university chair. I had been overlooked for the last vacancy in the faculty and was beginning to feel that maybe my future did not lie at Leiden. Perhaps I should quietly raise the question of a vacancy at Utrecht when I next saw Gijsbert Voet? But the old man was frail and not long for this world, so perhaps it would look like digging his grave for him; better to ask his grandson.

De Maets was a friendly fellow, and apologised at once for not shaking my hand, holding up his own to indicate some stains caused by his experiments with a solution of silver. 'I've seen you at the Academy, I think,' he said. 'You were at the funeral of that fellow yesterday, were you not?'

'I was,' I agreed, 'and it is in connection with his death that I have sought you out.'

'Me?' said de Maets. 'I thought he fell down the stairs?'

'He did. But someone encouraged him to do so.'

'I take it this encouragement went beyond mere exhortation?'

'It seems so. It took the form of a thump to the back of the head.'

'I see,' said de Maets. 'And may I ask what your part in this is?'

'Certainly. I have been asked by the Stadhouder to investigate the death.'

De Maets arched his eyebrows expressively. 'This Van Lucie chap obviously mixed in the right circles.'

'Van Looy — but, yes, his family were servants of the Orange household.'

'I must assume there is some discretion about all this.'

'There is. And I should therefore be grateful for your help on a confidential basis.'

De Maets indicated that we should sit and poured us each a little ale from an ornate flask with a small hinged lid. 'Never drink anything from an uncovered vessel in here,' he chuckled. 'You never know what may have fallen in it.'

I accepted gratefully and took a sip. It was much better than most of the beers sold in Delft, and I said so.

De Maets laughed again. 'If a school of chemistry cannot perfect the science of brewing, things have come to a sorry pass,' he said. 'It's all a matter of good water and carefully controlled temperatures, both of which we have here. But you didn't come here to discuss the brewmaster's art.'

'No, that's true. I must first swear you to secrecy.'

'Taken as read. I do so swear.'

'Thank you. Van Looy was not all he seemed. He was here undertaking some work for the Stadhouder in the course of which he had reason to make notes and reports. Of course, we have the completed reports, but we have not found much in the way of notes. Then it struck me that on Van Looy's desk there were plenty of pens, but nothing in the way of ink.'

De Maets laughed again. 'You suspect he was using invisible ink? In an invisible bottle?'

'Well, invisible ink anyway. But we haven't found any. So what could he use?'

De Maets took a long swallow and stared at the wall for a moment. 'Were these reports to many people, or just one?'

'Just one. Plus, I suppose, himself, because he would need to read his own notes.'

'Then it is reasonable to suppose that the recipient would know how to activate the ink. And I assume that Van Lucie would need to be able to write the notes at short notice, so it cannot be one of those preparations that are slow in the making.'

'Van Looy,' I corrected him again. 'That all seems plausible.'

'Well, Mercurius, there are broadly two types of invisible ink. Some are natural fluids and some are manmade stains.'

'If they're stains, wouldn't we see them?'

'They are formed of two parts. The author writes with one, which is invisible; the recipient washes the paper with the other, and the words can then be seen. The chemistry is trivial, but there are a number of possibilities.'

'And the natural fluids you mentioned?'

'The great advantage is that we always have them. Blood is readily visible, but there are others that are less so. Lemon juice, onion juice, vinegar, milk, saliva, urine or even a man's seed can be used.'

I felt a sudden and strong urge to wash my hands. 'So far as I know,' I said, 'Van Looy had not been gathering onions or lemons, so perhaps it is one of the others.'

'Do you have any paper that might bear such a message?'

I passed him a small sheaf of blank paper I had taken from Van Looy's chest. I suspected it because I could see no reason why a man would lock blank paper away, especially when a small store sat upon his desk.

De Maets took it to the window and fetched a glass flask. 'I don't have a lens here,' he explained, 'but this will serve to magnify the surface. You see, the act of writing will disorder the surface of the paper, whatever ink is used. We may not be able to read it, but we might see that something has been written.' He held the flask in front of each sheet in turn, slowly moving the paper so that the light fell on every part. I watched in silence as he sorted the sheets into two piles. 'I think they may all have been disturbed,' he finally declared, 'but perhaps some have just been under a sheet that has been pressed on. However, with these three I think I can see some evidence that a liquid has penetrated the surface fibres. Incidentally, I must compliment Van Lucie on his choice of paper. It is very good quality.'

I had given up correcting him by this point. I just wanted him to tell me what was on the paper. 'And is it possible to make the writing visible?'

'Oh, certainly! Well, almost certainly. Probably.'

'Then let us get on with it.'

'We just need some heat. Organic liquids mostly turn brown on the application of heat before the paper begins to char. If you will kindly open the small door of the stove in the corner, I will find some tongs to hold the paper.'

There was a small iron stove with a flat tiled surface. I opened the door while de Maets busied himself in moving some small pots from the nearer table to one on the far side of the chamber.

'I do not expect sparks,' he explained, 'but some of the items here do not take kindly to flame.'

'Is that the cause of the explosions we hear from time to time?' I asked innocently.

De Maets frowned darkly. 'No, Master, idiotic students are the cause of the explosions.'

'I thought students weren't allowed in here?'

'They aren't. That's why they come when I'm not around to put a stop to their high jinks.'

'Isn't there a lock?'

'There is, but it wouldn't delay an intelligent five year old with a bent nail. Ah, here we are!' De Maets lifted the paper away from the heat and held it at eye level. There was clear writing on it.

It said *MTXVI18*. And that was all.

We tried several other pages. One contained a list of dates, or so we thought. The other showed a cross such as Our Lord hung on, above a smaller cross with equal arms, and around them four six-pointed stars arranged in a square.

'It means nothing to me,' de Maets said.

'Nor me. But a man does not doodle with invisible ink, so we may assume that it meant something to him. And there is a precision about the size and arrangement of the stars. Is it a map, perhaps? Four landmarks between which something is hidden?'

'Something to do with four Jews and two Christians?'

'Then why would the two crosses be of different sizes?'

'Maybe one of the Christians is unusually tall? Master, you are a philosophy teacher. Conjecture is your art, not mine. But at least we know that Van Looy wrote these notes and kept them safe, so they must have been important to him.'

Indeed they must, I thought, but I had no idea why.

Returning to the Academy, I had the extreme pleasure of seeing a fuming Van Kamerik coming down the stairs, from which I divined that his efforts had not been crowned with success, a fact that he confirmed upon questioning.

'You have removed nothing from his room?' he said.

'Nothing that you do not know about.'

'The Rector tells me you found a message.'

'Yes — "you do not need to grind the nest" — written in English.'

'Which means?'

'We don't know. It sounds like nonsense to us. Why would you grind up a bird's nest?'

'But it must have meant something, or why would Van Looy have gone to the trouble of writing it down?'

'And why write it and hide it? If it's such nonsense, why not just leave it on his desk?'

Van Kamerik slapped his gloves into his open palm. Though it made a loud noise, he did not flinch. 'It would not matter if nobody else here would know what it meant,' he said.

'Well, clearly,' I agreed, thinking that was a statement of the utterly obvious.

'No, I mean we must work backwards. He concealed it because it needed concealing, therefore there must be somebody here to whom the message would have meant something.'

Van Kamerik's reasoning made sense. While the message was opaque to us, it must be transparent to someone, and whoever that was could conceivably have had access to Van Looy's office. That must be why he needed to hide it.

Then I had an alternative thought. 'But wouldn't that be equally true if he had no idea who the traitors were and therefore suspected everyone?'

Van Kamerik looked crestfallen. 'You mean I'm saying he hid it because the plotters would have recognised themselves and you're saying that doesn't mean that Van Looy would have recognised them?'

'Exactly. He didn't know whom to trust with the information.'

'He said he hadn't found them all yet.'

I hesitated about revealing anything to Van Kamerik who, after all, might have been one of the traitorous plotters, but if that was the case, why had he not stabbed the Stadhouder in his palace, where he had ample opportunity? True, he would have died himself immediately afterwards, but it was unlikely that he had never experienced a moment alone with the Stadhouder when he could have done violence to him. And we must not forget that Van Zuylestein, a man who enjoyed William's complete trust, had employed Van Kamerik in the first place.

'We found a sketch,' I began.

'A sketch?'

'Yes. It showed what looked like a pedigree. There was a grandfather, a father and three sons, but no names, just that shape.'

'Well, that could be anything,' Van Kamerik protested. 'It could be just a garden rake or a trident.'

I suppose it could have been; but I had a strange sense that it was describing some sort of relationship. I had no evidence for that; but then I do not have hard evidence for a lot of things that I believe. I just have faith, but that is no small matter.

When I told Beniamino that I was going to Utrecht on the day after tomorrow, I had forgotten that would mean having to travel on The Lord's Day. This would have earned me the censure of many of my colleagues, though not the Rector himself, and news of it would have thrown my dear grandmother into an apoplexy as a result of her complete conviction that those who profane the Sabbath are certain to be smitten with a heavenly thunderbolt. She can produce no conclusive evidence for this belief but says that it does not require evidence because it is something that "everybody knows".

I attended the Morning Service in the Pieterskerk, then hid myself in my room to say Mass. There are Catholic churches in Leiden, though they must be discreet and therefore operate in the back streets behind plain doors, but the people coming and going are watched and I could not afford to be identified as a

Catholic because my post at the university was dependent on my being a member of the Reformed Church.

To explain, I had not been deceitful, at least not when I took the job. I was converted to Catholicism and ordained a priest after I had agreed to take the position. This was possible because the Bishop who ordained me wanted to have a shadow church in place in case the visible church was persecuted, so I was under orders to keep my Catholicism secret and my training was truncated to fit it in over a summer.

His Grace was good enough to say that being an ordained minister of the Reformed Church had to count for something, and therefore he would take my biblical knowledge, my ancient language skills and my general understanding of theology for granted and only cause me to study the distinctively Catholic subject matter that was needed to complete my training.

I had therefore passed the last few years as both a Reformed minister and a Catholic priest who, aside from my personal spiritual life, did nothing of value for the Catholic church. When I was away from Leiden I might attend a Mass, having changed out of clerical clothing, but otherwise I kept my secret close.

I packed all my paraphernalia away and returned it to its usual hiding place in my room. The reader will forgive me if I keep its location to myself. One cannot be too careful.

I was in the process of packing for my trip to Utrecht when there came a knock at my door. I opened it to find myself faced by the unexpected sight of Molenaar.

'Forgive me, Master. Mijnheer Van der Horst told me you were looking for me and I am anxious to be of service.'

'I'm grateful to him for taking the trouble, but he has already satisfied my curiosity. I hope I haven't disordered your Sabbath.'

'Not at all. I had hoped I might see you at church, but our paths did not cross.'

'I attended the Pieterskerk this morning.'

'Ah, that explains it. I was at the Hooglandse Kerk as usual. No matter. I understand that there are unexplained circumstances surrounding mijnheer Van Looy's death?'

'Yes, there are. Were you in Leiden at the time of the death?'

'Yes, Master.'

'So you know when he died?'

'No, but since I have been nowhere else for some weeks, I can be sure that I was in Leiden when he passed away.'

I had the uncomfortable feeling that I was being teased or played with. 'But unlike your friend, you did not attend the funeral.'

'I did not know the gentleman. I should have felt myself to be an intruder.'

'That didn't seem to worry Van der Horst.'

'We do not agree on all matters at all times, Master. I respect his desire to join in the collective prayers of the university, but it is not something I would presume to do.'

I nodded. I was finding it hard to decide whether I was in the presence of a saint or a serpent. He sounded sincere, but I thought I might detect a censure in his description of his friend's actions. Young men do not usually speak in such a fashion. 'Forgive me if I appear inhospitable,' I said. 'I'm just packing to go to Utrecht for a little while.'

'Please don't concern yourself. I just wanted to offer myself for any questions that you might have. If there is nothing further to discuss, I'll leave you in peace.' He bowed politely. 'Enjoy your trip, Master.' I must admit to the unworthy thought that I would enjoy Utrecht all the more for knowing that mijnheer Molenaar would not be there.

CHAPTER THIRTEEN

Monday was a gloriously sunny morning, and it was with a light step that I walked to the quay to find a barge to Utrecht. My quest was immediately successful — as it should have been, because a regular barge to Utrecht was advertised there — and I found a place in the bow where I could enjoy the calm weather and the warm sunshine.

I had a large piece of bread and some ham for my breakfast and was just giving thanks over it when I heard a familiar voice addressing me.

'Master Mercurius! This is fun. We can travel together to Utrecht.'

I turned to see the appalling Beniamino standing over me. Even worse, he was carrying a lute.

'I hope you're not going to play that thing all the way to Utrecht,' I said. I am willing to concede that my tone may have been a little sour.

'I can't, I'm afraid,' he replied.

I hoped that this indicated that he had suffered a broken arm or some similar happy accident, but I was soon disabused of this idea.

'It's the water that sprays up. It gets into the strings and plays hell with the tuning. Oops — I probably shouldn't say "hell" to a minister. Still, I've said it now. No need to move along, there's plenty of space for me on this bench too.'

'I ought to say my morning prayers,' I said.

'Of course. I ought to practise my scales too. But you're probably much more diligent on your prayers than I am on my music.'

'If practice helps you play better, don't let me stop you.'

He strummed a few chords. 'Never had a lesson in my life,' he announced.

I can believe that, I thought.

It was a long journey. Beniamino described his travels in Italy — again — then began flirting with a young woman carrying a basket of apples who fortunately had the good sense not to respond to his blandishments. When we stopped briefly to find some lunch, Beniamino bought himself the stinkiest herring I had ever smelt and in a misplaced gesture of friendliness offered some to me.

'Thanks, but I'll stick to my bread roll,' I said.

Beniamino nudged me with his elbow. 'If you had five of those and I had two of these, you could get your mate to feed a few thousand.' He laughed uproariously until his eyes streamed with tears.

I opened my prayer book at the Ten Commandments just to check there was no footnote exempting lutenists from the prohibition on murder, but I was disappointed.

We finally arrived at Utrecht.

'Are you putting up at an inn, Master?' Beniamino asked.

'I don't know yet,' I replied. 'I have to report to the University, and someone there may have a room for me.'

'Does the University have a lutenist?'

'I don't know.'

'It should. Add a bit of tone to the place. Show an interest in the arts, you know. I may make enquiries.'

'If I find they have a vacancy, I'll be sure to let you know,' I said.

And I meant it; nothing could please me more than to know that Beniamino had a job in Utrecht — given that I lived in Leiden.

As I expected, Professor Voet insisted that I should stay at his house. He seemed a little stronger than when we had last met, and stood to greet me, walking a little towards me whilst leaning on the table for support.

I presented the Stadhouder's compliments and told Voet that the Stadhouder would be very pleased to have the help and support of his grandson and Van Leusden.

'I am very grateful for the Stadhouder for his continued confidence in my family,' Voet declared. 'Let us drink a toast to him together.' He tottered to the sideboard and poured us each a small glass of wine. 'To the Stadhouder and the House of Orange!' he proclaimed, and I repeated it with, perhaps, a little less fervour; not that I held any brief for the opposing faction, but those were days when avoiding alignment with either side seemed prudent. 'How do matters stand in Leiden?' Voet asked.

This took me by surprise and I was unsure how to answer. I did not want to mislead the old man, nor to alarm him. If the De Witt faction were bold enough to murder the Stadhouder's man in Leiden, who was to say that they would not do the same in Utrecht?

But if there was danger, it seemed to me that Voet had a right to know.

'I regret that one of the Stadhouder's servants in Leiden has been foully murdered since we last spoke,' I replied.

'Murdered? Dear me! By whom?'

'I do not know as yet. I am sure that I can trust in your discretion when I explain that the man was sent by the

Stadhouder to root out adherents to the opposition. It seems that he was on their trail when they arranged his death.'

'Poison?'

'No, Professor. He was struck on the head and pushed downstairs.'

'Stairs are dangerous places,' Voet murmured. 'The first Stadhouder died on a flight of stairs.'

Whilst undoubtedly true, the death of William of Nassau was due to his being shot at close quarters, and it can hardly be said that the stairs played a major role in his death. A man has to lie somewhere to die.

'It seems that this man had discovered a cell of five but did not know all their names. A diagram he left suggests that there was a captain, a lieutenant and three others. But then there was another diagram that seemed to show six conspirators, four shown as stars and two as crosses. Is one a later reworking of the other? Or, Heaven forbid, are there two such groups of villains in Leiden?'

'They are everywhere, Master. These are perilous times.'

'But you have none in Utrecht, Professor?'

For once, the Professor was not disposed to display excessive confidence. 'I will never say that there cannot be such conspiracies, but I have many pairs of eyes and ears at work and they report nothing to me. And you will permit me to remind you that, unlike Leiden, Utrecht was occupied by the French until very recently. The man responsible for our liberation therefore enjoys overwhelming support.'

It was rather hyperbolic to describe William as their liberator, because the French had actually pulled out of Utrecht before he got there. The flooding of the old waterline stopped their advance and a Dutch army threatened to advance into Germany and cut the French forces off, so they retreated; but I suppose in loose terms William had something to do with it and he was certainly not a man to refuse a laurel that was offered to him.

'Nevertheless,' Voet continued, 'by your leave I will ask my grandson and Van Leusden to join us here for supper this evening and we can discuss your information and decide upon our next steps.'

'Gladly,' I answered. 'I would much rather stifle an insurrection before it is born that try to round up the ringleaders afterwards, particularly as I have no powers to arrest anyone.'

'A small nicety,' sniffed Voet. 'If a man needs arresting, let me know and I'll get the Mayor to send the constables for him.'

Most Dutch cities have a Civic Guard to assist in their defence, consisting of local gentlemen and volunteers, but often with one or two professional soldiers to drill them. These full-time employees frequently double as Sergeants-at-arms for the Mayor and act as a police force, assisted in larger cities by a few constables. Unlike cities like Delft where the Civic Guard delighted in marching around the place, their Utrecht brethren seemed rather more subdued and I had seen no sign of them, but Voet clearly had confidence in their abilities.

There is a large painting by Rembrandt van Rijn that hangs in Amsterdam to this day showing a similar company of militia, and a more inveterate bunch of dandies and show-offs would be hard to imagine.

I do not think that it would have crossed Gijsbert Voet's mind that his grandson and Van Leusden might be otherwise engaged that evening, but his maid returned with the news that while his grandson would be delighted to wait upon us, Van

Leusden was away from home and not expected back until late; however, "late" would mean around sunset, because few men would venture outside the city after dark by choice, so there was a good chance that he would be able to join us eventually.

It remained a glorious summer's day, and Gijsbert Voet suggested that we might sit for a while under a nearby tree to enjoy the warm sun, not to mention a bowl of freshly picked strawberries. It was here that his grandson Johannes found us.

I find the idea of a young man bowing to his grandfather rather formal, but I think Gijsbert Voet expected it of Johannes, who removed his hat and performed an elegant sweeping bow.

'Sit ye down,' said the old man, 'and the Master will tell you what has been happening in Leiden. It shows the need for vigilance, for our enemy walketh about, seeking whom he may devour.'

'The fifth chapter of the first epistle of St Peter,' replied Johannes.

'Very good,' responded Gijsbert. 'We will make a churchman of you yet.'

I was only glad that he had not thrown the quotation at me. I recognised it, of course; it is from the passage that begins "Be sober, be vigilant", but I was a little vague about exactly where it was to be found.

Johannes sat and raised an eyebrow at me, whereupon I launched into an account such as I have set out in these pages.

When I finished, he sat stroking his chin in thought for a few moments. 'Such a shame! This Van Looy played a long game, I think. A lesser man would have had the small fry taken and lived on into old age. Instead he pitted his wits against theirs and paid a great price.'

'You think they moved against him because he was about to expose them?'

'What other construction can be put on events? He operates in safety for some months, then, when he is close to success, his enemies murder him.'

We sat in silence a short while, each of us lamenting that Van Looy had paid so dearly for an error of judgement; then the old man spoke quietly. 'When he is close to success indeed, but how did they know that?'

'I'm sorry, I don't follow,' I said.

'Killing Van Looy is a desperate act. Until then, they might have hoped to escape notice while their plans mature, but now the existence of the traitorous cell is known. They would only have done this if they felt that they had no alternative, that their discovery was imminent; so, I repeat, how did they know that?'

Johannes sprang to his feet and began pacing the garden, muttering as he went. It was clear that this line of thought excited him.

I was still struggling with the implications of this notion. I realise that this makes me look like a dullard, but I beg the reader to remember that I was sitting with two of the greatest minds the Netherlands has ever produced, so coming a distant third in such company is not so bad.

'Either Van Looy made a mistake and disclosed himself to them,' Johannes declared, 'or there is someone trusted by the Stadhouder who was able to tell them how matters stood.'

Gijsbert looked alarmed. 'A duplicitous scoundrel so close to the Stadhouder! Surely it is unthinkable. We must get word to him at once.'

Johannes spread his arms as if helpless. 'What can we tell him? We have no idea who it might be, or even which of the two alternatives that I suggested is the correct one. For all we know Van Looy may have summoned a plotter to his room, confronted him and been struck down.'

'That's true,' confessed Gijsbert. 'We can hardly tell the Stadhouder that someone in The Hague does not like him. He already knows that.'

The evening proved to be subdued thereafter. All of us were preoccupied with the question of how we might best ensure the Stadhouder's safety against an unknown threat. I described the time when I overheard Van Kamerik arguing with Van Looy, thinking that it showed that Van Kamerik's instincts, to round up the villains, were correct.

'If you overheard them, others may have done so,' remarked Gijsbert.

'I saw no-one else,' I answered.

'But did you really look?' asked Johannes. 'With respect, your attention was focussed on the unknown man with Van Looy.'

He had a point there.

'And why do you discount the possibility that Van Kamerik was himself responsible for the death of Van Looy?' added Gijsbert.

'Well, because his master is the Heer van Zuylestein, who is scrupulously loyal to the House of Orange.'

'Indeed he is,' replied Gijsbert, 'but he would not be the first man to have been deceived by one in whom he had placed his trust. Even Our Lord had his Judas.'

The difficulty with the particular example is, of course, that Our Lord, being one with God, shared in his omniscience and must therefore have known that Judas was going to betray him. Except, of course, that Judas had free will, otherwise he would have been acting under compulsion and would not have been subject to reproach for his actions, so if he had free will he could have avoided the betrayal. And here I must add that as a Calvinist I can see that Judas' free will is not incompatible with Jesus' foreknowledge of the choice that Judas would make; whereas the Catholic in me can see the necessity for Jesus' passion and therefore for his betrayal without which his purpose could not be achieved. But this was not the time to pursue these arguments.

We sat down to dine, still without any sign of Van Leusden, who finally appeared shortly before sunset, perhaps around nine o'clock. It was too late then to begin any lengthy discussion, for the professor was tiring, so we drank a glass together and agreed to meet again at six in the evening on Wednesday, the earliest time when all four of us were free of other commitments. If only one or other of us had changed our appointments, who knows how differently this story would have worked out?

CHAPTER FOURTEEN

Tuesday was another very warm day. Leiden, being nearer the coast and having many waterways, is often cooler than cities such as Utrecht which lack both of these features, and since Voet's house was close to the Dom Square, where there was little shelter from the sun, I passed a relatively uncomfortable day going back and forth between offices and explaining my report to the Senate of the University.

The Senate, being composed of intelligent men, quickly grasped that the Stadhouder's plan would give them something of a pay rise and were therefore in high spirits. The substance of my report having been leaked to them in advance by Professor Voet, they had resolved to feast me well at a banquet.

It took the gloss off the event a little to hear that they liked to find an excuse for these two or three times a year and would probably have thrown one to celebrate the end of the month of July if I had not been coming, but a convivial evening was had by us all. I am delighted to record that speeches were kept to a minimum, that no clergyman was permitted to deliver a sermon and that the burghers of Utrecht had a lutenist considerably more talented than Beniamino who played while we ate.

All in all it was a wonderful evening, and my resolve to see if there were any vacancies for teachers of moral philosophy was strengthened. There would, no doubt, be periods of prayer and fasting, but they are much more tolerable when one knows that nights like this will soon come along, especially if Albrecht is not involved in doing any of the cooking.

The centrepiece of the table was a pig's head with an apple in its mouth. The pig appeared to be smiling, as if to say that it was a privilege to be slaughtered and cooked for our pleasure. I drank rather more than was good for me, and found myself compelled to keep silent so as not to illustrate the fact by slurred speech or inopportune comments, but when the evening ended and we walked to our homes or lodgings, I was suffused with bonhomie and a general feeling that all was right with the world. This was not quite how I felt upon waking in the morning.

I knew of two paths to the Professor's house. I might have returned to the Dom Square and passed round two sides of the Dom to the street where he lived. It was not too long, but I had feasted rather well and was beginning to feel tired, so I chose the shorter route, which took me through a narrow passage and then along Achter de Dom.

I will remind the reader that I had drunk rather more excellent Rhenish wine than I was used to, but as I left the banquet I had the impression that I was being followed. I looked around, but saw nothing, though it was rather dark in the alleyway; thus I walked on, and the sense of being observed stayed with me.

I stopped abruptly, and heard one more step on the cobbles, but turning once more, the only person I could see was a man standing by one of the walls with his back to me. He had one arm stretched out against the brickwork so that his cloak formed a screen that prevented me seeing the woman he was undoubtedly propositioning, because I heard him speak in a low voice and she giggled in reply. I had, it seems, been so wrapped up in my own thoughts that I had failed to notice them as I passed by; but then, perhaps, they were taking care not to be noticed.

I thought of Janneke van Leusden and wished I had the liberty to walk with her that evening, though, of course, we could not have done so with propriety without a chaperone or a wedding ring. I did not care for the first, but the second appealed to me, and I went to my bed with happy dreams of what might be.

Gijsbert Voet was an early riser, so the household timetable was set to accommodate that, with the result that my shaving water arrived at some unearthly hour when even the birds in the trees were catching a little more sleep. I could see from the chamber window that it was another beautiful day. This fine weather cannot last, I thought.

I was sitting at breakfast when the door opened and an elderly lady walked in. From her mode of dress and her general air of superiority I guessed that this must be the professor's wife, so I sprang to my feet, banging my knee on the edge of the table as I did so.

'Are you one of my husband's students?' she enquired.

'No, mevrouw, I am Master Mercurius of the University of Leiden,' I replied, inclining my head politely.

'Ah, the Stadhouder's errand boy! I have been hoping to meet you,' she continued.

You had only to come downstairs and you would have done so, I thought, so I deduced that the desire to make my acquaintance was not quite as strong as she hinted.

I could have bridled at her description of me, but I decided to rise above that and simply asked her how I might be of service.

'Well, sit down and eat your breakfast, Master. I hope the Stadhouder has been mindful of my husband's exertions on his behalf — though I suppose you'll be sworn to secrecy on your mission.'

She bowed her head to mumble a prayer, so I waited until she had finished before speaking.

'On the contrary, mevrouw, I think I can safely say that the Stadhouder would wish it to be known that he has every reason to be grateful to the professor and has sent me to consult with him on lightening his load.'

'Good luck with that!' said the old lady. 'He'll die in harness. It is his conception of duty. His legs won't let him stand to preach any longer, but his mind remains sharp and he still writes his sermons, even if he cannot deliver them.'

'There is no desire to supplant him, mevrouw, but to consult with him on the appointment of assistants. I may say that we have identified two: your grandson Johannes, and a man named Van Leusden.'

The old lady paused in her chewing. The frown clouding her forehead had dissipated a little.

'Van Leusden is a good man. And Johannes is a very capable boy. You may be sure that neither will let the Stadhouder down.'

'I am grateful to you for your commendation of them.' And I was. In my — admittedly limited — experience, women are better judges of character than men, though I suspect a grandmother may take an overly rosy view of their grandson's accomplishments. My own dear grandmother has in the past attributed several gifts to me that I actually do not possess, the chief of them being a sense of diplomacy.

'And what do you have planned for today, while my husband is working?'

I sensed that I was being warned off disturbing him, and I resented the implication that I was taking a holiday from any labour myself. In fact, I had no plans before the meeting in the evening, but I did not propose to admit that lest I be accused of idleness. It was clear that Gijsbert Voet was addicted to work, and I did not want to appear any less committed to my duties.

'It may be some time before I see Utrecht again,' I said, 'so I thought I might explore the city.'

'It is worth the effort,' she averred, 'and if you will not be back, it would be good not to miss any of it.'

'Are there any places you would suggest I visit?' I asked.

Her face darkened again. 'I am sure an intelligent visitor like yourself can make perfectly adequate plans,' she snapped.

'Of course,' I added quickly.

'But I wouldn't wander too far. There is a storm brewing.'

I glanced out of the window at the bright blue sky. There was a slight breeze blowing, judging by the swaying of some saplings, which would be very welcome after such hot and still weather. 'I confess that I have never been good at reading the signs where weather is concerned.'

'Utrecht does not have the cooling winds from the sea you will have experienced in The Hague or Leiden. The weather is quite changeable, and after a run of hot days such as we have had, there is often a thunderstorm.'

I saw no sign of it, but I resolved to take my cloak with me; if nothing else, it would please the old lady that I had heeded her advice.

Later that morning, I was admiring the Pieterskerk. I am the last man to question the multiplication of churches, but since this fine old church could not have been more than a couple of hundred paces from the Dom, I was not clear why it was needed. A few minutes' conversation with the verger soon put me right, because he thought exactly the same thing, but pointed out that his church predated the cathedral. The Pieterskerk foundation can be dated to 1039, whereas the present cathedral was only begun in 1254, though he conceded that there had been a church or chapel on the site before that. Thus, he claimed, the proper question to ask was why Utrecht needed the cathedral.

I admired the pair of towers at the west end, the whole building seeming to my eye to be much better proportioned than some grander churches. When I said this, the verger's chest swelled with pride and he suggested I might care to ascend the pulpit and say a few words, where I would discover how fine the acoustics were. Not trusting myself to say anything extempore, I stuck to the Lord's Prayer and found that the verger's boast was not vain. I could make myself heard quite easily; and I will admit that the thought crossed my mind that if ever I were to have a parish of my own, this one would suit me very well.

The chances that such a thing might come to pass were not great, of course; while my bishop was keen that I should not advertise my Catholicism, I think he might have bridled a bit if I accepted a Reformed parish. And I will allow that my ideal had always been the academic life rather than parish duties, but in that sunny hour I found myself fantasising about having the care of souls in an agreeable city with a beautiful and accomplished wife to support me, and the leading candidate was less than five minutes' walk away.

It crossed my mind that Janneke and I might take a pleasant stroll together in the afternoon if she was at leisure, but I was not too sure what the etiquette might be for a gentleman calling upon a young lady when he knows her father is not at home, so instead of knocking at the door I fell upon the happy plan of walking back and forth along the street in the hope that we might bump into one another.

And so it proved. I was on my eighth passage in front of her house when she and her mother turned into the street. I feigned surprise at this felicitous accident and suggested that the two ladies might walk with me to a tea-house, if Utrecht boasted such a thing, and I would be honoured if they would join me in a pastry or two; or possibly six in her mother's case. This last thought went unsaid; even I am not so lacking in tact.

We wandered down to the waterside and walked through the park, I taking pains to converse with both the ladies equally, flattering the mother on the elegance of the lavender silk gloves I could see in her basket and complimenting the daughter on anything I could think of. I could see that the gloves had been newly bought, and I will not deny that I could not think when a married woman might wear a colour other than black with propriety, but I suppose we must allow the fairer sex their indulgences. Certainly if Janneke van Leusden had asked me for any number of pairs of gloves, I should have done my utmost to meet her desire without delay.

Speaking of desire, I suddenly became aware that I was very flushed and dabbed at my brow with my handkerchief.

'Why, Master,' said juffrouw Van Leusden, 'you must be very warm with your cloak on. Pray divest yourself of it, if it will make you more comfortable. I am sure neither of us will think it improper.'

I had completely forgotten that I was wearing it, and felt rather foolish. 'The Professor's wife suggested I might need it. She thought a summer storm was possible after so many hot, humid days.'

'Mevrouw Van Diest is a knowledgeable woman,' mevrouw Van Leusden allowed, 'but I think she may be mistaken. It is a fine afternoon.'

I shrugged off my cloak, rolled it and tucked it under my arm. 'Indeed it is,' I said. 'Now, what about some dainty sweetmeats?'

I walked the ladies home and returned to the Professor's house in good time to wash and tidy myself up before the planned meeting at six o'clock. The water was very welcome after being outside on such a sultry day, especially with a completely unnecessary cloak, and I dowsed myself thoroughly in it, giving my hair a good wash at the same time. I know that several eminent surgeons hold that washing one's hair is a sure way to induce fevers and mental disorders, but I have done it since I was a boy — or, more accurately, my mother and grandmother did it to me — and I believe my mental powers to have been unaffected as a result; there again, old Walther who kept the mill along our lane washed his hair regularly too and believed himself to be the brother of a donkey, so I suppose definitive disproof of the surgeons' hypothesis still eludes us.

The Professor was scribbling away when I entered the chamber, so I kept my silence until he laid down his pen.

'Master! Forgive me, I was deep in thought and did not notice you.'

'Not at all, Professor. I know how important it is to capture ideas while they are still fresh in your mind.'

'Quite so, quite so. I hope you have employed your time fruitfully?'

'I have indeed,' I answered, hoping that he would not ask exactly what I had been doing.

'Capital. So many men waste time, Master, and forget the wise maxim of Seneca — *non accipimus brevem vitam sed fecimus.*'

It is a strange feature of the human brain that where it achieves some tasks in one language perfectly well, and other tasks in a second language just as well, switching between the two can be very tricky. In my philosophical writings I use Latin, and I must admit that I do not translate anything into Dutch because I do not need to. I hear Latin and I reply in Latin, and all is well; and when I converse with colleagues, we will use Latin. But if I speak to my grandmother, who has no Latin, I use Dutch which is, after all, my mother tongue. Yet I often cannot easily translate the Latin into Dutch without feeling dissatisfied with the result. In this case, Seneca's maxim means something like "We don't start with a short life; rather we make it short," but I wish I could express it better.

Van Leusden and Johannes Voet arrived punctually and we began our meeting, which treated of the loyalty or otherwise of the important men of the city. Some names were readily assigned to one list or the other, but there was rather more discussion about others and in the end a third list had to be started where the three men did not agree.

I was pleased to note that although Van Leusden and Johannes showed every deference to the old man, they did not meekly allow him to have his way on all points. I forget the name, but when a brewer was mentioned, Gijsbert Voet would have placed him on the list of potential traitors whereas Van Leusden was convinced that the man was loyal to the House of Orange. Johannes whispered to me that if the man had pursued a more respectable trade there would have been less argument, but his grandfather believed that drunkenness was an appalling sin and blamed the brewers for it. This, it seemed to me, was much like blaming those who knitted blankets for the debauching of women, but I was maintaining a careful silence and casting the occasional glance at the street outside, where it seemed the Professor's wife's prediction was coming true, for there was a sharp, icy shower which seemed to be becoming more intense.

At one point the Professor became concerned that they may be overlooking someone, since they were producing names from memory, and Van Leusden remarked that this was easily overcome because they might borrow the alms register from the church vestry. This is not, as one might suppose, a list of the gifts received, but of the people from whom gifts might be expected, compiled on a systematic basis rather like a local census, and it seemed a very sensible idea. Van Leusden volunteered to fetch it, but he had not realised how foul the weather had become. I offered to go instead, since I had a cloak, but Van Leusden remarked that he was the best person to retrieve it, since he knew exactly where it was.

'Then by all means take my cloak,' I said. 'It will protect you from the storm.'

Van Leusden thanked me and donned it. Having checked that he had the keys he needed in his pocket, he stepped out into the rain and we watched him trot across the street and turn into the square that housed the Dom.

We returned to our seats when suddenly there was a mighty roar. It is not an easy noise to describe but, as I dictate these notes, it sounds as clear in my mind as it did then. We had no idea what had caused it — I think it must have been the towers of the Pieterskerk collapsing — but within moments there was a loud crack as a roof tile flew through the window of the room and several panes of glass were blown in. The noise was deafening as a mighty wind tore through the city from the south, and within a few minutes it was replaced by an even louder sound and a rumbling of the earth beneath our feet. I had never experienced an earthquake, and it would be idle to deny the fear I felt as the floor trembled.

Johannes reacted first, pushing his grandfather into a chair and lifting it bodily towards the back of the house. I ran to help and together we shielded the old man. We were bombarded by books flying off the shelves, and Johannes was struck by a wine bottle which cracked against his head, but he kept his post and by the grace of God the Professor was kept unscathed.

The storm must have persisted for above twenty minutes, though it seemed at the time to have been a good part of my life, not to mention the likely end of it, but finally the wind quieted and we could hear it move through the town to the north. The house had sustained considerable damage but it was intact. Tiles and glass had suffered badly, but those could be replaced. Johannes and I stepped outside, and we could at once see that the rest of the city had not fared so well.

The familiar twin towers of the Pieterskerk had fallen; the frontages of the houses to our right had tumbled inwards and whole roofs had vanished — one was found two streets behind — but the biggest shock was the sight of the Dom. Or, more accurately, where the Dom should have been.

Johannes and I stood open-mouthed. The bell tower had some damage, but was largely intact. The chancel towards the east end was in good order, apart from its glass. However, the entire nave, the long central section that joined the two ends of the cathedral, had vanished. Piles of stone littered the square, but we were spurred into action by the piteous cries of injured people.

We ran to the first we heard, a poor fellow who was pinned to the ground by a stone block that must have been at least four feet long in each direction. We could not lift it to give him any relief, and each attempt at movement caused him agony in his injured leg which lay beneath the block. It seems callous to rejoice that he soon died, but it must have been a blessing in view of the great pain he was suffering.

We next attempted to free a woman who had been fortunate enough to fall between a couple of pews, creating a small space and shielding her from the falling masonry that had landed on them. She was dusty and shaken but largely unharmed. As we lifted a section of wooden roof beam she crawled free, at which point Johannes suddenly cried out, 'Where is Van Leusden?'

If he had reached the vestry he should have been safe, because that part of the Dom was still sound, so that was where we first went, Johannes leading the way.

The door was unlocked and open, but there was no sign of Van Leusden. Johannes wanted to check the contents of the coffer, but it was locked, and it was some moments before he could find his own set of keys.

'The register is gone, so I deduce that Van Leusden arrived here safely. But he would never have left the door unlocked.'

'He would if he feared for his life,' I said. 'Perhaps he was here when the nave collapsed and ran outside to help.'

We searched around the wreckage as best we could. It seemed heartless to leave injured people while we looked for Van Leusden, but we needed to know what fate had befallen him.

It was growing dark before we found him. His body lay on a large stone at the south west corner of the nave. A large dent in his temple and a considerable amount of blood showed that death must have been instantaneous.

We stood and said a prayer over his corpse and then wondered what to do next.

'I don't suppose you want your cloak back urgently,' said Johannes.

We used the cloak as a sort of hammock to carry him back to the Professor's house, where the old man showed his distress at the loss of Van Leusden.

'Just an hour ago he was sitting opposite us,' he whispered. 'It is a reminder to us all that we know not the day nor the hour of our deaths.'

Since the Professor could reasonably expect to be closer to his own demise than I to mine, he could be forgiven for a morbid thought, but he was right. We cannot know when God will call us home, and therefore we must keep our lives in good repair lest we fall into the pit.

Deliana van Diest supervised Anna in the washing of the body, while Johannes said that he should go to inform Van Leusden's wife and daughter of the lamentable tidings. I had no appetite to join him, but I knew my duty, and we picked our way through the debris on the streets to his house.

A chimney lay on the ground in front of it and there was an ugly gash in its roof, but it was substantially unharmed. We could see the women looking anxiously from a window.

'It will come better from me,' murmured Johannes as we came to the gate, and he strode ahead.

The door was open before we knocked.

He bowed respectfully. 'May we come in?' he asked.

The women stepped back and we entered. I closed the door behind us to give them some privacy in their anguish.

'I am sorry to be the bearer of terrible news,' said Johannes, 'but I am afraid Bartholomeus has been killed in the storm.'

I am not unused to distress. As a clergyman I have often attended people at the hour of their death and seen the misery of their families, but rarely have I heard such a wailing as the two ladies produced. I had earlier felt uncharitable thoughts towards mevrouw Van Leusden which I now regretted as I watched the tears run down her cheeks; whilst I can hardly express my own pain at seeing Janneke's reddened eyes as she sobbed uncontrollably. Whatever the propriety of the situation, I felt the urge to wrap her in my arms. Johannes did the same to her mother, which made it feel less improper somehow.

At length we persuaded them to sit and we told them all we could of the circumstances attending his passing. We said we had found his body ourselves, which was being cared for by the Professor's wife personally; that he cannot have suffered since his wound was great, and that they should prepare themselves for a distressing sight if they wished to view him one last time, but that it might be better if we took one of the coffins from his store and bore him home therein, to which they agreed. We had not thought it then, but coffins were to be in short supply in Utrecht for some time to come.

We carried the empty coffin easily enough, but we had to find a couple of strong men to help us make the return journey with Van Leusden inside. We placed the coffin on a pair of trestles as would have been done for any other body delivered to the workshop. Despite our warning, Janneke insisted on lifting the lid to see her father one last time.

In truth, the Professor's wife and Anna had done a very good job of cleaning him up. With the blood washed off and his hair brushed over the wound, he looked quite peaceful. I was relieved to see that he was no longer wearing my cloak; it was not so much the expense of a replacement as the fact that I would be without one for a day or two that concerned me.

'Where is the wound?' Janneke asked me.

I pointed to the side of his head, whereupon she lifted the hair and examined it closely by candlelight.

'It has been well concealed,' she announced. 'I could not have done better. Mercurius, will you say a prayer for him?'

I did as I was asked, and we sat for a while in vigil. Johannes then excused himself, saying that he must see that his grandparents were attended to, and I was once more alone with the two women, neither of whom showed any indication of a desire to go to sleep.

'My father was a good man,' Janneke said simply. 'Why would God allow such a thing to befall him?'

This was neither the first nor the last time I would be asked such a question, and I still do not have an answer that entirely convinces me.

'God's ways are not our ways, and therefore we cannot presume to know the mind of God,' I offered.

'Perhaps there is no reason,' she continued. 'Perhaps there is no God.'

'Child! You cannot say such a thing!' her mother expostulated. 'You must forgive her, Master, she has —'

'There is nothing to forgive,' I interrupted. 'To doubt is natural in the circumstances. It will pass.'

'I find it easier to believe in no God than in a cruel one,' Janneke said, dabbing her copious tears from her cheeks while they continued to drip from her chin onto her gown.

'We live in hope that one day we will be admitted to Paradise,' I said. 'To do so, we must die; and though that will be hard for those left behind, we would not want our loved ones not to have the chance to enter Heaven.'

Janneke nodded dumbly. 'He will surely be admitted,' she said. 'There will be few more deserving.'

I was reminded of a passage, and opened my New Testament at the Book of Revelation, chapter 14. "'Then I heard a voice from heaven, saying unto me, Write, the dead which die in the Lord, are fully blessed. Even so saith the Spirit: for they rest from their labours, and their works follow them,'" I read.

It was a long night.

CHAPTER FIFTEEN

Morning came, and the three of us still sat around the coffin of Bartholomeus van Leusden.

Johannes appeared, bearing a small basket. 'I have brought some bread from my kitchen,' he said. 'You haven't eaten.'

'I cannot,' answered Janneke.

'You must,' he insisted gently. 'Your father would not want to see you neglecting yourself. His dearest wish would have been to see you happy in life, and we must do all we can to fulfil that desire.'

'How can I ever know happiness again?' she cried, but I noted that she took the bread at Johannes' urging, and ate a little.

'How is your own house?' I asked him.

'Some windows broken, a loose tile or two on the roof, but little damage, God be praised. The wind seems to have followed a very narrow track through the city. Of course, the taller buildings have suffered more.'

'Is it awful?' I enquired.

'Bad enough. The trees by the Janskerk are all gone. There are many barges lifted bodily out of the water and dashed on the banks. Barely a church still has a steeple or tower, though the Dom's tower has fared a little better. The towers of the Pieterskerk are now inside the church and it will need a new roof.'

I moved a little closer. 'Are there many dead?'

'I don't know,' Johannes replied. 'Too many, at any event, for one would be too many. And the dead may be the lucky ones, for some who yet live have fearful injuries. Some have lost arms or legs, or had their backs crushed by falling stones. I cannot imagine that they will live long. Grandfather wants to tend to them but he is too weak to walk. I will take him to see the Dom later, if he is strong enough. But now, you have not slept; I will stay with the ladies a while so you can refresh yourself.'

'I cannot leave them,' I said. 'While Janneke wants to pray, so must I.'

He could see that I was not to be dissuaded, but he turned his attention to the women and gently persuaded them to take a rest and try to sleep. We undertook to return later, and in a while we were outside in the warm daylight.

'Let's go to grandfather's and you can take some food. You must be exhausted.'

'My brain is dull,' I answered. 'I am not used to night vigils.'

'It is hard to concentrate for so long,' he agreed.

'I didn't,' I said. 'I found my mind wandering. And one of the things that it wandered to is nagging at me. What was Van Leusden doing at the south-west corner of the nave?'

Johannes stopped walking and stared at me, open-mouthed. 'Come!' he snapped, and ran towards the Dom.

He had locked the vestry door as we left it the night before and now fumbled for the keys to open it again. As he flung the door open, it presented a scene less orderly than I had remembered.

In the turmoil of the previous evening I had failed to notice anything except that Van Leusden was not there, but it took very little time in daylight to see that the register for which he had come, and which had not been in his grasp when he was found, was lying in front of the small window.

'I'm a fool!' announced Johannes, which summed up my own feelings very well. Not that he was a fool, you understand, but that I was.

'Don't worry,' I replied, 'I feel just as stupid. We sent Van Leusden to get a book, noted that he had taken it, but completely failed to remark on the fact that he didn't have it when we found him.'

'He must have taken it to the light to check he had the right one,' Johannes suggested. 'All the volumes in the coffer are very similar.'

'So the fact that he did not take it implies that he did not leave here voluntarily,' I said. I looked around the area where the book was sitting, and then I saw it: a splash of blood on the window ledge to the right, and a further smudge on the floor. 'Do you see it?' I asked excitedly.

'I do, Master. But what does it tell us?'

'This room is to the north-east of the church, so there would be very little light with heavy rain falling outside. Let us suppose Van Leusden had to come right up to the window to see the lettering on the spine. He is concentrating intently, and in his hurry he has left the door open behind him. An assailant sneaks in and swings a club or stick, using his right hand, and thus hits Van Leusden around the right temple. That causes him to slump sideways, his head bouncing on the ledge and then coming to rest just here on the floor.'

'That seems plausible.'

'I have no idea what motive the killer had, but let that pass a moment. The killer, for whatever reason, does not want to leave the body here. But the storm is now at its height, and he is safer here than he would be outside. So he shelters here until the storm begins to die down.'

'But he would have heard the mighty crash of the nave collapsing. Wouldn't that make him flee?'

'It has already happened when he hears the noise, and yet this small room is safe. Why risk leaving when you can see the havoc being wrought through the open door? Then, when the storm abates and he can hear the screams of the injured people, he realises that if he can just leave the body somewhere outside it will be assumed that Van Leusden died in the storm.'

'But why take it all the way to the opposite corner of the church?'

'I can only suppose that he wanted it as far from here as he could manage. After all, he does not know that it will arouse our suspicion because only we know where Van Leusden planned to go next, so he had no reason to be in the south-west corner.'

Johannes stood for a few moments in thought. 'I accept your conjecture,' he said, 'but we must search this room thoroughly for any other clue that helps us fix on the murderer.'

We knelt and searched the floor, then worked our way upwards. I could see nothing particularly helpful, except that it was likely that the attacker had brought his own weapon, there being no suitable object to hand there.

'We know its maximum length,' Johannes told me, 'because anything that comes higher than your hip would have been impossible to swing in this space.'

'Only if he grasped it at the end,' I replied. 'He might, perhaps, have held it partway up. But it does tell us where he must have been standing.'

We experimented with a brass candlestick that Johannes borrowed from the Dom. It is as well that I am a trusting soul, because I played the part of the victim while Johannes stood behind me and slowly clubbed me with the candlestick from various positions.

'Is there anything of value missing?' I asked.

'There is nothing of value here in the first place,' Johannes retorted. 'Although we call it the vestry, it was too small for the French priests when they took over the cathedral, so they kept their vestments and the Mass vessels elsewhere, and we use it only for storage.'

'Is that widely known, or might an opportunistic thief have supposed the valuables were here?'

'I'd have thought everyone in Utrecht would know. And surely an opportunist would first try inside the Dom, where there are plenty of things of value?'

'That leads me to suppose that Van Leusden himself was the target; and since he came straight here from your grandfather's house and was seemingly attacked very soon thereafter, it implies that someone was watching us and followed him here.'

Johannes was visibly shocked. 'I saw no-one!'

'Neither did I — no, wait! I had the idea that I was being followed as I left the banquet the other night. I didn't see anyone, but I thought I heard steps behind me.'

'But even if that is so, he was following you then, not Van Leusden; unless, of course, we are all being followed.'

It was a horrible thought. 'If so, then "all" now means you and me, Johannes.'

'That thought had not escaped me, Mercurius. We must take care. Do you have a weapon?'

'I'm a clergyman,' I answered. 'Of course I don't carry a weapon.'

'I'm sure God would understand if you carried a knife for a day or two.'

I dug deep into the pouch round my hips. 'I have a penknife!' I exclaimed. 'You never know when you might need to sharpen a quill.'

Johannes inspected it. 'You'd better get one for a bigger quill,' he smiled. 'To get close enough to use this on him, you'd need to be in his arms.'

'Let's keep together if we can, then we can each protect the other.'

I would do rather better out of such an arrangement than Johannes, since he was a tall man unencumbered by being a man of God, and I had no doubt he would fight ferociously to save me, whereas if our roles were reversed my best response would probably be to write the assailant a very stiff note.

'I think we should tell Grandfather what we have discovered.'

'I agree. You go first.'

Gijsbert Voet was put out of countenance by our news, but soon regained his composure. 'Master, you told me that a man was killed at Leiden. Could the murderer be the same man?'

This had not occurred to me. 'Well, both victims were apparently clubbed from behind on the right side of the head,' I mused. 'But one was in Leiden and the other in Utrecht. What could possibly connect them?'

'You could,' he replied.

'Me?'

'I don't mean that you attacked them. How could you? You were in our sight all last night.'

Somehow this grudging exoneration did not seem to me to do full justice to my complete innocence.

'What I mean,' the old man continued, 'is that two people loyal to the House of Orange have been killed in similar fashion. Perhaps someone knows of your mission here and is following you to see who is working against his cause.'

'Van Looy was killed because he was close to discovering the traitors in Leiden,' I said. 'Does this mean that they thought Van Leusden was likely to do the same here?'

'It must at least be possible. And we have no other explanation, do we?'

'That suggests that someone was in Leiden and is now in Utrecht. But who could that be?'

We sat in silence for a while, my tired brain looking for any hint.

Then it came to me. There was someone. A man with a lute.

Having marched around the city with Johannes, questioning all the innkeepers who might have employed an itinerant lutenist, all I can say is that the people of Utrecht must be thirsty folk, because it is hard to see how so many inns can remain in business otherwise. Sadly, some innkeepers could not be questioned because either they or their inns (or both) had perished in the storm, but nobody to whom we spoke could tell us anything about a lutenist answering Beniamino's description. Yet he must have been staying somewhere, and he needed to earn his keep.

'Could a man sleep in the fields?' I pondered.

'It's warm enough,' Johannes answered, 'but why come to Utrecht in the first place if not to play in the inns?'

'To kill loyal people.'

'Yes, but he has gone to some lengths to create a believable narrative. You said that in Leiden he could be seen playing his lute.'

'If we use the word "playing" in its loosest sense, that's true.'

'So if a man is seen around town with a lute that he never plays, wouldn't that just draw unwanted attention to him? Surely he would want to blend in and render himself forgettable?'

'If you'd ever heard him play, you wouldn't forget him in a hurry,' I said. I will now admit, with the passage of time, that I may have been unduly severe on his artistry. I have heard many worse lute players, but also many more melodious tomcats.

'We must check the casualties in case he was killed in the storm,' Johannes proposed.

'But if our theory is right, he moved the body after the storm abated,' I argued. 'And with his mission here accomplished, surely he would leave at the first opportunity?'

Johannes went off to check whether any barge-master had left with a lutenist on board, though it seemed unlikely given the debris still littering the canals, while I toured the city gates.

There was one gate each to the west, south and east of the city, and two to the north. At the time of the storm these had all been open because it was not yet dark, but they should have been manned; and by order of the city council all the gates had been closed after the storm so that an accurate count of those in the city could be completed and any looting prevented.

The guards were all sure that they had not seen a man with a lute leave the city since the storm. The only doubt was at the southern gate, because there were six windmills on the city wall in that area which had all been seriously damaged, and the guards had left their posts to help look for casualties there; but they assured me that the gate had never been out of their sight and that when the storm had passed, at least one of them had resumed his position. Since it would have taken Beniamino at least ten minutes to walk from the Dom square to the southern gate, it seemed unlikely that he could have escaped by that route.

We returned to the Professor's house to rest and refresh ourselves. I noticed that several of the missing panes of glass had been replaced with small rectangles of knitted wool, and the Professor's wife and maid were knitting by the fireplace. This was a better arrangement than hanging blankets over the casements, because it allowed light through the majority of the window. The glaziers and carpenters of Utrecht would be busy for a long time to come in repairing the buildings there, and glass would be in short supply, though the broken glass was carefully collected and melted to provide some additional raw material.

Anna paused in her knitting to prepare a beaker of herbal tea for each of us. It was warming, if rather pungent, and very welcome, as were the fresh bread and butter she set out. Johannes and I were enjoying these when the Professor spoilt my appetite.

'I have been thinking while you were gone,' he began. 'Why would anyone want to kill Van Leusden?'

Judging this to be a rhetorical question, I kept my peace, but Johannes filled the silence.

'Why, because he was your deputy here.'

'But nobody except us knew that!' the Professor exclaimed. 'And the Stadhouder, of course, who approved the arrangement. To everyone else, he was just a loyal man of the city. And even if someone wanted to kill him, wouldn't it be so much easier to do so in his workshop, where he was often to be found working alone?'

It could not be denied that there was good sense in the Professor's argument. Van Leusden was just a builder and coffin maker. Whoever killed Van Looy presumably knew who he really was, or at least the role he fulfilled secretly, but nobody could have known what Van Leusden was up to.

'Could Van Leusden have blurted it out himself?' I suggested.

The Professor snorted derisively. 'He was notoriously close-mouthed. A man could entrust him with any secret and know it would not be shared.'

'Then how do we explain what has happened?'

'Simple,' announced the Professor. 'The killer thought he was murdering you.'

'Me?' I do not know if you can stammer a monosyllable, but I found it difficult to utter it. 'Who would want to kill me?'

'Anyone who does not love the Stadhouder, whose man you are known to be.'

This did not seem the right time or place to say that I was lukewarm about politics in general and the Stadhouder's interests in particular, and that if I were done to death for my support of the House of Orange my soul would be entitled to feel highly aggrieved and would probably return to haunt my killer, if I knew whom to pursue.

'Grandfather,' asked Johannes, 'why do you think Master Mercurius was the intended victim?'

The Professor spread his hands as if the whole matter should be obvious to even the most obtuse mind. 'Consider what has happened since he came here. He believes himself to be followed. Perhaps he was, in which case that courting couple saved him because he could not be attacked in company. Then he passes an agreeable day visiting public places in the city, so he cannot easily be attacked then either. So the first chance the murderer has to attack him is when he leaves this house to go to the vestry.'

'But I didn't,' I said. 'Van Leusden went.'

'Indeed he did. But he was wearing your cloak.'

The ghastly truth hit me with as much force as if someone had buffeted me with their fist. Van Leusden had borrowed my cloak and had turned the collar up to protect his face from the rain. In fact, I had urged him to do so, never suspecting that by concealing his face from the attacker he would seal his fate. The murderer had hit him from behind and so had not seen whom he was belabouring.

'The murderer must have been discomfited to see that he had killed the wrong man,' I said.

'More than that,' said Johannes. 'He will know he has unfinished business.'

CHAPTER SIXTEEN

Any man of God knows that there are martyrs who willingly embrace death rather than deny their faith, and we honour them in perpetuity. Their example is placed before our congregations so that they will be stiffened in the face of adversity and remain steadfast in the faith.

I am not cut from that cloth. Faced with an angry Turk who demanded that I adopt the Mohammedan faith or pay with my life, I would at least consider temporary membership. I could always apologise later and throw myself on God's boundless mercy; and Mohammedans believe in God too, so it would not be as if I had denied Him. True, I am a priest and would have denied Jesus Christ, but then again, St Peter did that — and it did not seem to harm his future career.

You may be sure, therefore, that when the Voets begged me to take care, I needed no such encouragement. Were it not unmanly I should have retreated to my chamber and whimpered on the bed until someone else found the killer, but it was clear that unless I did so, there was nobody else to do it. The Professor could only walk a few paces at a time, and there was no reason for Johannes to put himself at risk on my account, though he was a fine fellow and would do all a man could ask of a friend, and more.

My first step was obvious. I had to put my cloak away and resolve not to wear it again. Johannes had promised to return to visit the Van Leusden women, but I did not feel I could do so now that I knew I was indirectly responsible for Bartholomeus' death. The incentive to find his killer was increased by that knowledge.

Since I could not remain in the house indefinitely, I accompanied Anna when she went to the market. She was shopping for vegetables and fish, while I had it in mind to buy the biggest knife I could lay my hands on. This ambition had to be tempered somewhat when I found such an instrument, since it could not have been concealed about my person, but I managed to buy a knife with a blade as long as my hand and a sheath in which to keep it. Thus equipped, I felt I stood a better chance against any murderous lutenist who might mean me harm.

Anna was not the brightest intellect with whom I might have conversed, but she was amused by this purchase. 'Forgive me, Master, but have you owned such a knife before?'

'Never.'

'But you know how to use one?'

'It cannot be difficult, Anna. If I am attacked, I produce it from my pouch and stab my assailant. What is difficult about that? But I hope that the fact that I have a knife will deter any attack.'

'But Master, if your big knife is going to stop people killing you, don't you have to wear it where the bad men will see you have one?'

'Ah — very good, Anna. I was wondering when you would notice that. But it is unthinkable for a clergyman to walk around carrying a weapon.'

'Then why are you doing it, Master?'

'To protect myself. And nobody will think ill of me, because nobody can see it.'

'God can see it,' she said.

'Well, yes, I suppose He can.'

'And aren't all clergymen answerable to Him?'

'Of course.'

'So what will He think of you having a big pointy dagger?'

'I am sure He will understand,' I answered, all the while thinking that I ought not to take that for granted. 'So long as I don't have to use it.'

'But if you're not going to use it, Master, what's the point of having one?'

'Well, in case I *have* to use it, despite my good intentions.'

'You mean, like, killing someone?'

'Yes.'

'Isn't that a sin?'

'Ordinarily, yes, technically… Look, aren't those splendid carrots? Perhaps we should have some?'

Later that day, I had a stroke of luck. Anna was talking to some of the other maids in the market and happened to mention that I was looking for a lute-player. I had told her that much, though not exactly why I wanted to find him.

You may be pretty sure that the collected maids of any town will have good intelligence on the whereabouts of any lute players, for the reasons I alluded to earlier, and one of them volunteered that such a man was staying at the inn in which she worked. When Anna passed this information to me, I asked to be introduced to the girl.

Her name was Marieke, and she proved to be a sturdy young woman with beautiful golden hair that flooded out from beneath her cap. Unfortunately, the rest of her countenance did not match the quality of her hair, but you cannot have everything.

'This lute-player,' I asked her, 'is he a man about my height, with brown eyes and a close-cropped beard?'

'Yes, Master.'

'Wearing a black jerkin?'

'Yes, Master.'

'And he came to you on Monday?'

'Yes, Master. But he spends very little time in the inn.'

'He does not play there for his supper?'

'On Monday, he came back late in the evening but played only for his own amusement. He did not play at all on Tuesday. In fact, Master, I did not see him in the evening at all. On Wednesday, likewise, I did not see him.'

This was promising. On Monday, I stayed in the Professor's house, so Beniamino could not attack me there. Obviously he gave up and went back to his inn. On Tuesday, I attended the banquet, where I was perfectly safe, but I had heard him following me as I left and, had it not been for that courting couple in the alleyway, who knows what might have happened? And on Wednesday, he lay in wait and thought to kill me, but actually killed Van Leusden, who was wearing my cloak. It was all falling into place.

It occurred to me that I had the element of surprise on my side. I could go with Marieke now, ascertain that Beniamino was in the inn, and no doubt Gijsbert Voet would instruct the city authorities to place some armed men at my disposal to arrest this desperate criminal before he did any more harm.

'Anna,' I said, 'I will go with Marieke now. Thank you for walking with me. Please tell your master that I believe I have found the man we are seeking and that when I return, I will discuss what further steps we must take.'

Anna appeared to be reciting the message to herself to fix it in her mind, but finally nodded and set off. I turned to Marieke, who was looking confused. 'Why are you looking for the lute-player, Master?' she asked.

I did not dare to tell a young woman that she may have been harbouring a murderer, so I said the first thing that came into my head. 'Oh, don't worry. The Professor has been looking for a lutenist to play at a family birthday.'

Marieke ducked her head towards me and spoke in a low voice. 'Maybe I ought not to say this, Master, but he isn't very good.'

As we walked across the town towards the inn, I rehearsed various possibilities that might face me. My plan was to discover whether Beniamino was there without alerting him to my interest. If he turned violent, I was armed. If not, I would get help and come back for him with a body of armed men. I would see him locked away somewhere, write to the Stadhouder to tell him where the assassin was, and get myself back to Leiden fast enough to ensure that I would not be in Utrecht to receive any reply. I would then do my level best to live happily ever after, pursuing a quiet academic life and having nothing to do with politicians for the rest of my days.

That did not happen. Indeed, the whole notion came under attack at once.

It was not surprising that we had overlooked the inn, because it was sandwiched amongst the warehouses that lined the two sides of the large canal that ran past the town hall. I had assumed they were all commercial cellars, but the inn was a big cave-like room with a kitchen behind, and a large communal sleeping room to one side. The best that might be said for it was that it may have been cheap, but the guests there appeared to be sailors and other low types. In short, it was exactly the kind of place where a lute-player would feel at home, and had I known of its existence this is where we would have looked first.

The difficulty was that it was impossible to make any discrete enquiry because it was noisy, busy and crowded. After a while Marieke managed to persuade the owner to come out to the street, where I learned that Beniamino had been staying there but was not in the building at that moment. The owner did not know if he would be back, because men paid for their places as they took them in the evening. It was, incidentally, reserved for men, not that any respectable lady would have dared to set foot in the place; and any less than respectable lady would have been shooed away, if the owner's account could be believed. I was surprised that Marieke's family would allow her to work in such a place, but I suppose poverty causes people to lower their standards. Even the poor must eat.

I thanked her for her help, instructed her firmly not to tell Beniamino of my cunning stratagem, and gave her a couple of stijvers for her trouble. She seemed surprised and grateful, and shoved them so far down the front of her bodice that only a man on the most intimate terms with her could ever hope to retrieve them.

I considered carefully what I might do next, and the idea came to me that I might pay my respects to Janneke and her mother, thus meeting up again with Johannes, and during this encounter I would find the opportunity to brief him on my discovery. No doubt he would then accompany me to his grandfather's house, carry whatever letter the old man wrote to the city fathers and march with me at the head of the armed band I hoped would effect the detention of the wicked Beniamino. Of course, if he chose not to return to the inn my plan would come to nothing; and I was not unmindful of the fact that he was probably at liberty in the city somewhere and was keen to see me dead. Somehow this intelligence weighed heavily on my mind, and I resolved to go to the Van Leusden house by the most public route.

Then I began to fret that I might easily be stabbed privily in a dense crowd, so I ought to walk by a less populated path; and, at length, I decided that my best course of action was to pay a strapping young sailor to walk with me, which he was very happy to do for a bigger fee than I had intended to pay him. Having read some works of political arithmetic in my time, I had expected that an ample supply of large sailors would lead to competition for my business, thus lowering the price, but several of the villains feigned a lack of interest in my money and encouraged the only willing one to ask a higher price. I suspect that he would then share the surplus with the others later, having first converted it into ale. However, I had no choice. I am not so miserly that I was going to risk a knife in the ribs for the sake of a few stijvers.

My mother would occasionally chastise me for a lack of sensitivity, but as I entered the Van Leusden home I could feel a certain chilliness in the greeting. Johannes had unfortunately just left, so we sat and prayed together for a while, then mevrouw Van Leusden said she must make arrangements for dinner with the cook. This allowed me a few moments alone with Janneke, but before I had the chance to say anything she took the wind out of my sails.

'Mijnheer Voet has told us that Father was murdered.'

'I am afraid that seems to be so.'

'Not an accident, then, as was thought?'

'No.'

'He also said that you were the intended victim.'

I hesitated to answer and decided to prevaricate a little. 'It may be, but until we catch the killer we cannot be sure what his wicked intentions were.'

Janneke appeared to be suppressing some strong emotion. 'But he was wearing your cloak?'

'Yes, he borrowed it when the sudden rain started and he needed to go to the Dom.'

She opened her mouth to say something, but I quickly continued.

'I offered to go, but he insisted.'

Her tears flowed as she shook her head at me. 'What have you done that makes someone hate you enough to kill you? If you hadn't come, my father would still be alive.'

'I didn't choose your father. Professor Voet suggested him and your lamented father agreed to help.'

'But he cannot have known that you were ushering death into our house!'

In a less emotionally charged setting I might have pointed out that it was the murderer who did that, not me, but I did not think that would go down well just at the moment.

'If you would prefer me to leave…' I began.

'Yes, I think I would,' she answered at once.

So I did.

Thus ended my foray into love.

I will not attempt to deny that this turn of events had disconcerted me considerably, nor that I was distressed that all my hopes had been so cruelly dashed, so the reader may imagine that it was with a heavy step that I walked out into the street, so wrapped up in my own thoughts that I completely forgot any notion of a bodyguard. In fact, at that hour I did not care if I lived or died, and I decided to go for a long and solitary walk to collect my thoughts.

I walked out past the Janskerk with the idea of heading out into the surrounding countryside where I would not have to concern myself with homicidal lutenists, but I had not realised that there was no gate in that direction, so I turned and walked round the city perimeter for a while, and in no time I was completely and utterly lost.

I felt sure that somewhere I would catch a glimpse of the Dom's tower and thus be able to navigate my way back to the centre, from which I knew my bearings, but the shock of finding that Janneke held me responsible for her father's death, however unjust that might be, made me want to run away altogether. I had never had much appetite for this sort of intrigue, and it certainly was not increasing. There are people who are born plotters, who love the complexities of public life and who enjoy spurring others to do that which they would not otherwise have done. I have read a play by the English writer Shakespeare in which a Moorish military leader is pricked into a jealous rage by one of his captains who alleges that his stainless wife has been unfaithful. Well, there is nothing of that Iago fellow about me. In fact, I empathise rather more with Desdemona.

I found myself outside an inn and decided that I would welcome a drink. After that drink I decided I would welcome several more, and all that curtailed my enthusiasm for getting blind drunk was the knowledge that I would have to present myself at the Professor's house in a state that would undoubtedly arouse his wrath and cause him to lower his opinion of me; though, truth to tell, the opinion that anyone who mattered in Utrecht had of me was already as low as it could get. Anyway, I had about three beakers of ale in all, and then a plate of herring to soak some of it up, and, thus refreshed, stumbled out into the evening air.

I must have been in there longer than I had thought, because it was actually growing dark when I emerged. Add to that the uncomfortable realisation that I was not yet quite as sober as I had imagined, and it is easy to see why I fell into what now happened.

As I had hoped, I spotted the Dom's tower and began to walk towards it in as straight a line as geography and my wayward legs would permit. When I look at a map of Utrecht now, I am not clear how I came to be in the neighbourhood of the fish market, but I was walking along a lane there when someone hailed me from behind. I turned and saw a dark figure silhouetted against the moonlight at the entrance of the alley.

He stood for a moment, his arms outstretched and his legs slightly bent as if about to wrestle someone. There was a curious asymmetry about the figure that I remarked but could not explain, and then it came to me. His right arm was longer than his left; and the reason that it was longer was that he was holding a large steel blade in his right hand.

Gentle reader, if ever you have overindulged in hop or grape, permit me to recommend a murderous assault as a fine way to sober up quickly. I began to rummage in my pouch for my knife and finally succeeded in extricating it, only to find that it was still enclosed in its scabbard, which seemed curiously reluctant to yield up its contents. The figure was now running towards me, and the most prudent course seemed to be to run like a frightened rabbit towards the other end of the lane.

Clerical garb is not made for sprinting, even when hitched up, and the assassin was gaining on me. I could only hope that there were plenty of witnesses in the street that crossed the end of the lane and, ideally, a crowd sufficient to allow me to melt into it and remain undiscovered.

I gained the end and tried to decide whether to turn left or right. There was much to be said for either option. The least successful course of action was to do what I was doing, namely to stand still whilst debating the matter with myself, and I now compounded this inactivity by turning to face my assailant rather than doing something useful such as diving into the canal and swimming for dear life.

The menacing shape advanced upon me, and I could see no prospect of deliverance. If my wits had not been so addled I would have recited an act of contrition, because I was horribly unprepared to meet my Maker. The glinting steel rose in the air as the attacker drew his arm back, and then…

There was a loud thud, followed by another, and a ghastly twanging sound as he slumped, first to his knees, then to the ground. This was caused by someone in a doorway near the end of the alleyway who had lashed out very hard with a large, bulbous object.

It was a lute, now lying in pieces on the cobbles, as Beniamino quickly removed his belt and lashed the man's arms together before repeating the action with a cord that he drew from a bag.

'I don't think you'll be able to fix that,' I heard myself say.

'Probably not,' agreed Beniamino. 'Not to worry. It needed a good tuning anyway.'

'I ought to thank you,' I began, 'for saving my life.'

'Yes, but not now. Let's get this man to a safe place.'

'Good idea. I'll see if I can find the city's sergeant to lock him away.'

'You'll do no such thing. This is a private matter.'

'He is a common murderer. Or attempted murderer, anyway. He tried to kill me. And I suspect he killed a man called Van Leusden.'

'I suspect so too. But we won't know unless we get a confession, will we?'

'Do you think he'll confess?'

'Mercurius, he'll confess. The only question is how much pain I'll have to subject him to before we arrive at that point. Now stop wittering and help me get him into the light where we can get a look at him.'

I took the man's legs while Beniamino grabbed him by the arms, and together we carried him into the street where the moonlight could play upon him.

I found myself looking into the battered face of Molenaar.

CHAPTER SEVENTEEN

Beniamino and I lifted Molenaar to his feet and looped his arms over our shoulders to give any observers the idea that we were escorting a drunk to his home. His unconscious state made this a difficult proposition, but fortunately Beniamino told me we had not far to go. He had the use of one of the riverside warehouses. I did not like to question how he had obtained this but was very glad when he propped Molenaar against the door while he unlocked it, then pushed it open so Molenaar fell inside.

'Careful!' I exclaimed. 'You'll hurt him.'

'Indeed I will, once he wakes up. But let's secure him to prevent any escape first.' He had a small crate full of ropes, which he used to tie Molenaar by his wrists and ankles to pillars. 'We need to prevent self-harm,' he explained.

'Self-harm?' I asked. 'Why would he harm himself?'

'To put an end to his misery. I've known it happen before, though not to one of my prisoners, I'm glad to say.'

'I may be going out on a limb here,' I said, 'but I suspect that you're not actually a lute-player.'

'I am,' he protested, 'but more of an enthusiastic amateur than a professional. Lute-players knock on many doors. Nobody is surprised to see them. And they're very quickly forgotten. When men are asked who was present in a room, they often overlook the servants and musicians.'

I could see the sense in that. 'And I suppose your name isn't actually Beniamino?'

'No.'

'What should I call you, then?'

'Best stick to Beniamino. You don't need to know my name, and if you found it out it might be unhealthy for you.'

I could feel my curiosity about his identity ebbing away at once. 'Forgive my nosiness, but — just to ensure you mean me no harm, I suppose — how do you fit into all this? For whom are you working?'

'That I can tell you. The Stadhouder asked the Heer van Zuylestein to arrange for me to follow you to see that you were kept safe.'

'Follow me?'

'The easiest way to follow someone is to openly go with them. How could I have followed you on the barge from Leiden except by pretending to be a fellow passenger? I couldn't wait for the next barge, could I? So, whenever possible I followed you by walking alongside.'

'I thought I was being followed a couple of days ago, but when I turned round there was only a courting couple there.'

Beniamino laughed heartily. 'One of my best!' he said. He stood up, turned his back to me and rested his arm against one of the posts so that his cloak dropped free. I then heard him propositioning a young woman and her giggling reply, even though I knew there was no girl there.

'How do you do that?'

'Necessary dissembling. Things you pick up in my line of business.'

'And what exactly is your line of business?'

'That's not important right now. Suffice it to say that I am a sort of civil servant working for the Stadhouder.'

What was going on inside Molenaar's head I did not know, but my own was spinning at this unexpected turn of events.

'That's a nice girl you're walking out with, by the way,' Beniamino declared.

'Was walking out with. She wants nothing to do with me now.'

'Well, that's women for you. A fickle bunch. Any particular reason?'

'She thinks it's my fault her father was murdered.'

Beniamino was, for once, at a loss for words, but only for a moment. 'So her father was the man who left the house in your cloak?'

'That's right. The murderer seems to have killed him, thinking it was me.'

Beniamino jerked his head in the direction of the man tied to the posts. 'That's the man who messed things up for you. If you want to give him a kicking later, just let me know.'

'I'm a minister of God. I can't go around kicking people.'

'Suit yourself. Nobody would know except me, and I'm trained to keep my mouth shut. If you change your mind, just speak up.'

'Thank you, but I won't.'

'If a man did that to me, I'd emasculate him at the very least.'

'I suspect that's a disciplinary offence for a university lecturer.'

'Well, you know best.'

A thought suddenly struck me. 'But if the murderer couldn't tell us apart, why didn't you follow Van Leusden when he left the house?'

'From where I was standing, I could see his face. I knew it wasn't you. I was very glad of that, because I wasn't dressed for heavy rain. Following someone in a downpour isn't fun, and people tend to notice you more readily. "Look at that idiot out in the rain," they say. I like to be unobserved whenever possible.'

I shivered. These man-made caves are not the most luxurious of surroundings.

'Are you cold? I'll light a fire in a minute,' Beniamino said. 'I'll need one anyway for my encouragers.'

'Encouragers?'

'Tools of the trade. Pokers, branding irons, whatever I can find around.'

'Is that strictly necessary?'

'That's not my decision. It's his. He can save himself a lot of anguish by confessing early. He's going to confess anyway, so why put himself through all that?' Beniamino put a hand on my shoulder. 'I understand that you have qualms. This isn't your world, Mercurius. It's the one I live in, and one day I may be the one tied up while someone heats the poker. You may rest assured I'll cause him the minimum pain necessary. But it's naïve to think that I can do this without hurting him. Why don't you go back to the Professor's house to let him know you're safe and let me get on with this? Come back here tomorrow, and I'll let you know what I've found out.'

'I have misgivings about this,' I said.

'Fine. Shall I let him go, then, and you can take your chances? Maybe he'll be grateful and he won't carry out his orders to kill you. But maybe he will.'

Put like that, I could see the advantages of Beniamino's way of doing things.

The Professor had gone to bed when I knocked at the door, so it was not until the morning that I was able to recount the events of the previous evening.

'I must admit that I do not like the thought of subjecting a man to violence to obtain a confession,' I said, fully expecting Gijsbert Voet to agree with me.

'We cannot be squeamish when a man's soul is at stake,' he replied. 'He was, as you describe matters, taken red-handed in attempting to kill you. That alone would earn him some severe earthly punishment. And, if our suspicions are correct, he is a traitor and must expect a traitor's death. Compared with that, and what awaits him after his death, this interlude will seem a trifle.'

'I fear he will be stubborn and suffer greatly, but Beniamino is sure he will confess in time.'

'Excellent. Confession of our sins is the first step towards righteousness. Without it he will surely be damned. And let us not forget that he is part of a conspiracy whose other members must be uncovered before they do further harm.' Voet rose unsteadily to his feet and tottered to his bookshelf, returning with a pamphlet. 'How is your French?'

'I manage,' I said, omitting to mention that I had been ordained priest in the Francophone part of Flanders.

'Read that. It's one of the ghastly scribblings that was circulated during the French occupation here. You will read that the population was well-disposed towards the invaders; that they refused to allow William of Orange to enter the city; that they committed unspeakable barbarities in the Dom and rejoiced in the fact; and that they were heard to say to the French authorities that they would rather be French than subjects of the Prince of Orange.'

There did not seem to be much point in reading the pamphlet after that. He must have covered the content quite comprehensively.

'Is it true?' I enquired.

'True? What does the truth have to do with it? It is propaganda. The point is that it was believable. Undoubtedly some of the population, being Catholics, found the French occupation congenial. They probably did renounce any allegiance to the Prince of Orange, and some of them hoped the French would stay. They burned most of the fittings of the Dom, which we are only just finding the money to replace, and we have had to remove the most offensive papist images. And it is true that the regent, that idiot Martens, refused to open the city gates to William. He said he feared the troops would loot the place — as if the French troops wouldn't.' He took a deep breath and flopped into his chair. The anger he felt was exhausting him. 'That is what we are guarding against. Those days must not be allowed to return. Under the De Witts, Catholics were allowed too much latitude. I have nothing against them myself, you understand. They are heretics and will pay for their heresy in the fires of Hell, but at least they are Christians, and it is easier to convert Christians than heathens. The House of Orange has been pleased to grant toleration to Catholics and we are bound by our loyalty to accept that. I make no complaint. But without William, I have no doubt that this country will divide on religious lines and there will be great bloodshed. Your work, Mercurius, is of the greatest importance, do you see? It is not just a matter of the murder of two men. It is preventing the slaying of many more.'

I began to see how things were. I had thought that those ranged against William were all adherents of the De Witt faction and proponents of democracy, but they were surely not numerous enough to be a real threat. They had loud voices, of course; protesters often have. But when you added to them the large number of Catholics and other non-Reformed inhabitants, you could see why William's rule was thought precarious. These were volatile times. Just look at the English, as dull a nation as you could wish to meet; in barely a quarter of a century they had beheaded their king, set up a republic, brought back the king's son, who had been in exile in the Netherlands, which he then showed his gratitude towards by declaring war on us, made peace, started another war, pretended that they had ended that war and made it impossible for the French to attack our coast by sending their navy to get in the way. If these things could happen, who was to say that the Netherlands might not become French, or Spanish, or even English?

I begged leave of the Professor to go to see how Beniamino's work was progressing. The Professor entreated me earnestly to get Molenaar to confess his sins and throw himself on the mercy of Almighty God. I undertook to do so without having the least belief that it would prove possible.

The warehouse door was shut, but I knocked and announced my name in a loud hiss. Beniamino opened the door with a smile.

'You don't think skulking up to a door and whispering furtively might draw attention to the place?' he asked in a tone that suggested amusement at my folly.

'I don't know what the form is for all this cloak and dagger stuff,' I snapped, and pushed past him.

A horrible sight presented itself to me. Molenaar was sitting on a chair, his legs bound to the chair's legs. He was naked apart from some smallclothes and his chest was a mass of torn flesh — as if he had been flogged. His face was battered, and one eye was closed by swelling which extended down his cheek and up to the corner of his mouth. His wrists were tied to the arms of the chair and I suddenly realised the top of one of his fingers was missing.

'Was that necessary?' I snarled at Beniamino.

'Yes,' he answered coolly. 'You see, each hand has fourteen such joints, so he knows I can put him through that pain twenty-seven more times if I have to. Cut an ear off, and I can only do it twice. Fingers are much more effective. For a start, before removing the top joint I can pull out the finger nails and give the exposed area a few minutes' work with a hammer. Compared with the pain of that, losing an ear is a trifle.' He lifted some papers from the top of a barrel. 'However, that will not be necessary, because, as I predicted, Molenaar has told me what we need to know, I think. I'll tell you what he said, and you can see if there are any more questions we need to ask before I nail him in a crate and transport him to The Hague. I think the Stadhouder will want to supervise his execution himself.'

The jovial, vulgar, boisterous lutenist I had known had been repulsive company, but there was something yet more appalling about this cold, mechanical tormentor. He seemed completely detached from his work and, having obtained the intelligence he required, he was now showing considerable solicitude towards Molenaar, offering him a cup of water and holding it for him as one would a child's beaker with great patience and gentleness.

'How can you use him so roughly and then nurture him like that?' I whispered.

'He is a man,' said Beniamino. 'He has played the game and lost, and he will pay a heavy penalty. He knew that would be the case if he did not triumph. We all do. But we can be magnanimous to a vanquished opponent.' He motioned to me to sit on a barrel while he did the same. 'Molenaar has admitted that he is one of a cell of three.'

'With Van der Horst and Terhoeven?'

'If you already knew that, you could have saved Molenaar a deal of pain.'

'I did not know. I suspected,' I said haughtily.

'Their task was to work amongst the students at Leiden discovering those who were well-disposed towards the De Witt faction, and to foment unrest there, but in particular to discover fanatics who would join them in an attack on the Stadhouder's person.'

'An assassination attempt? But surely they would pay with their lives?'

'They did not expect to survive. So long as the Stadhouder died, they did not mind if they did the same.'

'Van Looy suspected that there were three of them. He even wrote a cryptic secret note.'

'Which said?'

'"You do not need to grind the nest."'

Beniamino laughed immoderately before wiping eyes with a kerchief and looking at me with some amazement in his face. 'You don't see it, do you?'

'Whatever "it" is, no.'

'Van Looy was giving you the names. He wrote it in English, but if you translate it the right way into Dutch, it's clear enough. Who grinds things?'

'Why, a miller I...'

Of course. The English word "miller" is "molenaar" in Dutch. To need can be translated as "hoeven", as when we say that it behoves us to do something. And horst is a rather poetic or archaic word for a bird's nest. I do not mind saying that I felt a complete fool, and the really galling aspect was that this thug had worked it out on the spot. No doubt he was one of those fellows who always gets the answers to riddles quicker than I do, of whom they are many, because I am not good at riddles.

'Who gives them their orders?' I asked.

'He doesn't know. And I think that's genuine, because he carried on sobbing that he didn't know while I was pouring burning candle wax on his genitals. That's a great loosener of tongues, by the way. You may find it handy to know that someday.'

For the record, I have never had occasion to use that trick, though sometimes during university Senate meetings I have been sorely tempted.

'What he will say is that Van der Horst was their leader, but he was very cautious. Terhoeven was always encouraging more action.'

'We should arrest them both quickly, before they realise that Molenaar has spoken.'

'He says Terhoeven has vanished.'

'Van der Horst planned to spend the summer in Leiden. We may find him there.'

'We'll go there as soon as we have concluded matters here.'

'Does he admit to killing Van Looy and Van Leusden?'

'Yes and no. Or, more accurately, no and yes. He killed Van Leusden thinking it was you. His orders were to end your life, so when he killed the wrong person he stayed here to have another go. But he denies killing Van Looy. He says Terhoeven did that. Van der Horst and Molenaar were furious because he had received no orders to do so. He acted on his own initiative.'

'I must report at once to the Stadhouder,' I said. 'What else must we do?'

'Not so fast. This man has committed a murder in Utrecht. He should be tried here. We have to persuade the city authorities to send him to The Hague for examination there first. Then, if he survives further questioning from servants of the Stadhouder who lack my finesse, he can be brought back here to hang for murder.'

Looking at Molenaar's face, I would not have dared to use a word like finesse myself. 'Won't he be tried for treason?'

'Maybe, maybe not. The Stadhouder may not want to draw public attention to the fact that there are any disloyal elements in his realm. A nice quiet execution in Utrecht for a completely unrelated crime might suit him very well. So long as Molenaar dies, the Stadhouder won't mind too much how it comes about.'

This attitude made my blood boil. 'There is such a thing,' I expostulated, 'as justice!'

'Is there?' said Beniamino. 'Let me know when you find it.'

CHAPTER EIGHTEEN

Beniamino declined to accompany me when I attempted to solicit the Professor's support to have Molenaar shipped to The Hague, citing the importance to his future usefulness of maintaining a very low profile. This seemed a bit rich if, like me, you had seen him standing on a tavern table singing a vile song about a Frisian milkmaid and her excessively friendly approach to livestock, but I suppose I could understand what he meant. There was always the chance that a traitor would see him and recognise him at some time in the future when he needed to remain incognito.

I decided not to go to the Professor single-handed, and found my way to Johannes' home to lay the matter before him first. He was very welcoming and listened intently to my account of the arrest and interrogation of Molenaar.

'What do you propose to do now, Master?' he asked.

'Well, we must somehow get Molenaar to The Hague. I assume Beniamino will have some idea about how best to do that. Then we must arrest Van der Horst and look for Terhoeven.'

Johannes contemplated the contents of his glass of madeira wine. We Dutch drink a lot of Portuguese wines, if only to annoy the Spanish.

'Why do you suppose Terhoeven killed Van Looy? Assuming, of course, that Molenaar is telling the truth.'

'Why wouldn't he tell the truth?'

'Well, if he has regard to the future state of his soul after his inevitable execution, then of course he will tell the truth. He would be stupid to do otherwise. But if his desire is merely to stop the pain of his torture, he might say anything that came into his head that may satisfy our curiosity.'

'Beniamino is convinced of his sincerity.'

'Beniamino will want to be thought effective, so he would say that, wouldn't he? But think for a moment. Suppose you and I had not met, and Molenaar had blurted out my name, would you think that enough to arrest me?'

It was a good question. Without further evidence, why would we arrest someone on the basis of an allegation?

'We need more, don't we?' I conceded reluctantly.

'I think we do,' agreed Johannes. 'But we cannot ignore what we have either. However, I repeat my question: why do you suppose Terhoeven killed Van Looy?'

'Presumably because Van Looy was about to expose them.'

'And how could they know that?'

The Voets had asked this before, and I still had no answer. Van Looy was a clever and prudent man. A complete pain in the posterior too, but that does not detract from his intelligence. He would hardly have told his quarry that he was hunting them down, so how did they know? I could only assume that, like me, they had overheard something said.

At this point, the university lecturer in me took over. It is a standard technique in my profession, when you are surprised by a question, to answer it with a question of your own, and the most common response came to my mind now.

'What do you think the answer is?'

Johannes rolled the wine round his glass slowly, as if considering whether to say something unwelcome. 'Somebody told them.'

'And how did that somebody know?'

'Because they were in a position to hear the reports of Van Looy. There is a traitor somewhere in The Hague.'

'But they are all vouched for. Van Looy himself was loyal. He passed his reports to Van Kamerik, who is the servant of the Heer van Zuylestein, a man whose loyalty is beyond reproach. The Stadhouder was careful to construct a completely secure pathway.'

'I understand that, but can you think of a better explanation than the presence of a traitor near to the Stadhouder?'

'Put in those terms, no, I can't.'

'Then we must be exceptionally careful what we say. I would urge you to speak in person to the Stadhouder and only to the Stadhouder.'

That made sense to me. One cannot be too careful where the security of the nation is at stake. 'I confess that I detest this sort of work,' I said. 'I can't wait to get back to teaching cocky and insubordinate students as usual.'

Johannes laughed. 'I don't think Leiden has a monopoly on those.'

'The sooner this is over, the sooner that day will arise. At least now we can explain one of the diagrams Van Looy drew.'

'Could I see them?'

I passed them to him. Johannes flicked through them, pausing to absorb the content of each.

'So if the trident or family tree shows us the three members of the Leiden cell, this suggests they were led by another who took his orders from someone else. Is it too fanciful to assume the man at the top of the tree is the traitor in The Hague?'

'It wouldn't be easy for him to communicate directly with the students, and probably not safe either, given their lack of sobriety and loose tongues. But who is the intermediary?'

This was a question that Beniamino had repeatedly put to Molenaar, as evidenced by several burns on Molenaar's hands.

'The palms are very sensitive,' explained Beniamino. 'Obviously the privities are more sensitive still, but there is a limit to how many times you can use a hot iron on them.'

I winced. It seemed crystal clear to me that a man who was not talking when his penis was being grilled was probably a man who had nothing useful to say. 'Is this strictly necessary?' I asked, waving my hand in the general direction of the hellish instruments.

'Not now,' said Beniamino. 'I think we have gone as far as we can go. It is time to put him out of his misery.'

'You plan to kill him?' I gasped.

'No, of course not. I'll deliver him to the Stadhouder, and he'll die, either at The Hague or here in Utrecht.'

'Is there no place in your world for mercy?'

'Not for the Stadhouder's enemies. But consider this, Master. When we reach The Hague, I will tell the Stadhouder what has been done, and there will be no further torture because it has already achieved all it can here. When I say no more torture, I mean apart from his actual execution, of course.'

'Won't he just be hanged?'

'Maybe if he is returned to Utrecht, but if he dies at The Hague, I doubt it. The man who killed William the Silent had his hand burned off and was quartered and disembowelled alive. Of course, that was ninety years ago. We're not as cruel these days. They probably won't bother burning his hand off.'

I felt conflicting passions roiling within my breast. I looked at the bruised and bleeding body slumped in the chair and wished he could just be told to go away and sin no more. Jesus said that to the woman taken in adultery, who herself faced a horrid execution by stoning, so there were precedents. On the other hand, Molenaar would not have shown me any mercy. He intended my death, and perhaps if he had the means he would still murder me. 'I don't have the stomach for your work, Beniamino. In fact, I despise all this undercover stuff. I just want to have done with it and go home.'

'Home? Now, there's a nice idea.'

'Don't you have a home somewhere?'

'No. I had one once, but I'm a soldier, albeit one who doesn't wear a uniform. One day, if God wills, I'll retire and buy a cottage somewhere.'

'Don't you want a wife and children?'

'Do you?'

'I'm a university lecturer and a minister.' I almost said priest. 'I'm not in a position to marry.'

'Attachments would make me useless. Any woman for whom I felt love would ruin my career because I could not put her through what may one day happen to me. I'm not without female company, and I've spent many a night between —'

'Yes, I see what you mean!' I interrupted. 'To return to our work, has Molenaar said anything about how he gets his orders?'

'They're relayed to him by Van der Horst, who is the only one that their master speaks to. And Molenaar doesn't know whether actual speech is involved, or written orders, because he never sees them being delivered.'

'Then it looks as if my next task is to find Van der Horst, which means returning to Leiden.'

'We can't do that.'

'Why not?'

'Because my orders are to keep close to you to see that you come to no harm, so if you go to Leiden, I have to go too, and I have to bring him with me. And frankly, he is no shape to make the journey. Added to which, it would give him an opportunity to escape.'

'But surely the danger is past now. You have trapped the would-be assassin.'

'How do you know he's the only one who wants to kill you?'

I stood amazed and aghast. My mouth moved, but I could make no sound. It was true. If Van der Horst had told Molenaar to kill me, perhaps he had said the same to Terhoeven. In any case, I dared not take any chances until we knew where Terhoeven was.

Beniamino laughed again and clapped his hand on my shoulder. 'I've come pretty close to feeling like killing you myself.'

The city fathers of Utrecht were unhappy, and they let me know it in clear terms. They wanted to hang Molenaar in their city, for killing one of their people. It was not until Johannes arrived with a letter from his grandfather that their mood changed.

After the usual introductory pleasantries, it continued:

Gentlemen,

I hear from my grandson that there is dissension amongst you about the best way of proceeding now that the self-confessed murderer of our late and lamented colleague, mijnheer Bartholomeus van Leusden, has been taken and is imprisoned.

It is not my place to dictate the city's response. I write merely to ensure that certain arguments are placed before you which, I think, you will come to agree have some weight.

Ignore that bit about not dictating the city's response. That was exactly what he wanted to do.

First, I draw to your attention the fact that we do not know where this man is imprisoned. I suppose that it might be discovered, but Master Mercurius and his associate are servants of the Stadhouder and are under no obligation to inform us. If they leave without him, how does it profit us unless they vouchsafe to tell us his whereabouts?

They could follow me, no doubt, so I made a mental note to take a roundabout route every time I visited the warehouse in future.

It is entirely reasonable that we should wish to see this man suffer for his crime. The soul of our dear friend Van Leusden cries out to be avenged. However, he can be avenged just as well at The Hague as in Utrecht. What matters is that this criminal undergoes punishment to expiate his crime. The Stadhouder's agents have requested his release into their custody for onward passage to The Hague, where we may be sure that our beloved Stadhouder's passion for justice will see a fit doom bestowed upon the prisoner.

I hesitate to tell you what you must already know, but the loyalty of the people of Utrecht has been in question since the late occupation, and it would be well if no cause were given to the Stadhouder to consider us less than good Dutchmen.

If I may make a suggestion, it would not be unreasonable if the burghers of the city agreed to the Stadhouder's request, but imposed a condition of their own, namely, that the widow and daughter of mijnheer Van Leusden, and a delegation from this city, should be welcomed at The Hague as witnesses when the killer is executed so that they may verify for themselves that justice has been done.

Given so clear a hint, the city council finally managed to pass the necessary resolution, unsurprisingly exactly in the terms that Professor Voet suggested, and further undertook to offer four guards to accompany Beniamino and myself as we escorted the prisoner. When I returned to Beniamino to inform him of this, he appeared vexed.

'We can hardly refuse, and it will increase the security of the journey, but it exposes me to their scrutiny. I'll have to disguise myself and you'll have to do most of the talking. In fact, if we can manage it, it might be better if they don't realise I'm on the barge with you.'

I wanted to ensure that the Stadhouder was prepared to receive our prisoner, but at the same time I did not want to commit anything to paper that might alert our adversaries, so I wrote a note telling him that we were returning with one of the traitors to deliver him into safe custody. By courtesy of the mayor, one of the civic guard's lieutenants was despatched on horseback to deliver the message, which I had sealed on the reverse with a special seal given to me by the Stadhouder's office for this purpose.

In the evening we transferred Molenaar to the city's jail, and thus relieved of the duty of guarding him, Beniamino and I were able to pass our last evening in Utrecht in a more relaxed frame of mind. I returned to the Professor's house to keep him informed of our plans and to pack for my journey, and to thank him for his abundant hospitality.

Unexpectedly, he asked if he could meet Beniamino to thank him for his efforts in person. I explained that Beniamino guarded his privacy jealously, but undertook to see if he would attend upon the Professor, and so I hunted out the place where he had said he proposed to sup.

He was in high spirits. A young wench sat on his lap, he had a large tankard of beer (and had obviously had several before that) and all seemed well with him. Then I noticed something that made my heart sink.

He had bought a new lute.

When we arrived at The Hague, another bunch of soldiers were there to meet us. The Utrecht guards came too because they needed somewhere to stay overnight before making the return journey, so we looked a formidable troop as we walked from the quay to the Binnenhof.

The buildings included a dungeon, so it was convenient to take Molenaar there first and see him secured before we presented ourselves to the Stadhouder. Pieters came down to tell us that the Stadhouder would see us in half an hour. Meanwhile, we might take some food and drink in the hall, and select some for the prisoner. This we did, sending him some bread and beef, just as we had, and a jug of beer. I drank sparingly because I was tired and wanted to keep a clear head, but Beniamino more than made up for my limited use of the Stadhouder's hospitality.

Half an hour extended to almost an hour, but at last we were admitted to the Stadhouder's chamber.

'Gentlemen, welcome! And my congratulations on your success thus far. Pieters, I won't need you for a while. Now, sit and tell me what you have discovered.'

I was going to let Beniamino do the talking, but he showed no inclination to open his mouth and simply nodded to me to indicate that I should start.

'The prisoner's name is Molenaar. He is a student at Leiden, one of three who form a cell there. The others are called Van der Horst, whose father is a clergyman and known malcontent living in Haarlem, and a man called Terhoeven, of whom we as yet know little. They received their orders from an intermediary, not yet identified, who in turn received his from someone here.'

The Stadhouder sat up abruptly. 'How do you know this?'

'To be strictly truthful, we don't. But it seems that someone knew that Van Looy was close to exposing the trio in Leiden. We don't know who that could be if not someone here.'

'Perhaps someone overheard something in Leiden?'

'Van Looy was a very secretive man. He even kept his own notes in invisible ink. It is possible that someone overheard him arguing with Van Kamerik, as I did myself, or that Van Kamerik said something that was overheard.'

'Van Kamerik could be the traitor himself. Van Zuylestein trusts him implicitly, but men have been wrong before. Except me, of course.' He smiled gently as he said this, so I did not believe him to be claiming infallibility, but you never knew with the Stadhouder. Despite appearances to the contrary, he had a sense of humour. More or less, on a good day.

'Molenaar says that Van Looy was killed by Terhoeven acting on his own initiative. He then fled, and so far as I can tell he must have left Leiden at once.'

'Do we know where he lives?'

'Molenaar doesn't know. I can check the university records when I return to Leiden.'

'Do so. We need to find this man so we can have both killers publicly executed together and perhaps discourage anyone following their demented paths. If you need help to find and detain this Terhoeven villain, let me know and I'll send a troop of soldiers. I'm not going to pussyfoot around this, Mercurius. Anyone who harms one of my people can expect the full force of my power directed against them.'

'Thank you, Stadhouder. I certainly won't attempt to tackle him on my own.'

Beniamino stifled a laugh. The Stadhouder did not bother with any stifling.

'That's probably for the best,' he said.

This disparagement of my physique was becoming wearisome. I grant that I do not possess the muscles of a wrestler, but I was a young man, abstemious in my habits and very similar in constitution to my older brother Laurentius, who served with distinction in our navy until an English bullet ended his life at the Battle of Lowestoft. Nobody ever sniggered at him.

'It is too early to nominate another man to replace Van Leusden as Professor Voet's deputy in Utrecht, Stadhouder, but I am pleased to report that the Professor is strengthening. And, in the light of services rendered to me, I am much more confident that his grandson Johannes would be a fitting replacement if one were needed.'

'Excellent. I may go to Utrecht myself soon, once this conspiracy is squashed.' He turned to Beniamino. 'Thank you again for your service. Pieters has your fee ready outside.'

Beniamino stood, and the men shook hands. He gave me a playful clap on the upper arm as he walked past. 'We probably won't meet again, Master. It's been fun.'

The door closed, but for some reason we continued to look at it for some moments after Beniamino had departed.

'A fine servant to me,' said William, 'loyal and capable. But awful on the lute.'

I was about to agree when the door opened and the captain of the guard ran in.

'Stadhouder — it's the prisoner. He's dead.'

CHAPTER NINETEEN

'Mercurius, don't let the lute-player leave!' the Stadhouder yelled, picking up his pistol and following the captain.

I caught up with Beniamino and quickly told him what had happened.

'You let the Stadhouder go alone! Fool! Suppose it's a trap!'

We ran to the dungeon as fast as we could, which, in Beniamino's case, was much faster than me, but then he wasn't wearing clerical garb.

'A trap?' I called out breathlessly.

'How do we know the captain isn't a traitor and that Molenaar is really dead?'

'The Stadhouder took his pistol.'

'Let's hope he keeps it loaded. This way is quicker.'

He led me down a small set of stairs behind a curtain and we found ourselves in some kind of pantry. We ran through an arch, which led to an ante-room at the back of the kitchen, and suddenly we were in the courtyard.

'It's where the food is delivered,' Beniamino explained.

We could see a commotion to our left as someone was fumbling with a ring of keys.

'Faster, man!' barked the Stadhouder.

By the time we arrived, the door was being flung back and the Stadhouder led the way in.

'Everybody out except the captain!' he yelled.

I stood back to let the others drift out and was about to follow when I was called back.

'Not you, Mercurius. And bring your friend.'

Beniamino and I entered the gloomy, narrow room. The captain called for light and someone handed him a lantern, by which we could see the body of Molenaar spread-eagled on the floor. He had vomited copiously and lay in an awkward position with one arm thrown back behind him.

'Send for my physician,' William instructed. 'And if he has gone to bed, don't let him waste time dressing.'

I knelt and said a prayer over Molenaar. Just for form's sake, I checked the side of his neck for any sign of a pulse, but it was fairly clear that there was not going to be one. 'He's dead,' I said.

'Thank you, but I think we knew that,' growled the Stadhouder. He turned angrily to the captain. 'Which of your imbeciles were on guard?'

The captain pointed out two men in the courtyard who were doing their best to blend into the crowd.

'You two, here!' For a small man with a bad chest, William could be remarkably loud when he wanted. 'Who entered this man's cell?'

'Nobody, Excellency.'

'Nobody? Did you check him for concealed poison?'

'There was nothing, Excellency. Not a blade, not a string he could strangle himself with, nothing in his clothes.'

Beniamino muttered in the Stadhouder's ear. 'My Lord, if he had such poison he would have used it when I was questioning him. And I searched him thoroughly when he was first detained. He has not harmed himself.'

William took this in and stomped around the cell for a while, kicking the door in annoyance. 'So we are to assume that if these two half-wits are right, somebody managed to poison him through the bars of his cell?'

If ever I saw men looking uncomfortable, I saw it then. They knew that they were being held responsible for Molenaar's death, and faced summary punishment.

'Perhaps the answer is simple,' William continued. 'Perhaps you poisoned him yourselves.'

'No, Excellency,' stammered one, dropping to his knees in terror.

'I could question them if you like,' said Beniamino. His eyes betrayed too much relish for my liking, and the two guards saw it too. One wet himself where he stood.

His kneeling companion looked pleadingly up at the Stadhouder. 'We're telling the truth, Excellency. From the moment we locked the door and stood outside to the moment he collapsed, nobody went in. In fact, nobody even approached. Perhaps it is God's hand.'

Being of a religious turn of mind, I am very happy to ascribe miracles to God, but when He smites wrongdoers He normally prefers fire and lightning, not to mention making it very plain that He is responsible and why He did it. Read the Old Testament and you will see what I mean. He does not go around slipping people nasty drinks.

At this point the physician arrived, looking bemused and dishevelled. Despite the Stadhouder's instructions he had obviously insisted on putting his breeches on, since his shirt was half in and half out.

He knelt by Molenaar, held a mirror to the corpse's nose and mouth, and tried tickling him with a feather. 'He's dead, Excellency,' he announced at length.

'God's wounds, your years at the Sorbonne weren't wasted!' William shouted. 'Of course he's dead. I could see that. What did he die of?'

The physician dipped a finger in the vomit and sniffed it. Rolling Molenaar onto his back, he tried to straighten him out. 'The corpse is uncommonly stiff, Excellency. I cannot be sure, but I suspect the poison nut.'

'Poison nut? What on earth is a poison nut?'

'A plant from Africa and Asia, which gives a fruit. In small quantities the grated seed is a stimulant, sometimes used in medicine to stir those who are failing. But in larger amounts it causes the muscles to tighten. The victim suffocates, being unable to breathe due to the tightness of his chest.'

'I know that feeling only too well,' the Stadhouder replied.

'If you will look, you see that his back is lifted off the floor in a shallow arch. A larger amount would have produced more curvature, something akin to lockjaw.'

I interrupted. 'Do you think that this was just a warning, and his weakened state led to death?'

'It is too imprecise a weapon to use as a warning, Dominie,' the doctor answered. 'If so little was used, I surmise that it must be because so little was close at hand.'

'And he could not have administered it to himself?'

The physician spread his arms. 'Self-murder by poison is not unknown. But where is the phial?'

'That's true,' said the Stadhouder. 'The door was locked when we got here and there is no phial.'

'Maybe he threw it through the grille when he'd taken the poison,' suggested the kneeling guard.

'Search the yard!' snapped William. 'But if, as I suspect, it isn't there, you two have some explaining to do.'

Their colleagues scoured the ground assiduously. One suggested that if Molenaar had thrown it underarm, he might have lobbed it onto the roof of the guardhouse.

'God give me strength,' muttered William, but ordered a ladder to be brought anyway. After half an hour, it was clear that there was no sign of a phial.

'Maybe he swallowed the phial…' began the other guard, but his voice tailed off in the face of a fierce glare from William. It seemed to me that the more agitated the guards became, the less logical their train of thought. If we could relax them, we might get more sense out of them.

'May I question them?' I asked.

'As far as I'm concerned, you can set them on fire if you want,' the Stadhouder answered. 'I've done with them.'

'Think carefully,' I began. 'Let's go back to the moment when we all arrived from the barge. What happened then?'

The kneeling one seemed to be reflecting, rerunning the events in his head. 'The captain directed the guards from Utrecht to the barracks to find a place to sleep and told them to sup there.'

'Yes, I remember that too. Then?' I asked in as encouraging a tone as I could.

'Well, we were ordered to put the prisoner in this dungeon, so I went to fetch the keys. His wrists were loosed and he was led inside. He didn't resist. Then we fastened one of his ankles in the irons.'

'And he received no visitors?'

'Well, just the one, obviously. You brought him his dinner.'

I suddenly felt very uncomfortable, and very aware of the Stadhouder's aggressive gaze.

As is often the case, once you have freed a mental block, the idiots became very vocal.

'That's right,' the other guard said. 'You brought his dinner. I remember now.'

'I brought his platter from the kitchen, that's true. But he had the same food that we did.'

I was grateful when Beniamino chipped in. 'That's true. I saw the Master putting the food on the platter, and it was exactly the same as ours. In fact, I just picked up any of the platters. If it had been poisoned, it might have been me lying dead.'

I relaxed.

'Of course, he could have poisoned it on the way down the stairs…' Beniamino unhelpfully added.

'But why wait until now to do that?' William asked. 'He had abundant opportunities to kill Molenaar on the journey, presumably.'

'Certainly,' Beniamino agreed. 'Well, not on the barge, obviously, because the Utrecht men were guarding him. But in the warehouse he could have done it. I would have known it was him, but he could have fled, I suppose.'

William looked me up and down. I hoped he saw someone who patently was not a murderer. 'Let's go inside,' he finally said. 'Clear up this mess, put this villain somewhere and get back to work.'

I trudged back into the building, feeling that I ought to be grateful that they were cleaning the dungeon of vomit and corpses before throwing me into it and wishing Beniamino would keep his mouth shut. As if in apology for his half-hearted — some would say half-witted — defence of me, he patted me across the shoulders as we climbed the stairs. I am sorry to say that my suspicious nature only made me wish I had not gone in front of him. I would rather have kept Beniamino where I could see him.

The Stadhouder paced back and forth in his chamber. 'Well, this is a damnable mess!' he said at length.

I felt the need to get something off my chest. 'Stadhouder, I realise appearances are against me, but I want you to know that I did not kill Molenaar,' I said.

'You would say that, wouldn't you?' he replied. 'But by the time the fellow beside you has finished with you, you'll be confessing to killing people who aren't even dead yet.'

I gulped. Actually, all I seemed to be able to do was gulp, because I kept doing it.

'Oh, stop looking so miserable. I never thought you did,' he added. 'You're not stupid enough to embarrass me by killing someone in my custody for a start.'

I had not considered that very welcome way of viewing the matter.

'But who could have poisoned the food?' asked Beniamino.

'I can't think,' I said. 'It was all so ordinary and everyday. I wasn't really paying attention. We were shown into the kitchen, then we collected our dinners and I had a second platter for Molenaar.'

'You can't have held both and still had a hand free to pick things up,' the Stadhouder pointed out.

'No, I filled one at a time.'

'Therefore you must have put one down.'

'I prepared my own plate, put it on the table next to Beniamino's, then went back to get something for Molenaar.'

'And did you take it straight to him?'

A bright light shone inside my head; belatedly, admittedly, but still there. 'No! I thought one of the servants would take it, so I put it on the table near the door. It was only when we'd eaten ours that I realised Molenaar's plate was still there.'

'I remember you said you'd better take it if nobody else was going to,' Beniamino added in his first helpful contribution to discussion for some time.

'So there was a considerable time when that food, which was known to be for Molenaar, could have been poisoned,' concluded William.

'Yes,' I readily agreed.

'But you didn't see who did it?'

'I had my back to the door,' I said. 'Beniamino was facing it.' I was rewarded for this comment with a hard stare from the man beside me. Good; it was payback for failing to exonerate me at once.

'I didn't see anyone,' said Beniamino, 'but people were coming and going all the time.'

'But who could have known that food was intended for Molenaar?' I asked. I did not intend it as a rhetorical question, but since nobody answered that is what it became.

William broke the lengthy silence. 'So what happens next?'

'We have to find Van der Horst and Terhoeven, which means going back to Leiden,' I said. 'We can go to the University Registry to get their addresses. Should we take some soldiers?'

'The trouble with that idea is that if people see soldiers marching through town, word will soon get back to the people we're trying to arrest,' William commented.

'I have great respect for your abilities,' I said to Beniamino, 'but as you have pointed out in the past, I'm not much use when it comes to rough stuff.'

'No,' agreed Beniamino. 'I agree we should take someone. I just don't think it should be soldiers, or even the Utrechters who came with us. Give me an hour and I'll round up some irregulars. I know where to look.'

William nodded his agreement, so Beniamino left us to make his arrangements.

'Even if you don't know the individual who killed Molenaar, what was the point of doing so?'

'He was going to be executed, so there was no point in any of your followers doing it. I assume his fellow conspirators did it to prevent his betraying them.'

'But he already had.'

'He hadn't really. He only knew the two he'd met. But the others may have worried that he had learned more somehow. Killing him here was a very risky option, which makes me think that they were desperate to silence him. They must have believed that they would never get a better chance.'

The Stadhouder stood up, so I did the same. 'Can you amuse yourself for a few minutes? I need to give Pieters some instructions.'

I did not think I had any option in the matter, so I agreed.

'Why not take a look at my library? There may be some books in there of interest.'

I doubted that William could have told me which books those were likely to be. Some men have shelves of books where others hang tapestries, purely as decoration, but I have never been able to resist an hour in a library, so I was very happy to do as bidden, especially as William called in one of the guards outside the door and told him to go with me and see that I came to no harm.

The library was, at that time, not in the best condition because when the French left they took a number of the choicest volumes with them, and despite repeated diplomatic protests they had not been returned, nor were they likely to be given that the dastardly French refused to admit that they had them; but there were some books there that I had never seen, and I spent a few minutes scanning the titles to see which I should like to inspect further.

William had a desk between two of the bookcases. It was an unostentatious, dark wood table with an inlaid leather top, tasteful but definitely for use rather than for show. It was against the wall near one corner of the room and appeared to be where he did his serious work rather than simply signing documents. Diplomatic despatches littered its surface which I was careful to avoid reading, and over the desk there hung a beautiful pen and ink map of the Netherlands. The sea had been given a light blue wash, and there was a margin which enclosed the coats of arms of the major towns and cities.

And then I saw it.

On the left side, the fourth shield down: four six pointed stars, a small cross with equal arms and a sword pointing up the shield to the cross. I feverishly rummaged in my pouch to find Van Looy's secret papers, smoothed them out on the desk top and found the one I wanted. Holding it up to the map, this time having it the right way up, it was crystal clear. Van Looy had drawn the arms of the city of Haarlem.

The obvious reason for that was that Van der Horst came from Haarlem, so it was perhaps from Haarlem that he was receiving his instructions; and since his father was a minister there, and was known not to be well disposed to the House of Orange, his father might be the intermediary who was relaying the commands from the leader of the rebels.

On the other hand, Van der Horst made no secret of the fact that he and his father did not see eye to eye and he had made no effort to travel to Haarlem during the vacation, choosing to remain in Leiden. It was at least possible that there was someone else in Haarlem who was actually his contact.

My first thought was that we would never know, but then I came round to thinking that we could know if I went there to speak to Van der Horst senior. If a man knew that his son faced a public execution, surely he would confess himself or attempt a rescue. Either way, we would know what was behind this.

I sat on tenterhooks waiting for either the Stadhouder or Beniamino to return, itching to share the result of my research. Admittedly "research" is quite a pompous word to use for looking at a large wall map, but at least I had made the link from my memory.

The time dragged. I tried saying a few prayers, but my excitement was such that I could not concentrate, and then a happy idea occurred to me. I could now explain two of the pieces of paper; what about the third?

I looked at it again.

MTXVI18.

I turned it upside down, which had worked for the arms of Haarlem, but made no sense at all with this one. I tried to picture it in lower case. I thought it might be a cipher, but why would it mix letters and numbers?

Maybe if I diverted my mind by concentrating on something else for a while it would be clearer when I returned to the problem. I thought I would read a portion of my bible. There are systems under which you read a small section each day, completing the whole bible in a year or two. Unfortunately I could not remember where I had left off, and my ribbon marker had fallen out, so I closed my eyes and tried to picture the place where I had finished reading.

If I ever doubt that God watches over me, remind me of this moment. For whatever reason, the riddle that had beset me was suddenly no riddle at all. MTXVI18 was the kind of thing I had written many times; it was a reference to a bible text. MT XVI 18: the gospel according to St Matthew, chapter sixteen, the eighteenth verse. Some of us use roman numerals for the chapter and Arabic numerals for the verses so as not to confuse the two. Out came my New Testament once more, and I could barely control my fingers as I found the relevant verse.

Et ego dico tibi quia tu es Petrus et super hanc petram aedificabo ecclesiam meam et portae inferi non praevalebunt adversum eam.

Tu es Petrus.

You are Peter. Or, more likely, you are Pieters.

Beniamino said that nobody notices the musician, but neither do they notice the secretary. Dredging the past up from the sludgy parts of my brain, I was sure he had been in and out of the room when we had discussed this case. It was certain that when I wrote to the Stadhouder to tell him that we were bringing Molenaar to The Hague, the letter would have been given to Pieters to give to his master. Pieters dared not discard it, because I would mention it when I arrived and the Stadhouder was unprepared, but he could make some arrangement to ensure that Molenaar gave nothing more away.

It was Pieters who had taken us to get some food, and had checked that we were well provided for before he left, but by that time I was eating and Molenaar's food was set out on a platter. He could easily have poisoned it.

The part that was causing the feeling of spiders on my spine was that it was so perfect a plot. Who better to know everything the Stadhouder was doing than his secretary, who could pull the strings of any number of plots around the country, watch them mature, protect them from discovery and ultimately assassinate his master? A simple murder now would not guarantee victory because nothing was prepared; but if there were to be uprisings in a few large cities and then the Stadhouder were stabbed to death, who knows what chaos would result?

The Stadhouder returned. 'I hope you have not been bored,' he said. 'Unfortunately, it took rather longer than I expected.'

'Not at all, Stadhouder,' I said as I walked past him and checked the door was firmly closed. I motioned to him to keep quiet and came very close so that I could whisper. 'I have solved the mystery of the secret writings,' I said.

The Stadhouder was about to speak so I did something unforgivable. I clapped my hand over his mouth. He was surprised but, give him his due, he did not get angry or beat it away. 'And?' he whispered.

'I believe the mastermind behind your opponents' plans is none other than your secretary Pieters.'

That this came as a shock to him was plain to see from the look on his face. 'Are you certain?'

'No. I would like to place the evidence before you and Beniamino to see if you agree, but we must do it without any risk of being overheard.'

William nodded. 'Alternatively we do it where there is plenty of chance of being overheard, but not by Pieters. Come!' He strode to the door, threw it open and marched boldly up to the table where Pieters was sorting letters. 'Mercurius and I will be gone for an hour or so. When you've done that, go to bed, Pieters.'

'As you wish, Stadhouder,' he replied.

We continued down the stairs and across the court to the guardroom. Beniamino was not there, which surprised me because I could think of no other place where he could find the soldiers we were to take to Leiden.

There came a hammering at the gates, and the sentry reported to the captain that the lute-player had returned with four cut-throats who were seeking admittance. William interrupted to order them to be brought to him. When they were ranged in front of him, he asked Beniamino to explain.

'Retired mercenaries, Stadhouder,' said Beniamino. 'Desperate, violent, malodorous but scrupulously loyal to you.'

'Three cheers for the Stadhouder!' shouted one, and they all joined in. I suspect they had been plied with copious amounts of drink.

Beniamino approached and spoke to William in a low voice. 'Five guilders a man, but I guarantee worth every stijver.'

'If they aren't, you'll pay the twenty guilders,' William coolly retorted. 'Get them equipped and ready to move at once, and come with me.'

Beniamino issued some terse orders which saw the four men equipped with pistols and ammunition, coats and boots. These were not military in appearance, which led me to wonder why they were so readily to hand, but I had more important things to consider.

William led us to the upper floor, closed the door, and retreated to the far side of the room. 'Tell him what you told me,' he barked.

I hastily explained my discoveries.

'It makes sense,' Beniamino conceded, 'but how do we prove it? If we get it wrong, we alert the true traitor to our knowledge.'

'I have an idea,' William answered. 'I want the two of you to go to Leiden right now.'

'Now, Stadhouder? It's dark,' I objected.

'Good. Nobody will see you going, will they? Go now, do your work in the registry and give the addresses to these four. They can't arrest them, but at least they can see if they're around or go looking for them. The pair of you will travel straight on to Haarlem to find the minister Van der Horst.'

I did not like the sound of this.

'Meanwhile,' said the Stadhouder, 'I will tell Pieters tomorrow evening to prepare a letter to the mayor of Haarlem telling him that I want him to send some men to help you arrest Van der Horst senior. If Pieters is our man, he is likely to send a warning to the minister, and you will already be there to see it arrive and, if possible, to intercept it. I, on the other hand, will watch Pieters to see if he shows any sign of anxiety. If the mayor's men turn up to arrest Van der Horst and there has been no interference in that plan, we may take it that Pieters is innocent.'

It seemed a clever plan to me. People said lots of unpleasant things about William, but I never heard a man say that he was stupid. Rather the opposite; even his enemies conceded that he was cunning.

Beniamino and I descended the stairs, collected our belongings and wondered how we were meant to get to Leiden at this time of night, when no barges were available. You can walk the route in an afternoon in good summer weather, but in the dark you are as likely to plunge into a canal or a bog.

As we formed into a group and waited for the gate to be opened, the lieutenant of the watch murmured to us. 'The Stadhouder says you're to walk to the Kloosterkerk. It's just a few minutes away.'

'I know it,' said one of the mercenaries.

'Good. There are six fast horses waiting for you there.'

Had the opportunity arisen, I would have pointed out that clerical gentlemen do not ride horses, especially when in their gowns, but I was bustled outside and the gates were closed behind us. Discretion dictated that we moved quietly through the streets, and I will allow that I was impressed with how silently the other five moved. I, on the other hand, might as well have been a pedlar advertising his wares, because every move I made seemed to echo in the night-blackened streets.

When we reached the Kloosterkerk a couple of men were waiting with some fine horses, already saddled in preparation. It was a long time since I had ridden a horse, but I vaguely recalled my riding master instructing me on the importance of building a rapport with your steed before attempting to ride him, so I patted his muzzle a few times while telling him what a fine animal he was.

'There's no time for that now,' said Beniamino. 'Besides, you don't want to make juffrouw Van Leusden jealous.'

I could have done without that reminder of my lost love.

CHAPTER TWENTY

Beniamino and I set out along the road on a fine night with bright stars above, though there was little moon. The horses were strong and kept up a good pace without any prompting from me, which was just as well as I was struggling to keep my knees locked against my mount's sides.

'There's not much point in the Stadhouder lending us fast horses if you're going to keep yours at a fast walk,' Beniamino commented.

'Fast walk? This is a trot,' I replied indignantly.

'Hang on,' he answered. 'Let me count its legs. No, it has four. It can go faster than that.'

Thus saying he flicked my horse's rear quarter with his hand and cantered off on his own. My horse took the hint and tried to keep up despite my furious tugging at the reins. Since I was rocking in the saddle, the poor animal became confused about which direction I wanted him to go, my knees taking it in turns to buffet him, so we zigzagged along for about an hour before Beniamino indicated a pause and slowed his horse to a walk so it could approach the river bank and take a drink and rest for a while. I took the opportunity to adjust my dress, which had become disordered in several respects, and to take a mouthful from the flask I was offered. I thought it contained water, but it was actually genever which scorched the back of my throat as it went down.

'Bit rough for your palate, dominie?' laughed the mercenary who gave it to me.

I tried to think of a witty rejoinder, but there was little point since I had temporarily lost the power of speech.

We remounted and completed our journey at a trot, arriving at Leiden to find the gates firmly shut and nobody around to open them. This did not concern the soldiers in the least, who seemed happy to camp in the fields, but I have an attraction to a proper bed, so I hammered on the gates once more.

'Open in the name of the Stadhouder!' I bellowed.

'Is he with you?' came a cry from inside.

'No.'

'Then go away.'

The guard did not actually say "Go away" but that was the gist of his comment.

'I am Master Mercurius of the University,' I shouted, 'and I demand that you open this gate.'

Beniamino smiled and walked up to the gate, pushing himself flat against one. 'You men pile the faggots up against the gate,' he bellowed, 'and I'll get the fire.'

The small inspection window in the gate opened briefly, and a worried face appeared. Before he had the chance to say anything, Beniamino extended his arm from the side and grabbed him by the hair, almost pulling his head through the small window.

'Ah, it won't go through!' Beniamino announced. 'Perhaps if we cut the ears off we could make a difference.' He brandished his knife.

'I don't think so,' said one of the other mercenaries. 'It'll still be too tall. We could take a chunk out of the scalp, I suppose.'

'Or he could be a nice man and tell his colleague to open the gate so we don't need to pull him through the hole bit by bit,' Beniamino suggested.

'Open the gate! Open the gate!' the sentry shouted.

There was the sound of a beam being withdrawn from its cradle, and then the gate creaked open.

We walked our horses through in single file.

'Thank you, lads,' said Beniamino. 'Don't forget to lock it again. There are some bad types out there.'

Considering how much noise we had made in seeking entry, I confess I did not see the point in our reversion to quiet movement, but we walked the horses slowly through the city. I had given no thought at all to where the horses might be stabled, but the soldiers scouted round the University buildings and finally spotted a place where they could tether the horses. It was a dry, mild night, so there was no need to take them inside, and the soldiers settled down to have a nap in the garden.

I headed for my room and was taken aback when Beniamino followed.

'Where are you going?' I asked.

'To the Registry. Isn't that where you're going?'

'I was planning to go to my bed.'

'There's no time for that now. We've got to get those addresses and be on our way before sunrise.'

That would give us about three hours, at best; I was losing enthusiasm for this mission by the moment, and since I had never had a great deal of it in the first place I was in danger of reaching zero enthusiasm fairly soon.

'The Registry is closed, Beniamino,' I explained.

'Closed, aye; but is it locked?'

'I don't know,' I confessed.

'Neither do I, so let's go and find out.'

I led him to the door, took a deep breath and turned the handle. It was open. I was shocked; the Registry contains all manner of confidential information, but it seemed that anyone could just walk in during the night and help themselves. I decided I must make a point of drawing this to the Rector's attention. It was as well that Van Looy was dead, because if he hadn't been his anger at finding this door unlocked might have killed him.

I had only the slightest acquaintance with the Registry's layout, but I knew that the records of current students were kept in loose-leaf form. This was logical, because students come and go and if you had a bound book you would have to read right from the start if you were looking for someone. Each student had his own leaf on which his personal details, his payments and his achievements were recorded, and to my great relief I found that someone had placed them in alphabetical order, so I soon found the pages for Molenaar, Van der Horst and Terhoeven. I copied out the addresses for the three men, reasoning that there may be something worth finding in Molenaar's papers, and was about to return them to the drawer when something on Terhoeven's record caught my eye. I took the paper to the window so that I could be sure that I was reading it right.

'What is it?' asked Beniamino.

'Hm? Oh, nothing. At least, just an administrative oddity,' I said.

But I wasn't sure that was all it was. I just didn't yet know what to make of it.

Beniamino gave the addresses to the mercenaries, having checked that at least one of them could read, and instructed them just to find the men and, if successful, to follow them, detaining them only if they looked like leaving the city.

'We expect to be back in about two days,' he told them, swinging his leg effortlessly over his horse and waiting for me to do the same. With the kind assistance of one of the soldiers, I finally did likewise and we set out as dawn broke, which meant that the city gates were being unlocked as we followed the road north and there was no need to maltreat any more guards.

This time we kept at a fast walk, because the horses had to cover about eight leagues to get to Haarlem. I found the rhythm soporific and was probably asleep when I was woken by a shove on my shoulder.

'A horse is no place to cat-nap,' Beniamino said.

'I'm sorry. It seems so long since I slept,' I moaned.

'Well, once we've found the minister's home we can get a little sleep. If Pieters is going to get a message to him, it can't set out before this evening when the Stadhouder tells him what we're up to, so we can go to bed early and be bright-eyed at two in the morning to take up position outside.'

I have never been bright-eyed at two in the morning. I have enough trouble getting up for the early prayers before breakfast, even when I am supposed to be the man saying them, so the prospect of another disturbed night did not appeal. Nights are for sleeping. I am told that there are officers who delight in marching their armies about by night to put them in more advantageous positions before the morning battle, which seems to me to be very near cheating.

The horses bore up well, so as the morning wore on we broke into a gentle trot and found ourselves in Haarlem before midday. I had never been there before, so I was keen to look around, but Beniamino insisted that we must find the church where Van der Horst senior was minister.

It took little finding, and the verger who was sweeping the front path was happy to confirm that this was the church of the celebrated mijnheer Van der Horst. Beniamino laid it on a bit thick, telling how he had heard great things of Van der Horst's preaching and that we hoped, God willing, to attend church on Sunday to hear him.

'There's no need to wait that long, bless you, gentlemen,' said the verger, 'for there is a prayer preparation service on Saturday afternoon at five o'clock.'

Beniamino's ability to fake enthusiasm was truly impressive. I felt hardly any excitement at this prospect, and I am ordained, so he must have felt even less, but you would never have known it by the way he reached into his saddlebag for a notebook and carefully wrote down the details of the service before thanking the verger and riding on.

We found an inn, stabled the horses and climbed the stairs to a private room. There was only one bed, but I did not care. If I could only get some sleep I did not mind if I had to share it with Beniamino, though I hoped his predilections ran only to wenches, because one hears some things about lute-players that make one wonder.

'You can have the bed,' Beniamino charitably offered. 'I'll just fold up a blanket as a pillow and doss down on the floor by the hearth.'

He appeared to be one of those people who could sleep just about anywhere. I have long envied them. I have never had a lot of money, but the one luxury I have always tried to secure for myself is a good bed. We spend a third of our lives in it after all, so a man should be prepared to pay for the best he can afford. As I write this now, I have the happiest thoughts of a bed I bought in 1693 which was beyond comparison. We were very happy together until it developed woodworm and fell to bits one Saturday night not long ago. It was a good servant, and I shall not see its like again.

I was woken after dark by a violent shaking of my shoulder.

'What time is it?' I yawned.

'Past midnight. Come — I've got us both some dinner before the kitchen shut below. Eat it while it's still hot.' He took a bite of chicken. 'While it's still lukewarm,' he said.

I was not especially hungry, but who knew when the chance to eat would come round again, so I tucked in while wishing that it was possible to sleep and chew at the same time.

'Don't drink too much,' he counselled. 'A soldier is vulnerable when he's peeing. It tends to put you off your guard.'

I resolved to remember this in case it was ever useful in my life, and it never has been.

We extinguished the candle for safety and Beniamino opened the window slightly, just enough to get your fingers behind it from the outside.

'We may need to let ourselves in when we get back,' he explained.

'Beniamino, this room is on the upper floor,' I protested.

'Yes. And your point is…?'

'How will we get into an upstairs room?'

'Simple. I'll climb on your shoulders, open the window and climb in. Then I'll let down a sheet to you and you can walk up the side of the building using the sheet as a rope.'

I admired his resourcefulness without ever feeling the need to emulate it.

'We'll go out through the back door. The front one has a heavy bolt and opening it will wake the household.'

I followed him through the kitchen and we slipped out into an alleyway, then into a road. It was quite a long walk across town, but at length we came into the square where the church was and Beniamino led us to a small archway between two houses.

'The chat this afternoon was just a subterfuge to inspect the surroundings for a good vantage point,' he explained. 'I don't actually have much interest in hearing Van der Horst preach.'

'I never thought you did,' I answered. 'Tell me, do you believe in God?'

He looked at me long and hard. 'Of course I do,' he said at length. 'What sort of question is that? Only a fool doesn't believe.'

'I just wondered,' I said. 'Don't you get pangs of conscience when you're — oh, I don't know — cutting off part of someone's finger or searing their genitalia with a red hot iron?'

'I'm a seeker after truth, in my own way,' he protested. 'I value it as much as you do. I just have a more direct way of getting hold of it. Now keep quiet so we don't draw attention to ourselves.'

We crouched down behind the house wall and listened, Beniamino having explained that at this time of night we could hear anyone approaching, so we did not need to keep peeking out.

'Take a nap if you want,' he said, 'so long as you wake as soon as I nudge you.'

I did as I was bid, and somehow drifted off, but was soon awakened once more.

'Is something happening?' I whispered urgently.

'No, you were snoring.'

'Oh, sorry.'

'Very loud.'

'Sorry again.'

Dawn was approaching, and the city would soon come to life. I was beginning to think that our vigil had been wasted when there was a clatter on the cobbles and a horse was tied up outside the minister's house.

Beniamino walked briskly up to the rider as he tethered his animal. 'You have a letter for mijnheer Van der Horst, I believe. I'll take it for you.'

'My orders are to give it directly into the minister's hand,' said the messenger.

Beniamino levelled a pistol at his head. 'They've just changed,' he said.

'So they have,' agreed the messenger, handing over the missive.

'Now, no doubt you are tired and hungry. Why don't you go and have a bite to eat and take your time about the trip back to The Hague?' Beniamino suggested, holding a couple of coins in the air.

'No skin off my nose,' said the horseman. 'Can I leave the horse here?'

'We'll take good care of it,' Beniamino said. 'Give us an hour or so. When the horse is tied to the other side of the gateway, you'll know we've finished.'

'Haven't I seen you before somewhere?' the horseman mused. Beniamino cocked the pistol. 'No, I'm wrong, never seen you before in my life. In fact, I haven't even seen you now.'

'Good man... That's the way I like it. Off you go.'

The rider loped off across the square in search of breakfast, which was an enticing prospect, but we had work to do. Beniamino slit the letter open with his knife, glanced at the contents and passed it to me.

'It's not signed,' I noted.

'Of course it's not signed. Who in their right mind signs a treasonous letter? But we know where it has come from. The rider didn't argue when I told him to go slowly back to The Hague. And we know the message in the letter — "Flee, for all is discovered. Warn the others if you can. Men are coming to arrest you." What a shame we got here first,' he chuckled. 'Stay here,' he ordered, 'and stop anyone coming out.'

'How?'

'It'll be a middle-aged man and a maid,' said Beniamino. 'How hard can it be? In fact, don't bother stopping the maid. Just stop the minister. Use reasonable force.'

'A minister can't manhandle another minister!' I expostulated.

'He may kill you if you don't.'

'Ah. That changes things.'

'I thought it might.'

Beniamino went along the passage to the back of the house. Moments later I heard the door being kicked in, a maid screaming and the sound of Beniamino running up the stairs. There was some shouting, then Beniamino called to me from the upper window.

'Let yourself in at the back. It's open.'

If "open" is a synonym for "hanging off its hinges" Beniamino was right. I made my way upstairs, ignoring the whimpering maid in the kitchen. I am not good with maids. I don't mean that I molest them. Rather, I tend to pity them and hold conversations with them, as a result of which I find myself promising to try to improve their lot. It is a lifelong weakness of mine.

Van der Horst was sitting on the edge of his bed in his nightwear. He did not appear frightened in the least. 'What is this intrusion about?'

Beniamino unfolded the note and held it so that the minister could read it, for which purpose he donned a pair of eyeglasses.

'I see. And you are…'

'The Stadhouder's men. You are to come with us to The Hague.'

'And if I refuse?'

'You'll still come with us, but in a box.'

I had to admire the old fellow's poise.

'May I dress first?'

'Naturally. We can't have you going out like that. It wouldn't be decent.'

Van der Horst dressed carefully, selecting a clean shirt and arranging his collar precisely. 'I must look my best for the Stadhouder.'

Beniamino indicated the stairs and told me to go down first in case the prisoner decided to throw himself down in an attempt to break his own neck.

Having gained the street we walked across town. The minister was addressed by several people who must have wondered where he was being taken, but eventually we found the inn. The front door was now open, so we all entered and proceeded up to our room. I took the opportunity to ask the innkeeper's wife if breakfast for three could be sent up. Even a traitor is entitled to some basic hospitality.

He pronounced a blessing over it and we ate together. That seems astonishing to me as I say it now, but it is the case; I asked him questions, and he told me the truth.

'I do not repent of my belief that this country does not need or want a Stadhouder,' he said. 'I have been open and honest about that, as befits a Christian man.'

'Your views seem to be widely known,' I agreed.

'Nor have I countenanced violence against his person. I hate the office, not the man.'

'That may weigh in your favour.'

'I doubt it,' he grimaced. 'The Stadhouder is not of a forgiving nature. I shall hang.'

'The more you confess openly, the better your chances,' I told him.

'Do you think I want to spare my life?' he asked. 'Why should I want to live a moment longer in a world that will never be the world I want?'

'Because it is God's world and there is no other. Because an execution would tarnish your reputation. Because your son will be on the scaffold with you.'

'He has done nothing. He refused to join us.'

'That is the impression you have both attempted to give. Your supposed antipathy would be protective if one or other of you were to be arrested, but it won't do. It's only a sham.'

Van der Horst smiled slightly. 'I see you are a minister too. How do you come to be doing the Stadhouder's dirty work?'

'I have been investigating the death of two men, one in Leiden, and one in Utrecht, both killed by members of your cell.'

'My son?' he asked, unable to disguise his strong emotion.

'Innocent of both, so far as I know. Molenaar confessed to killing Van Leusden and Terhoeven has been named as the murderer of Van Looy.'

He waved his hand dismissively. 'I know neither of those names.'

'I'm sure that is so. You would not need to know them, and it is safer if you do not. They were fellow students of your son in Leiden.'

'Will I see him again before we suffer?'

'I cannot make any promises, but I will do what I can.'

He seemed genuinely moved. 'Thank you, Dominie,' he said.

The absence of a third horse troubled me, but Beniamino had a plan. We found a barge whose master, for a certain sum, agreed to leave a little cargo behind to accommodate three men and two horses. I cannot say that the horses enjoyed the voyage, any more than we enjoyed sitting behind them and watching for any sign of intestinal activity on their part.

'How much money do you have?' I asked.

'The Stadhouder is very liberal when it comes to hunting down traitors,' he replied.

This liberality was tested again when we switched to a second barge to take us to Leiden. We climbed out onto the quay there and were met by one of the mercenaries who informed us that they could not find Terhoeven, but young Van der Horst was in his room.

We trooped off to corner the young man and effect a family reunion of sorts.

Two men were left to guard the father while the rest of us arrested his son, who came without resistance. When the two men came face to face, I watched their reaction closely. Neither showed the dislike that they claimed to profess for the other.

'Do we stay here to look for Terhoeven, or do we take this pair to The Hague?' Beniamino asked me.

'I think I know where Terhoeven may be, and it isn't here,' I said. 'We may as well take them to the Stadhouder now. If we set off now, we may just arrive before nightfall.'

'Let's make sure that we do,' said Beniamino, telling two of his men to walk the horses back to The Hague while the other two accompanied us and the prisoners on yet another barge. Barge travel is a way of life in our country, but I cannot say that I relish it. There are some cargoes that make the journey less pleasant, manure being one of them, which was what we were sitting beside. I would almost have preferred the lute which, I am pleased to report, had been stowed away somewhere in the Binnenhof at The Hague. Was it too much to hope that it might have gone missing by the time we arrived?

CHAPTER TWENTY-ONE

The first thing I noticed when we disembarked at The Hague was that Molenaar was hanging from the gallows in front of the Prison Gate.

'Isn't hanging a dead person rather pointless?' I asked.

'Not at all,' Beniamino replied. 'Hanging is a punishment for the offender and a deterrent for the rest of us. They don't need to know he was already dead when he was strung up.'

'How long will he stay there?'

Beniamino paused to inspect the hanging corpse. 'Till he falls to bits or they need the gallows again. Which is likely to be quite soon, thanks to us.' He smiled broadly, probably in contemplation of some kind of bonus, and pushed our prisoners through the gate first.

We were greeted by a slim, ascetic looking young man at the top of the stairs.

'I am Bouwman,' he told us, 'temporarily acting as the Stadhouder's personal secretary in the continued indisposition of mijnheer Pieters.'

Mijnheer Pieters was currently in the same dungeon that Molenaar had occupied and if not yet indisposed he soon would be, because the Stadhouder told Beniamino to question him as soon as we were finished in the main hall.

The Van der Horsts were forced to kneel in front of the Stadhouder. To my surprise, he was very restrained, and did not kick either of them. In fact, he ordered chairs brought for them both.

'You have plotted against me,' he said baldly.

'Not against you; against the office of Stadhouder,' said the minister.

'You think those are different?'

'You have always been you, but there was a time when you were not Stadhouder, and such a time may come again. But I would be just as opposed whoever the Stadhouder is. Resign your place, and I will wish you a long life and happiness.'

'And you?' he addressed the student.

'I am my father's dutiful son in all things,' he replied simply.

'Even illegal ones?'

'I am not convinced that it is illegal to want a republic without a Stadhouder. The people should choose their own leader.'

'Remind me again — how often were the De Witts elected? How much say did the people have in that?'

William had a point there. Johan de Witt had been elected Pensionary by the States of Holland, effectively the salaried leader of the government chosen by delegates to the States. There was no popular vote. And Holland was only one province; small groups of men in the other provinces agreed to acknowledge him as the leader of all the provinces.

Young Van der Horst said nothing.

'Shall I put them to the question?' asked Beniamino, which was a euphemism for employing all those loathsome gadgets he had in the hope of eliciting a confession.

'Not yet. They may volunteer what we need to know without the need for brutality, but thank you for reminding us all that it is an option,' William answered. 'You need to know that Pieters is in custody downstairs. His life expectancy is not long, but what does scripture tell us? "Man that is born of a woman hath but a short time to live, and is full of misery." For Pieters the short time will certainly be full of misery. My inquisitor here will see to that.'

Beniamino inclined his head to acknowledge the testimonial to his powers.

'Master Mercurius, please explain to us all what you have discovered. Bouwman, I think we would all like some wine.'

'As you please, Stadhouder,' I said, 'but may I first ask that the Treasurer joins us?'

'De Ring? What does he have to do with it? Very well, Bouwman, fetch him.'

We sat for some minutes in silence before the door opened and Cornelis de Ring entered. He was dressed in an old-fashioned style with a long fur-trimmed gown which concealed his feet so that he appeared to glide across the floor. He bowed to the Stadhouder, who told him to take a seat.

'Thank you,' I began. 'The man we knew as Van Looy worked for the University of Leiden. After he was murdered, we discovered that he was actually called Dekkers and was a servant of the Stadhouder, sent to Leiden to hunt out malcontents and rebels. It seemed likely that one of them was responsible for his death, particularly as we found among his papers certain secret writings that indicated a cell of three receiving orders from an intermediary who was himself directed by another. Let us call these two unknown individuals the intermediary and the director.'

I paused to collect my thoughts.

'I was then sent by the Stadhouder to Utrecht...'

'Mercurius, when I said I wanted you to tell us all you know, I didn't mean literally everything. Be selective, man.'

'As you wish, Stadhouder. At Utrecht an attempt was made upon my life, which was unsuccessful.'

'Obviously,' William sighed, causing me to blush.

'When a further attempt was made, the attacker was seized. He proved to be Molenaar, one of a group of three students at Leiden of whom this Van der Horst before us was another. The third was a man called Terhoeven, who vanished after Van Looy's death. According to Molenaar, Terhoeven was responsible for the death of Van Looy and did this without orders from others. Is that correct, mijnheer Van der Horst?'

The student stood to reply. 'It is, master. We did not order it, nor did we approve it.'

I turned to Cornelis de Ring, who was sitting impassively. 'Where is Terhoeven, Master Treasurer?'

I felt quite proud of myself as I surveyed the astonished faces. It was what I believe the French call a *coup de théâtre*.

'I discovered in the University Registry that you meet his fees.'

The Treasurer rose slowly to his feet. 'Terhoeven is my godson, Stadhouder, the son of a younger sister whose parents died when he was yet a minor. He came to live in my house and, so far as I know, is currently at my country estate.'

'Have you spoken to him since the death of Van Looy?' I asked.

'Yes. He admits his part but urges that he was on the Stadhouder's business at the time.'

'On my business?' the Stadhouder exploded. 'How dare he bring me into this!'

Leaving aside the question of whether the Stadhouder was already in the business as the intended victim of a plot, it seemed reasonable to request an explanation of Terhoeven's extraordinary statement.

'It is my fault, Stadhouder. I beg that I will suffer the punishment and disgrace that would otherwise fall to my godson.'

The Stadhouder had calmed down somewhat. There was no more exemplary servant of the nation than De Ring, which fact earned him some consideration.

'Please sit, Master Treasurer, and explain yourself.'

'Thank you, Stadhouder. I am not as supple as I was, however much I try to deny the fact to myself. There was talk some time ago of plots against you. My godson entered the University at Leiden last year. When he told me that he had heard disloyal talk there, I urged him to give the appearance of enthusiasm for the cause in the hope that he would garner firm evidence that I could bring to you. He reported that he had made common cause with two colleagues but that, while Molenaar was eager to act, Van der Horst was very cautious. My godson therefore took it upon himself to goad them into action, his idea being that once a plot was about to hatch, he would inform on them.'

'That does not explain the death of Van Looy,' I prompted.

'I did not know that Van Looy was active in the University,' De Ring claimed.

'But you paid him?'

'Indeed I did; but you will permit me to remind you, Master, that I explained the process to you. In order to enhance the security of the agent, I knew only that he was somewhere, and only under his real name. I confess it never crossed my mind that the Stadhouder might not have ignored my warnings as I thought, but have secretly dispatched Van Looy to investigate.'

He took a sip from the goblet of wine he had been given.

'At some point my godson spotted Van Kamerik, who is a neighbour of ours, visiting the University and followed him. Discovering that he was in conversation with Van Looy, and knowing Van Kamerik's role here, he deduced that Van Looy must be in communication with The Hague and approached him. By his account, he told Van Looy that he was acting for the Stadhouder and offered to share information; to his surprise, Van Looy called him a liar, argued that if there were other agents in Leiden he would have been told about them, and told him this was a feeble attempt to save his pitiful neck. He said that the three students were all named in the report he was writing. Terhoeven panicked and struck him, his intention being to find and steal the report to avoid exposure. If he was declared a traitor, he risked the noose if he could not establish his motive, but if he did so he would be hunted down by other traitors and killed. The only safe way was to prevent the report being sent. He searched for it but failed to find it, and his delay in getting help meant that mijnheer Van Looy died for want of care. In case he had been seen entering Van Looy's room, my godson tipped the body down the stairs, which was disrespectful of him.'

I might have suggested that hitting somebody over the head with a heavy object was more disrespectful, but I held my peace.

'At a later time, Terhoeven returned to make a more thorough search. Not finding the report, and fearing that his colleagues disapproved his actions, he fled to my house for safety. I give you my word, Stadhouder, that if I had been at home I would have brought him back here to throw himself on your mercy.'

William gnawed his thumb and said nothing.

'May I continue?' I asked. Receiving a nod, I launched into the second part of my account. 'I was then sent to Utrecht to confirm whether there were plots afoot there. I need not describe what occurred in that city, except that I was followed by Molenaar. Molenaar and Van der Horst had been watching me to see whether Terhoeven's actions had drawn attention to their cell.'

Van der Horst interjected. 'We had the greatest respect for your mental abilities, Master. Molenaar was convinced that if you had not yet made the connection, you soon would, and therefore that you must be dealt with.'

'I foolishly told Molenaar where I was going. He must have followed at the first opportunity, and on Wednesday evening, during the great storm, he made his move. Unfortunately the victim was not me; I had lent my clerical cloak to Bartholomeus van Leusden, whom Molenaar battered to death in my stead. Thus disappointed, he resolved to try again, but Beniamino here prevented him, and he was arrested. Brought here, he was poisoned before he could speak.'

It was my turn to take a drink now. My mouth was drying up as I ran out of things to say.

'But how could this be, since we had been at pains to ensure that only the Stadhouder knew that we were coming? This was where we benefited from having discovered some papers left by Van Looy. On three sheets he described the structure of the treasonous band, their link to Haarlem and the fact that their leader was Pieters. This explained how Molenaar had been poisoned; Pieters knew because he handles the Stadhouder's correspondence.'

I bowed to the Stadhouder to indicate that I had finished.

William said nothing, but was clearly thinking very hard. 'Bouwman, summon the captain and have these two locked away, separate from each other and from Pieters. I'll deal with them later. We must deliberate on their fate.'

I have to say that I did not like the sound of that "we". I would have preferred "I"; or, at a pinch "everyone except Mercurius".

The Van der Horsts were led away, and the Stadhouder topped up his wine before passing the flagon to the rest of us. De Ring made as if to leave but was ordered to keep his place.

'What am I to do?' asked William. 'If I do nothing and just ignore the attempted treachery, it only encourages others to do the same.'

'If I may comment,' I began tentatively, 'it seems to me that they are only encouraged if these matters are made public.'

'We can hardly hide the fact that Van Looy and Van Leusden are dead,' the Stadhouder pointed out.

'No, and their killers must pay some sort of penalty,' I agreed, 'but as for the Van der Horsts, they have been ineffectual. They may have thought many things, but they have done nothing practical about them.'

'And Molenaar has already been hanged,' Beniamino contributed, 'albeit he was already dead. But it's the thought that counts.'

'You have Pieters in custody,' I added, 'who seems to me to be the real villain.'

I may not have made sufficiently clear that I am deeply uneasy about capital punishment. I know many people believe it to be sanctioned by God, but life is precious and I would prefer that it was not taken. Hanging Molenaar had not brought Van Leusden back, and I did not believe that it would give Janneke much comfort when she heard about it. Anyway, I was not going to recommend execution, even for Pieters. I acknowledge, though, the inconsistency in feeling that Pieters, who did nothing violent personally, was more of a criminal than Terhoeven, who had killed in a panic. Still, this was something for the Stadhouder to decide, and I was heartily glad that it was not my decision.

'What would you do with them, Mercurius?' William demanded.

Those who say honesty is always the best policy haven't met some of the people I've met. However, I decided just to speak my mind and let him take or ignore my advice as he thought fit.

'If the Van der Horsts do not want to live under a Stadhouder, let them be banished, forbidden to return under pain of death. Pieters has betrayed your trust in the most flagrant way, accepting your gold and your hospitality whilst plotting against you, and so deserves severe punishment. As for Terhoeven, I am inclined to mercy because of his youth and stupidity, but we cannot overlook that he is a murderer.'

William nodded as if slowly processing my suggestions. 'And you?' he asked Beniamino.

'I would hang the lot of them,' he said. 'I would just drag it out for Pieters. Maybe a bit of drawing and quartering after the English fashion. Or we could break him on the wheel.'

'Master Treasurer?'

De Ring started as if he had not expected to be asked his opinion. 'I cannot judge these men while my own godson is among them, Stadhouder. It grieves me to say so, but I fear that someone must pay for my godson's crime. I would do so myself if it were possible. Blood should have blood.'

I could not help but admire the old man.

'Perhaps we could avoid the humiliation of a public execution for him,' William muttered.

'But if we put him to death privately, justice is not seen to be done,' Beniamino pointed out. 'I suppose we could hang him quietly and then announce it, but that spares no humiliation.'

With the interval that has elapsed I have developed the idea that my next comment was fuelled by too much of the

Stadhouder's excellent burgundy wine. I cannot otherwise account for my plain rudeness.

'Stadhouder, there is another way of looking at this,' I said boldly. 'You sent a man to look into a half-baked plot. Because you didn't tell De Ring that you were acting on his intelligence he, out of a care for your safety, recruited his own godson who was willing to pretend to be disloyal, an act which must have been deeply abhorrent to him and which carried great danger if he were discovered. You worried about plots in Utrecht so you had Van Leusden prepared to deputize for Professor Voet, which, indirectly, cost him his life.'

'Are you seriously saying this is all my fault?' William asked me. He was a small man, but very threatening when he wanted to be.

'No. Well, yes, in a way.' I was floundering when a happy thought came to me. 'A man who fears plots breeds plots. He encourages conspiracies. He looks about him, and he finds evidence of treason because he sees treason in every heart. But I think of the English preacher, George Fox, who says that if we look we will see a little of God in every man. *Circumspice*, Stadhouder. Look about you, but look for the good. Stop seeing plots, for men are so well-disposed towards you that they will denounce any conspiracy they find; and the Low Countries will be a happier place for it.'

William announced that he needed to be alone to pray and think, and bade us rest in the castle and wait upon him in the morning when he would announce his decision. As we bowed and left, I could hear him muttering to himself *circumspice*, *circumspice*.

CHAPTER TWENTY-TWO

When morning came I was surprised to find that Beniamino had left. He did not choose to wait for the announcement. The rest of us filed into the hall, where William was sitting in his most imposing chair. The Van der Horsts were led in and made to kneel before him. De Ring made to do the same as proxy for his godson, but William ordered him to remain standing.

'If you do not wish to live under a Stadhouder, then live somewhere else,' he pronounced. 'Our colonies in the East Indies need ministers of religion and competent young men. If you will undertake not to return for the rest of your lives, you may live in peace there.'

The two men agreed and were taken away to await transportation.

'Pieters will hang presently,' said William, 'but I have no relish for barbarities. He has spent a night with my inquisitor and has suffered enough.'

I wondered what exactly Beniamino had done to him, but decided it was probably better if I never discovered that. I did not propose to stay to watch him hang.

'That leaves us with Terhoeven,' William continued. 'De Ring, Van Looy had no wife or children, but if he supported any aged relatives you and your godson will provide the same support so long as they live. It is my pleasure that your godson should serve in my army, where he will have the opportunity to demonstrate his zeal for our House of Orange and redeem his honour. I will review his position in five years.'

De Ring fell to his knees. 'Your Excellency is merciful indeed,' he said. I could see tears on his old cheeks.

'Now leave us. Not you, Mercurius.'

We were left alone. The Stadhouder rose from his chair and walked behind a curtain, returning with a bowl.

'Apple?' he said.

I took one and muttered my thanks.

'You have done well. I won't forget this.'

If it's all the same to you, I'd rather you did, I thought. *I never want another job like this again.*

'I have written a letter to the Rector expressing my satisfaction. It also tells him he may retire at the end of the year, as he has been wishing to do for some time. Have you ever thought of becoming Rector, Mercurius?'

'No more than I have thought of becoming a nun,' I said. 'And I am equally suited to both roles.'

He handed me two envelopes.

'What is the other, Stadhouder?' I asked.

'It tells anyone who reads it that you are my trusted servant and that if you are in need of any assistance, it must be rendered or the person concerned will answer to me.'

I had not expected that. Unworthily, my first thought was to march into Jan Steen's inn with it and declare that I was thirsty and needed a free beer, but I supposed that the Stadhouder intended me to use it for more suitable reasons.

'Goodbye, Mercurius.' He offered me his hand, which I took.

'Goodbye, Stadhouder.'

'Bouwman has a pouch for you, and my carriage will return you to Leiden. And now, farewell.'

I enjoyed the journey. The carriage was very grand and comfortable. If I became a bishop I would travel like this all the time, I thought, but then dismissed the thought and returned to counting the contents of the pouch. Gold is heavy if you have enough of it, I discovered.

Heads turned as we rode into Leiden and pulled up outside the Academy building. This must be what it is like to be a great man, I told myself; but there is a price to be paid for power.

Circumspice, Mercurius.

Look about you, and be content with what you see.

A NOTE TO THE READER

Dear Reader,

It is a curious but very welcome discovery that sometimes a story is given a welcome prod by a new fact that presents itself.

I had begun this story and decided that part of the action would take place in Utrecht in 1674. To gather some useful background my wife and I went there. (Strictly speaking, we went to see the Miffy museum, but I wanted to walk the city too.) It was then that I found out that on the first day of August 1674 the Dom fell down in the middle of some strange meteorological event. That just had to be worked in somehow.

Ben Salfield is a much better lute-player than Beniamino, though probably not much of a torturer. I encourage you to seek out his music. His brother Jon plays the guitar but, more importantly, taught me to fence, at which I am about as useful as Mercurius.

If you have enjoyed this novel I'd be really grateful if you would leave a review on **Amazon** and **Goodreads**. I love to hear from readers, so please keep in touch through **Facebook** or **Twitter**, or leave a message on my **website**.

Dank je wel!

Graham Brack

Sapere Books is an exciting new publisher of brilliant fiction and popular history.

To find out more about our latest releases and our monthly bargain books visit our website: **saperebooks.com**

Printed in Great Britain
by Amazon